HER ENEMY

LEENA LEHTOLAINEN

Translated by Owen F. Witesman

amazoncrossing

Text copyright © 1994 by Leena Lehtolainen
English translation copyright © 2012 Owen Witesman

Published by agreement with Tammi Publishers and Elina Ahlbäck Literary Agency, Helsinki, Finland.

Printed in the United States of America.

Published by AmazonCrossing
PO Box 400818
Las Vegas, NV 89140

ISBN-13: 9781611099645
ISBN-10: 1611099641
Library of Congress Control Number: 2012922284

For Mari

CAST OF CHARACTERS

THE INVESTIGATORS

Maria Kallio..Legal counselor, ex-cop
Pekka Koivu........................Maria's old partner at Helsinki VCU
Pertti Ström...Espoo police detective
Ville "Dennis the Menace" Puupponen...............Espoo police officer

THE FAMILIES

Annamari Hänninen..Kimmo's mother
Henrik Hänninen...Kimmo's father
Kimmo Hänninen...Armi's fiancé
Marita Sarkela Hänninen.......................Antti's sister, Risto's wife
Matti and Mikko.............................Risto and Marita's twin sons
Risto Hänninen..Kimmo's half brother
Sanna Hänninen...Kimmo's dead sister
Antti Sarkela..Maria's boyfriend
Marjatta Sarkela...Antti's mother
Tauno Sarkela..Antti's father
Armi Mäenpää.......................................Kimmo's fiancée, nurse
Marja "Mallu" Laaksonen...Armi's sister
Paavo Mäenpää...Armi's father
Taisto Laaksonen...Teemu's father
Teemu Laaksonen...Mallu's husband

SUPPORTING CAST

Out of the ash
I rise with my red hair
And I eat men like air.

— Sylvia Plath

1

The cherry trees were the first thing I saw when I woke up. The spring had been warm, and now the trees were blossoming with fluffy, fragrant bunches of flowers. Antti always wanted to sleep with the curtains open so we could see the curled branches against the night sky. It made it hard for me to sleep, but I'd gradually gotten used to it.

Antti was still sleeping, and Einstein was stretching contentedly in a puddle of sunshine at the foot of the bed. It was already eight o'clock, and I needed to get ready for work.

Shuffling from the bedroom to the kitchen, I started the coffeemaker. I'm useless before my morning coffee. After rinsing my face with ice-cold water, I walked across the yard to pick up the paper. The grass tickled my bare feet, and, as I breathed in the scent of cherry blossoms, I could already sense the coming heat of the day. The only thing disturbing my idyllic moment was the noise from the constant construction on the West Highway.

Taking longer than I should have, I leisurely ate my breakfast and read the paper before letting Einstein out for his morning rounds along the shoreline. Pulling on cotton capri pants and a clean shirt, I threw on some mascara and a dab of lip gloss, then headed out to my bike. Antti was still in bed, one foot poking

out from under the sheet like a child's. He'd been up late strug-
gling with his dissertation again and hadn't crawled into bed
until nearly dawn.

We had been living together for a little over a month, and so
far, we'd managed to avoid any serious blowups, despite my occasional anxiety. New place, new job, new routines, no real sense of
direction after graduating...plenty of stress for one woman.

I'd known Antti for a long time—he was friends with
my roommate's boyfriend years ago, and I remember there
being electricity between us even then. We'd lost touch until
last summer, when that boyfriend was murdered and I'd been
assigned to the investigation. After I solved the case, Antti and
I found we were still interested in each other. A romance didn't
fit in with either of our plans: I was grinding away like a madwoman at my master's thesis, and Antti was working on his
dissertation and teaching math courses. But then our lunches
at the university started lasting longer, and after a while, we'd
skip the food to make love on the couch in Antti's office.

I eventually finished my thesis and started looking for work,
which was much harder than I had imagined. For a moment, I
even considered calling my old boss at the police department,
though begging for another temporary posting would have
meant swallowing my pride.

Then everything shifted: Antti received a large fellowship
that made it possible for him to work on his dissertation full
time for the next year. I found a job in a small law office with
a laid-back atmosphere in the North Tapiola area of Espoo, and
the same week, my great-aunt's heirs told me they'd decided to
sell the apartment I'd been living in for four years.

At first, neither of us suggested moving in together. Antti's
one-bedroom apartment would have been entirely too small

since he was working at home. I started searching for a new place of my own, but then Antti found out that his building would be undergoing an extensive exterior renovation.

"I'm never going to be able to concentrate with all that racket," he told me over the phone. "My parents are planning to spend the whole summer at their cabin in Inkoo, so I'll probably move into their place in Tapiola while they're away. When are you supposed to be out of your place?"

"Beginning of June, at the latest. Why?"

"I was just thinking…what if you came with me to Tapiola for the summer? We could just see how it goes, if we get along."

I pulled the phone away from my ear for a moment and stared at it.

"You don't decide this kind of thing over the phone," I finally said, trying to stall him. Moving in together felt too final. Too frightening.

After hours of talking at his place that night, I had eventually agreed. Antti's parents were going to move to Inkoo on May Day and stay until the end of September, maybe longer. Antti's father had retired in the spring, and it seemed likely they might even move to Inkoo permanently. I hadn't thought through anything past the summer, but I knew that with my new salary from Henttonen & Associates, I could afford to find an apartment if things didn't work out with Antti.

I nearly always rode to work on the north side of Tapiola, keeping to the shoreline and grassy meadows along the way as much as I could. As I was passing the shopping center downtown, I spotted a familiar blond head. Makke Ruosteenoja was next to a dumpster, breaking down a huge pile of cardboard boxes from his sporting goods store.

"Hey, Makke. Did you get tired of building your fort?" I brought my bike to a stop next to him.

"Just organizing the stockroom for our summer clearance sale. You don't need a new swimsuit, do you? You could get a good one cheap."

"Ugh, trying on swimsuits first thing in the morning—no thanks. So will we see you tonight at the Hänninens'?"

"Yeah, they invited me, although I don't understand why," Makke said, letting the top of the dumpster slam shut. "See you there."

As I continued my ride to work, just a quarter of a mile away, I thought about my first meeting with Makke.

A couple of days after starting my new job, I'd gone to buy some bicycle saddlebags I'd seen in the window of Makke's shop. I'd been the only customer in the store, so Makke spent a long time going over all the various models.

The next night, we happened to be at the local gym at the same time. While I was working my triceps on one of the machines, Makke sat down on the military press bench next to me. We continued our conversation, talking about bikes, whenever we were at adjacent stations. We seemed to be in sync: as I walked out of the women's dressing room after unwinding in the sauna, Makke was just coming out of the men's side.

"I could go for a beer right about now," he said. "You?"

I nodded, and we walked a block to a café and took a seat on the patio. Makke insisted on buying the round, and I watched him as he walked inside to get the drinks. The silhouette created by his worn jeans and tight purple T-shirt revealed a surprising mass of muscle. His straight straw-colored hair was a little longer in the front than the back, and it swung in front of his eyes as he turned back. There was something about those eyes, something there that seemed more than rambunctious.

"This is typical for me: first sports, and then a sports drink," I said. "My name is Maria Kallio, by the way."

"I know. I looked when you signed your credit card receipt yesterday. Markku Ruosteenoja, but most people just call me Makke. I live in Hakalehto, in the apartment buildings behind the tennis center. Are you from around here?"

"No. I just started working here last month, in a law office."

"For Eki Henttonen? He said he'd just landed a feisty new lady lawyer. That must be you. Eki helped me out with some stuff last year."

Even though it was nearly nine o'clock at night, the sun was still in my face, the light bouncing off the windows of the five-story office building that also housed the café. Ducks were splashing in the reflecting pool, and an energetic golden retriever plunged in, chasing them away. The beer tasted too good—half of mine was already gone.

Makke lifted his own to his lips. He was the sort of well-built jock I probably wouldn't have looked at twice if I'd just seen him walking down the street, unless I had noticed that flash of something deeper in his eyes.

"Lawyer, gym rat, biker—what else are you?" he asked, teasing.

"Ex-cop and punk till I die," I rattled off. "And you?"

"Well, not much of anything. Sporting goods salesman. Do you live close?"

"I don't really know where I live. This summer I'm staying in my possible future in-laws' row house on the shore in Itäranta, but I don't have a clue what's going to happen after September."

"Possible future in-laws?" Makke said sadly. "So you're taken. Of course you are." Then he drained his glass, and for a second I thought he was going to get up and leave right then and there. When he instead stayed sitting, it seemed as though continuing the conversation was now my responsibility.

"'Taken' sounds depressing. Let's just say I've been dating the same guy for almost a year. Which is a pretty big accomplishment for me."

Makke grinned, although he probably didn't realize exactly how serious I was.

"So this boyfriend of yours doesn't mind if you go out for a beer with another guy?"

"I wouldn't be going out with the kind of man who wanted me sitting at home. Even if we were married and had five kids, I'd still need to have the right to go out for a beer with whoever I chose."

"You want another?" Makke had emptied his glass and was getting up to fetch more.

"Bring a bottle, but it's my turn to pay now."

Makke had already gone, and when he came back, he wouldn't take any money. We continued our slightly stiff conversation about bicycles and bodybuilding, until Makke suddenly asked, "Were you joking when you said you were an ex-cop?"

"No. I went to the police academy and then worked for a couple of years before going to law school. I've done some temporary stints on the force too, including last summer."

"You don't really seem like a cop. Or like a lawyer, for that matter." Makke looked at my sweatpants and at my red hair twisted into a messy swirl on top of my head. No, my freckles and snub nose don't exactly give the impression of a sober defender of the law.

"Although I guess there isn't much point judging people on how they look," Makke continued. "Winter before last I was still drinking pretty damn hard, but now two pints in the evening is plenty."

I felt a life story coming on. Oh well, I was used to listening to life stories. But no—Makke fell silent, sipping his beer and looking off somewhere in the distance. He suddenly came to, and raised his arm in a wave as Kimmo Hänninen biked past.

"Hey, guys!" Kimmo yelled as his bike curved down the underpass and disappeared from sight.

"You know Kimmo too?" Makke asked, rotating his beer glass.

"Kimmo lived in the same small town as me for a couple of years when we were in high school. I didn't really know him; he's four years younger than me, but I hung out with his sister sometimes. Sanna, the one who died last spring. And Kimmo's brother is married to Antti's—my boyfriend's—sister."

Makke looked at me as if he were expecting a punch in the teeth.

"I was Sanna's boyfriend. I was on the beach when she drowned."

I didn't know what to say. Sanna drowned on her thirtieth birthday in the cold March waters of the Baltic Sea. Her blood-alcohol level was considerable, and tests also showed traces of sedatives. Her boyfriend had been found drunk out of his mind and half-frozen on the beach, with no memory of what had happened. According to the official explanation, Sanna tried to go swimming and drowned. A lot of people, including Antti, thought she did it on purpose.

"So your Antti is Antti Sarkela," Makke said quietly.

"Yeah." I drained my beer, trying to decide if I should give in to my desire for another.

"So this little date we're having is perfect payback. I was always jealous when Sanna talked about how smart Antti was." Makke forced a smile, and I grinned too, although nothing about the conversation made me feel good.

Three weeks had passed since that conversation. Afterward, I would see Makke at the gym sometimes and joke with him in the weight room. We didn't talk about Sanna, or anything else serious, but there was always something more under the surface of his wisecracks. I liked Makke, but he also frightened me a bit.

Anyway, I was surprised how quickly I was meeting people in Tapiola, and they all seemed to know each other—my boss was a friend of the Sarkela family and of Kimmo Hänninen's parents. Sometimes I wondered whether my job offer had come thanks to Antti's dad helping me out, but with the amount of student debt I had, there was no room for moralizing.

The day turned out hot, and to be able to walk out the back door and jump straight into the water after work was heavenly. Although I had my doubts about the purity of Otsolahti Bay, I risked it, bobbing in the seawater for fifteen minutes before going in to bother Antti.

He was sitting at the kitchen table chewing on a sandwich.

"Were you swimming? I'll come too if you're going back out. What time are we supposed to be at Risto and Marita's?"

"Seven. We still have a couple of hours. Are you going to work anymore?"

"Well, not if you have a better suggestion," Antti said hopefully, brushing his hand against my body. I let my towel fall to the floor. We weren't in any hurry.

We didn't realize it was time to start getting dressed until after six. Antti mixed us cocktails from his parents' generously stocked bar while I tried to calm down with a cold shower. The birthday party, for Antti's brother-in-law's fortieth, had me tied up in knots.

Usually I don't care much about how I'm dressed—I'm happiest in jeans—but I'd bought a new dress in honor of the occasion. I'd liked it at the time, but staring at myself in the entryway mirror, I thought the bright-green fabric seemed too garish, the hem too high, the neckline too open. The cap sleeves barely fit over my shoulders, making me look like a drag queen.

"Wow." Antti looked at me admiringly. Clearly, he didn't think the dress was too revealing. Antti's idea of formalwear was a flower-print dress shirt with a violet leather bow tie and his best black jeans. As far as I knew, the only suit he'd ever worn was on his confirmation. The purple suede shoes were new to me.

"I found them for three pounds in London. Overstock, I guess," Antti said in reply to my incredulous look.

Well, demand for that particular style in men's size twelve probably wasn't all that high.

I slipped into my own size six-and-a-half black stilettos, which made me walk like a newly birthed calf. Three inches isn't much these days—plenty of style gurus think a five-foot-three woman should wear at least four-inch heels—but these still weren't made for walking.

Suddenly we were out of time and had to make the trip by bike. Unfortunately, my dress got in the way. The police-auction eighteen-speed I had was a men's model, not designed for use with a narrow skirt and high heels. After my third attempt to mount ended with threatening sounds from the hem of my skirt, that was it.

"You could ride on my rack," Antti suggested.

"And sit sidesaddle! Fat chance!" Flustered, I marched inside and put on my running shoes and a pair of bike shorts. Then I hitched my skirt up around my waist, hoping the resulting wrinkles wouldn't be a complete catastrophe. I brought the heels, deciding I could smarten up once we got to the house.

"Nervous?" Antti asked as I stepped back into my shoes along the shoulder of the Hänninens' street.

"I hate being shown off like this."

Of course, I had met all the close relatives in small batches—but the idea of a public inspection, where they would probably all be trading comments about me, was irritating.

"I'll get you back, though. My Uncle Pena's sixtieth birthday is in the fall," I said as we walked in.

Built in that ostentatious style popular in the mideighties, the Hänninens' house featured white plastered brick, columns, and arbors, making it clear the owners wanted us all to know they had spent time in southern Europe. The woman of the house was Antti's sister, Marita Hänninen, née Sarkela, a math teacher who spent her summer vacation tending her immaculate geometric garden. Well-dressed partygoers mingled through, filling the linear spaces between the flowerbeds. I wished I had drunk a stiffer cocktail before leaving.

A champagne glass in his hand and a rose at his breast, the man of the hour was standing in front of the buffet table. Risto Hänninen was wearing a well-cut summer suit, with an expensive-looking red silk tie that perfectly matched the rose in his lapel. My dress, picked out at a thrift store, suddenly felt more secondhand than vintage. Marita was standing next to him, dressed in a gauzy navy number that softened the angles of her slender frame. I had heard rumors that Risto's company was doing just as poorly as every other engineering firm during the recession, but you couldn't have guessed it by looking at the two of them.

We presented our gift, a leather-bound book about nine-teenth-century hunting firearms. Antti had paid an arm and a leg for it at a used-book shop, and the volume was beautiful, with each individual illustration a small work of art. Although I find hunting revolting, I had flipped through the pages of gun diagrams out of sheer professional curiosity. As an ex-cop, I mean.

Instead of letting us slip away after drinking to his health, Risto insisted on presenting us to the other guests—"the cream of Tapiola." He really said that, and I honestly couldn't tell whether he meant it ironically. I met a couple of local politicians, the director of a major bank, a famous conductor, my own boss, and a local gynecologist who glanced at my pelvic area with a professional eye, making my dress feel not only secondhand but also too short.

"Hey, Antti! Maria!" Kimmo called out from across the grass. Wearing a beige three-piece suit more appropriate for an older man and with his cherubic curls uncombed as usual, Kimmo was disarming, even with his acne-scarred face. Nearly fifteen years separated Risto and Kimmo. After the death of his first wife, Risto's father, Henrik Hänninen, had remarried. He and his second wife, Annamari, had Sanna, and then, several years later, Kimmo.

"Maria, this is my fiancée, Armi," Kimmo said enthusiastically as we made it over to him. About my height, with a round face, wide hips, and thin blonde hair the stylist had wound too tight while doing her last perm, the girl looked sweet. Her poofy, flowery dress was woefully out-of-date. Maybe she'd gone to a thrift shop too, but she clearly wasn't even trying to look vintage.

"Armi Mäenpää," she said, smiling warmly. The blue of her eyes was so bright that I wondered whether she might be wearing tinted contacts.

We traded news and complained about the heat wave, and then said hello to Antti's parents, who had come all the way in from Inkoo just for this party. I had already emptied my glass of Champagne—with a capital C, because judging from the label on the bottle, this was the real stuff—and started scanning the room, hoping for something stronger. Antti was telling Kimmo about his progress on his thesis, so I tried to chat with Armi.

Actually, I didn't have to chat at all. Armi took care of the talking.

"I hear you're working in Eki Henttonen's law office. I'm a nurse, in Dr. Hellström's clinic. He's a gynecologist with a private practice. Actually, I'd like to specialize in obstetrics as well as gynecology, but after nursing school I'd had enough studying for a while. I hear you have two degrees—Marita told me—that you were a police officer first and then went to law school. Didn't you like being a cop?"

"Well, it was sort of—" I managed to say before Armi interrupted.

"It was probably pretty dangerous…I guess handling legal cases pays better too and works better for a woman. But I've never known a policewoman before. I have all kinds of questions for you."

Antti's parents appeared with two wriggling little boys in tow. Completely spoiled, the Hänninen twins—Matti and Mikko—were terrors well known to our cat, Einstein. Whenever he saw them, the poor thing usually scaled the highest bookcase he could find. At first, Einstein had tried hiding under the bed but had found that it was too easy to end up boxed in, with a twin on either side.

"Uncle Antti! Uncle Kimmo!" the boys whooped. "Come look! We got a Nintendo for our tree house!"

"Maria, you haven't even seen the boys' tree house yet! Kimmo and I built it last summer. Come on," Antti said, laughing as one of the shrieking boys dragged him and Kimmo toward a pine in the backyard with a handsome playhouse perched in its branches.

I swallowed. When I was little, I'd always wanted a tree house just like that. All the most exciting books featured one as a fort or clubhouse. However, building a tree house would have required the help of an adult, and my father didn't think girls needed tree houses.

"Can we climb up and look?" I asked, genuinely excited.

The little boys looked abashed.

"No girls allowed," Kimmo explained. "But Maria used to be a police officer. You have to let police officers into tree houses, don't you?"

"You used to be a cop?" Unconvinced, Matti looked me up and down just as pointedly as Dr. Hellström had. "Cops don't wear dresses."

"They wear all kinds of clothes on TV," Mikko said. "Do you have a gun too? A revolver? Dad has hunting rifles, but he never lets us touch them."

"I did have a gun when I was a police officer, but not anymore."

Despite this, the boys gave me permission to climb up with Antti to look at what might have been the first game console ever installed in a tree. Antti seemed almost hurt when I asked him whether the tree house would hold our combined weight.

"Hey, we do good work. Kimmo and I have built plenty of forts in our day."

Imagining them running around with just as much energy as Matti and Mikko was easy, with Armi under the tree playing the mother, telling them to be careful and passing up cups of juice. Maybe it was time for someone to teach the Hänninen twins that women liked tree houses too. I kicked off my shoes, and, despite the narrow skirt, succeeded in climbing up the wooden ladder.

Although the tree house was only a few yards off the ground, it gave a bird's-eye view, revealing the degrees of baldness of the men at the party. Behind the illusion of the curls, Kimmo's hair had started to thin on top, while Risto had skillfully combed his own hair to cover a bare spot. Audible from below, Armi was giggling a little too loudly, standing with Makke, who had just arrived at the party.

"Sanna always made fun of Armi's name," said Mikko, appearing at my side. "She said she should wear boots and be a soldier."

"'Cause her name sounds like 'army' in English," Matti added. "Did you know Sanna, Maria?"

"We went to the same school."

"Sanna drank too much vodka and then she died," Matti continued. "She was really good at Nintendo too."

The boys started showing off their video games, and I crouched with them, safe in the tree house, until I realized that I needed to find a bathroom.

I had visited the Hänninens a couple of times already, so I easily found my way. However, there was a line. I got behind Armi, was also waiting in the hallway.

"I like your dress," she said nicely.

"I feel like maybe it's too short," I replied.

"No way. You have great legs; you should show them off."

I tried not to bristle at such a personal comment as she continued to chatter.

"Actually, I just bought a leather miniskirt," I blurted out. Why was I telling her this? "I just need to let out the waist a little, but I don't have a sewing machine."

"I do!" Armi said. "It has a good leather needle too. You can come over any time and use it. Really. Tomorrow? I just live over behind the sports park. Maybe about two o'clock? It would be a nice opportunity to talk."

The bathroom door opened, and Makke stepped out. As Armi slipped inside, Makke smiled and whispered, "Looks like 'the Army' has decided to draft you."

I laughed, although the idea of poking fun at someone because of her name made me vaguely uneasy—reliving high school was the last thing I wanted to do as an adult.

After I got out of the bathroom, I couldn't find Antti, so I walked around the house to the front yard. There I found a handful of older gentlemen sitting in a circle of chairs: Risto, Antti's father, my boss, Dr. Hellström, and the principal from the school where Marita taught. When I realized they were talking about me, I stopped short and stayed behind the shrubbery.

"You sure lucked out, Eki, getting a young chick like that to replace Parviainen," Dr. Hellström said. "I'm guessing these days you'd rather be in your office than at home with your wife."

To my astonishment, my boss grinned.

"Having a little eye candy around the office is nice," he agreed. "But you have Armi. She's not so bad-looking either."

"Oh, I get to see plenty of naked women during business hours," Hellström said with a laugh.

"As far as I can tell, Maria isn't just a 'chick,'" Antti's father broke in dryly. "I might even call her a feminist."

"She has the calves of a feminist anyway. She's got muscles like a man," Hellström continued. "I prefer something more slender and feminine."

"Listen, you boys don't have any idea how masculine my calves would be if I hadn't shaved my legs," I observed loudly, stepping out from behind the bushes. "Any more, comments about my body? Why not make them to my face?"

The furious expression on my face silenced them. "I'm pretty sure you hired me for my specialty in criminal law, Eki. You could have paid a lot less for tits and ass."

I hadn't known my boss long enough to read him very well, and I had no idea how he would react to a reaming like this. For about two seconds, I was bracing myself to be fired, right then and there. I was relieved when Eki burst out laughing and turned to Antti's father.

"Forget your diplomas and forget your calves, Maria; you got the job because you don't take guff from anyone. I can't stand women who knuckle under."

I snorted and headed toward the drinks table, where a bottle of the best cognac available from the state liquor store had appeared. The recession was definitely not bothering the Hänninens. I was pouring myself a good stiff drink when Antti appeared by my side.

"Do you really need a drink that badly?"

I told him about my eavesdropping, but Antti just laughed.

"There's no doubt Erik Hellström makes too much noise about how thoroughly he knows the women of Tapiola. Mom stopped going to him because of it. But I've heard he's one hell of a good doctor. Without him, Armi's sister, Mallu, would be dead. So I don't know."

"What happened? What was wrong with her?"

"Bad miscarriage, real bad. Ask Armi. But don't ask now— that's Mallu right there behind Armi."

Armi was leading a thinner and darker-haired version of herself toward us. I tossed the rest of the cognac down my gullet and poured myself another. I had already had my fill of new people and obligatory smiles. I spoke politely with Armi and Mallu, but Mallu didn't seem any more interested in talking than I did. Armi dominated the conversation, with Kimmo and Antti throwing in a comment when they could get a word in edgewise. Someone refilled my cognac. I was starting to get drunk. When we heard dance music start coming from inside, Kimmo said that three musicians from a local big-band orchestra had been hired for the party and were playing in the living room.

"Shall we dance?" Makke had appeared and was bowing to me somewhat ironically. When I nodded, he led me inside. Under his dress shirt, I could feel Makke's hard shoulder muscles. His hand was on my back, sweaty from the warm night and cognac. Makke smelled of too much aftershave, but he was the perfect-height dance partner for me. Antti and I always have trouble because he's a full foot taller than me. Other couples slid past us: Kimmo and Armi, my boss and his wife, Antti with his mother. The cognac was pulsing from my head down to my feet as the trio turned to tango music and Makke bent me into a perfect dip.

Dancing past the mantelpiece, I caught sight of a large graduation picture of Sanna, wearing that bored smile of hers. I'd been a freshman in high school when she graduated, and, after the ceremony, half of the school had been drinking at the only park in my little hometown. Sanna was falling-down drunk and some people were whispering that she had taken something stronger too. I remembered how a bottle of rowanberry wine slipped from her lips and the red liquid stained her jacket. Sanna took it off, and the skimpy camisole she had underneath revealed arms adorned with cigarette burns and slashes, maybe from a razor blade. I had heard rumors about her arms before, but that was the first time I'd seen them in all their gruesome glory.

Makke noticed the picture too.

"I'm surprised they invited me here," he whispered in my ear. "I guess they wanted to show that they forgive me."

"Sanna's death wasn't your fault," I whispered back.

"If I hadn't been so drunk, I would have been able to stop her from going swimming," Makke replied.

"And if you hadn't been drunk, Sanna wouldn't have been either. Listen, Makke, if there's one thing I've learned in life, it's that there's no point what-if-ing."

If only I could have remembered that myself the next day.

The rest of the evening was actually fun. Perhaps I had the cognac to thank or perhaps the skill of the musicians. We headed home at around one thirty, about the same time as Armi and Kimmo. We were already down the driveway when I heard Armi yell from the Hänninens' front gate.

"See you tomorrow at two with your skirt! And we can talk; I have so much to ask you!"

2

When I woke up, around noon, my mouth felt sticky, and even after my morning coffee and a long, cold shower, my temples still throbbed. As I took two ibuprofen in preparation for my ride to Armi's house, Antti declared he was taking the day off and went out into the yard to read a collection of French poetry. I would have liked to stay and lie next to him, perhaps lazily making love under the cherry blossoms.

"If I'm not here when you get back," he said, "I'll be over swimming at the breakwater."

"Wait for me. We'll go together. This will only take about an hour."

"Don't count on it. Armi's quite a gossip—you'll be stuck there forever," Antti said.

As I pedaled across town, I thought about how little interest I had in trading girlish secrets with Armi. It was oppressively hot, and though the bike path was relatively flat most of the way, I started sweating immediately and desperately needed something to drink by the time I made it to Armi's street.

Armi lived in a rented one-bedroom row house. I remembered Kimmo explaining the day before, his mildly drunk eyes amorously gazing at Armi, that she had two homes: this little place and a house she shared with her parents in Haukilahti, on the other side of the freeway. I hoped Kimmo would be here too; it would take some of the pressure off me.

I rang the doorbell three times, but no one answered. Strange. Could Armi be in the shower? She didn't seem like the type to dally in the shower in the middle of the day, but then again, it had been a late night. Just to be sure, I checked my watch. Two o'clock. That was what we'd arranged, and I didn't think Armi had been so drunk as not to remember. Perhaps she was sitting in the backyard and couldn't hear the doorbell.

When I walked around the building, I discovered a lush backyard, bordering a small stand of trees. Creeping vines hung over the gate, and a high fence, also covered in vines, prevented any view into the neighboring yards. I peeked carefully through the gate.

"Armi?"

No answer. I stepped through into the yard. After the shadows of the trees, it was a hangover nightmare: the bright sunshine stabbed at my temples, and the red of the flowers blazing in the beds felt excessive. A garden table and a couple of chairs stood surrounded by flowering yellow forsythia bushes. A pitcher of juice and two glasses sat invitingly on the table. I noticed something else behind one of the bushes and stepped toward it.

A foot. Judging from the pink nail polish on the toes, a woman's foot.

There was Armi, lying on her stomach with her face buried in the grass. I walked closer, repeating her name, but she neither stood nor answered. In my police work, I'd seen enough dead bodies to know one when I saw one, but I still checked her pulse and carefully turned her head.

Her swollen, purple tongue lolled out of her mouth like a child pretending to be a dog. The face was Armi's, but it was still grotesquely unfamiliar. I wanted to close the eyes that stared back at me in terror, but I knew I shouldn't.

I tried not to vomit. Luckily, the back door to the house was open. I found the telephone in the entryway. Holding the receiver with a paper towel, I called the police. Next, I rushed to the bathroom and, still using the paper towel, turned on the shower and plunged my head under the running water. After that and drinking nearly a liter of water, I felt ready to go back out to the yard to meet the police.

Every detail burned into my brain. The little black-and-white bird hopping around in the flowerbeds. The bumblebee buzzing from one red blossom to another. The iridescent fly that had parked itself on the lip of the juice pitcher, gleaming in the hot sun. I didn't want to look at Armi, but I couldn't help it. And why wouldn't I look? The movie running in my brain was superimposing her mottled face over the other images the whole time anyway.

I was used to registering the details of a crime scene. And this was most certainly a crime scene. Judging from the marks on the ground, Armi had put up stiff resistance while she was being strangled. I couldn't make out any actual footprints in the grass, but maybe the forensic laboratory would be able to get more out of the jumble of scrapes and gouges.

The patrol cars were quick in coming, the local officers' eager eyes saying that a murder was clearly a welcome break in their usual routine of rounding up drunks. The ranking officer introduced himself as Detective Makkonen and started asking me questions, but the rest of his squad just stood there, wondering what they were supposed to do. Their dithering irritated me, and I had to exercise serious restraint to keep myself from ordering them to start taking pictures and looking for fingerprints.

However, these were just beat cops—they didn't even have the proper equipment or investigative training.

The medical examiner and county forensics team took longer to show up. The lead detective was familiar to me from my time at the police academy: Detective Sergeant Pertti Ström. He, Tapsa Helminen—who worked in the Helsinki Narcotics Unit now—and I were all at the top of our class. The men were rising through the ranks nicely now, I thought, while I'd bailed out of the profession. Though, Ström had spent some time in law school too—in Turku, if I remembered correctly.

"Hi, Kallio," Ström said, seemingly a little thrown off guard when he saw me. "When did you transfer to the Espoo?"

"I didn't. I found the body."

"Do you know her?"

"Not very well. She's my...my boyfriend's brother-in-law's stepbrother's fiancée," I explained, confusing even myself. "I met her yesterday for the first time, and I was only coming to borrow her sewing machine."

Once Ström took the lead, things started to roll along in the usual rhythm. The medical examiner arrived at two forty-five, and his initial opinion was that Armi had died one to three hours earlier. The killer had stood behind her, he said, and choked her with his hands. Judging from the size and location of the bruises, the murderer had relatively large hands and was more likely a man than a woman. There was something strange about the marks, though, which indicated that the hands had not been bare.

"Possibly rubber gloves," he said. "Let's see if we can find some dishwashing gloves in the house."

At this point, it dawned on Ström that he shouldn't be letting me listen in on the results of the investigation. As he asked me to leave, he requested that I refrain from telling anyone but Antti about Armi's death. He didn't have to explain—I knew the drill.

Once I got out of the neighborhood and back onto the main bike path, I started feeling ill again, and vomited up the water and my breakfast in a ditch carpeted with buttercups. A few passersby glanced at me pityingly. My legs were shaking so badly that I could barely pedal home. Luckily, the end of the trip was downhill.

Nothing had changed in the yard. Antti was still lounging in the yard with his book of poems. Einstein was sleeping with his tail in the sun and the rest of his body in the shade, and neither of them seemed to notice me.

"You're back soon," Antti lazily observed. "Still want to go swimming? Hey, what's wrong?" He had finally lifted his eyes from his book.

I explained briefly. Antti's face took on a strange expression, and, for a little while, he couldn't say anything. Suddenly the day felt cold, and even the cat was tense, awakening with a swish of his tail and hissing angrily at a swallow that flew low over him.

"You mean Armi is dead…murdered?" Antti finally said. The words came out slowly, as if he were punching at a piano with stuck keys. "Are you sure?"

"I wasn't the only one who checked her pulse. Half of the cops in the county were there."

"Does Kimmo know?"

"I suppose the police have gone to tell him. They asked about next of kin, and I told them Kimmo."

"I'm going to his place." Antti stood up.

"No, you are not! Let the police do their jobs. And don't tell anyone yet either, not the Hänninens…or…"

"Why?"

"This is a murder. Someone did this to Armi, probably someone she knew. Someone she had served juice to."

"Goddamn it! I can't do this again! Last summer my friends, and now my relatives! You and your murders can go to hell!" Antti rushed inside, and I heard through the open window as his feet pounded down the stairs to his basement office. We had agreed that the office was off-limits to me; I would go down there only in extreme circumstances, so Antti could have somewhere to be in peace if he wanted.

I felt abandoned. I mean, I was the one who needed comforting here. I was the one who had found the body. I couldn't say I would mourn for Armi, because I barely knew her, but finding a body is traumatic, even for someone with experience on the police force. Indignation and anger won out over my nausea, so I marched out to the shed and started chopping wood.

After splitting a few logs' worth, I had managed to calm down. I took a shower to wash off the sweat, and started getting hungry and thirsty. Of course, I understood Antti. The previous summer, one of his childhood friends had murdered another. That had been a hard experience for Antti and still haunted us both. That case had been more than routine police work for me too, but it had turned Antti's life completely upside down. I guess our relationship was the only good thing to come out of it.

I made myself a couple of open-faced salami sandwiches and emptied a bottle of pilsner. Still, Antti was being a stupid ass. Was it supposed to be my fault that someone killed Armi?

Unless…unless Armi's parting words the previous night had meant something other than her wanting to gossip and ask me nosy questions about my relationship with Antti. What if Armi had wanted to talk to the lawyer and former police officer, not

compare wedding plans? Maybe someone who didn't want us talking had gotten to her first. Someone who was at the Hänninens'
garden party and heard us arranging our two o'clock get-together.

I was trying to think of who might have been listening,
when the phone rang.

"Hi, it's Kimmo," said a frightened voice.

"Kimmo! I'm so sorry. Do you want to come over? Or do
you want to talk to Antti?"

"No, I want to talk to you. They've arrested me for Armi's
murder. Will you be my lawyer?"

"Arrested? Did you do it?"

"No!" I could hear he was crying. "But I…Come here,
Maria, and I'll explain."

"Come where?"

"The Espoo police station."

"Is there a police officer close? Give the phone to him for a
minute. I'll be there as soon as I can, hopefully in about half an
hour. Try to keep it together that long. Don't say anything to them."

The officer guarding Kimmo was terse but would at least
tell me that Kimmo was under arrest for suspicion of the murder
of Armi Mäenpää, with sufficient evidence to hold him.

"Is Detective Sergeant Ström available?"

"He's at the suspect's apartment."

I didn't bother calling Ström. The most important thing was
to get to Kimmo and calm him down. Arrested for murder, sufficient evidence. Kimmo being the murderer was logical. It was
usually someone close to the victim. Did they have a fight? Was
he drunk? But picturing Kimmo as a strangler was a stretch.

Figuring this was an extreme circumstance, I headed down
to Antti's office and knocked on the door before entering. He
was lying on the sofa staring at the ceiling.

"I'm sorry for bothering you, but Kimmo called. He's under arrest and needs a lawyer. I'm going to the police station."

"Kimmo? I'm coming with you."

"They won't let you see him. Stay here. You can probably call the Hänninens now, since Kimmo is in custody."

"But it doesn't make any sense. Kimmo! Are they complete idiots?"

"Can you call me a taxi? I have to change clothes."

I dressed, did my hair, and threw on some makeup in record time. After five minutes of furious activity, I stood in front of the mirror with a competent young lawyer staring back at me, the hungover party girl buried under a layer of concealer and blush. I penciled in my eyebrows, preparing for battle. The taxi was waiting in the driveway, and within a quarter of an hour from receiving Kimmo's call, I was in the police station.

Detective Sergeant Ström had arrived in the meantime. I explained my position, and he sized me up as he would an enemy.

"Well, your common sense is going to tell you Hänninen is guilty too, when you see him and hear what he was doing when we found him," Ström said ominously. "He claims he left Mäenpää's place at twelve fifteen, that she was alive and painting her nails, but of course she was already dead by then. And the jerkoff was celebrating what he'd done!"

Now I was lost. Ström's harsh language was surprisingly unprofessional. But I started to catch on to what he meant by "jerkoff" once he led me to the small interview room.

After the bright sunshine outside and in the glassed-in lobby, the interview room felt dark, with dim overhead lights. Kimmo sat in the gloom like a shiny black shadow, his curls standing out in a frizzy golden halo.

Then I realized what Kimmo was wearing: a rubber suit, overalls that looked like a wetsuit, only thinner. I thought he must be cold, because his face looked blue and withdrawn.

"What the hell are you wearing?" I asked Kimmo. I snapped at Ström, "Were you in such a damn hurry to arrest him that you couldn't even let him put on some decent clothes? Do you still have someone at his house? If you don't, then send one of your boys to get him some clothes. Otherwise, I'll file a complaint for inhumane treatment of a prisoner. Kimmo, is there anyone at home at your house?"

"Mom is with Matti and Mikko in Helsinki, and Dad is on his way to Ecuador."

"Ström, give me the phone."

Antti answered after two rings. I asked him to go get clothes for Kimmo. When I hung up, Ström was staring at me angrily.

"You really have switched camps," he said, lighting a cigarette.

"What do you mean 'switched camps'? As I recall, the academy taught us both the same fundamentals of how to treat someone in custody. And smoke your cancer stick outside. You've fumigated this room quite enough already."

"So you're a tight-ass now too?" Ström ground his cigarette into the floor, dangerously close to my left shoe. "When we went to interview the victim's boyfriend here, we found him jacking off in that rubber suit, surrounded by sadist porn magazines. I can show you the evidence if you want! The girl's fingerprints were all over the suit, and do you see the rip on the left calf? We found the missing piece in her yard. Looks like his little sex game got out of hand."

"Did you find any evidence of sexual assault?"

"Guess he didn't have time. He got cold feet and went home to rub one out!"

Ström left, slamming the door behind him. The guard left with us scowled. Kimmo's attire probably wasn't helping my mood, but Ström's behavior was infuriating. He'd always been cocky, but his quick advancement through the ranks was obviously going to his head. Tapsa Helminen had almost made me break his elbow before he'd started treating me as an equal, and with Ström, I'd had to wipe the floor with him repeatedly on our theory exams. He found comfort in being the best sharpshooter in our class, though.

"Kimmo! I'm really sorry about this whole mess."

The guard didn't try to stop me from wrapping my arms around Kimmo, although technically it was against the rules. As if I hadn't broken any other rules in my life. The rubber surrounding him felt surprisingly warm and smooth, and my hands slid easily across it.

"Can you tell me what happened? When did you last see Armi?" I sat down next to him and dug my notepad out of my bag.

"I saw her this morning...I spent the night there. I was a little hungover, but I was up by nine a.m. Armi was still sleeping. I put this on and went out to lounge in the sun in Armi's backyard. I guess I fell asleep again. Armi came out around ten thirty and woke me up. She startled me, and I guess that's when I ripped my suit. I took it off and we made coffee. We talked for a while, and then I went home. She wanted me to leave—she said she wanted to speak to you privately and that she still had some calls to make before you got there."

"Did she tell you what she wanted to talk to me about? Or who she needed to call?"

"No, she didn't. She was a little...crabby."

"Did you have a fight? About what?"

"We weren't really fighting. Armi just didn't like this rubber suit." Kimmo blushed, his cheeks turning the same cherry color as the trees in my yard. "We had...an agreement. That I wouldn't...when she could see. And then I asked her to touch me..." Kimmo labored over every word, his face turning redder and redder, until he finally started crying. I dug out a tissue and let him cry.

"If I would have known I was seeing her for the last time..." He sniffed. "Is she really dead? Did you see that she was dead?"

"Yes, Armi is dead. But she was alive when you left. What did you talk about?"

"We were supposed to be getting married this fall when my thesis is done. I even have a job all lined up. We were talking about how I...I can't..." Kimmo burst into tears again, and, at the same moment, Ström opened the door and walked in with a bundle of clothes.

"Get dressed, Hänninen. That pervert suit is staying with us."

I stood to leave so he could change clothes. I seemed to remember being in a sauna once with Kimmo, but I wanted to show an example of how to respect the dignity of a detainee. Ström and the guard stayed inside.

Antti was standing in the hallway looking confused.

"Why are you still here?" I sounded more unfriendly than I meant to.

"It would be nice to know why you sent me running all over Espoo looking for Kimmo's clothes. And then Kimmo's mom came home while I was there, and the cops scared her out of her wits. What am I supposed to tell Annamari? And what about Risto and Marita? Did Kimmo do it?"

"I don't think so. Tell them that. But in any case, someone did kill her. Not me and not you, but maybe one of the others."

"Why do you say that?"

"We'll talk about it at home. You can't do any good here now. They won't let you in to see Kimmo. I'll tell him you were here." I wrapped my arm around Antti's waist for a moment, trying to relieve the stiffness between us.

"Annamari went to see Marita and Risto. I guess I should go there too, although I'd rather be alone."

"Once I finish up here, I'll swing by the Hänninens' house and then come get you so we can go home together."

Getting dressed in normal clothing had clearly calmed Kimmo down. Ström left to take the rubber suit somewhere, pinching it with gloved fingers and holding it away from him like a leper's garment. I wondered whether they had dusted it for fingerprints while it was still on Kimmo.

"Antti says he's sorry for your loss and wishes he could see you. Do you feel up to answering some more questions?"

Kimmo nodded feebly.

"So what were you and Armi talking about this morning?"

"Our sex life. I like dressing up in rubber, and I thought making love in it sometimes would be nice, but Armi didn't want to. We agreed a long time ago that I can do whatever I want by myself so long as I don't get Armi involved. This morning, I just wanted to make love, but she got mad at me for breaking our agreement. We were talking about what we were going to do about it after we were married, but we couldn't agree on anything. Then we both felt like it would be better for me to go home. That was about twelve fifteen."

I glanced at the guard, who was listening with open interest. Professional confidentiality or not, it was a sure bet that half of Espoo would soon know about Kimmo Hänninen's curious sexual proclivities. He'd gotten himself into a real bind. Every new thing he told me just made his situation seem worse. I wished I could talk to him alone, because I was going to have to make him reveal more about his sexual interests.

"So you weren't actually fighting?"

"Well, no. We've talked about this so many times; it didn't go that far."

"And then you went home?"

"Yeah. Mom was going into the city with the twins, and since I was left home alone..."

"You put the rubber suit back on and browsed through some of the...uh...appropriate magazines." For some reason I was blushing too.

"Yeah. And I didn't hear anything. Maybe the police rang the doorbell, but I guess Mom left the door open, and suddenly a crowd of guys was standing at my bedroom door and I..."

"And they arrested you, just like that?"

"At first, they didn't even say why they had barged into the house. They just started going through my magazines and digging around in the closets. Then someone told me that Armi was dead. Then they brought me here. I still don't completely understand. When we got here, they asked if I wanted a lawyer, and I remembered you."

"Well, they did a hell of a job! Listen, Kimmo, I don't think there is any conclusive evidence here. Legally they can't hold you here any longer than forty-eight hours. I know this is a nightmare for you, with Armi gone and you accused of a murder you didn't commit. But just try to hold on, and you'll be a free man again soon."

I could hear how empty that cliché sounded. Things would never go back to the way they had been. Armi was dead, there would be no fall wedding, and soon the courts and the media would publicly be discussing the most intimate aspects of Kimmo's personal life. Right now, I couldn't do anything but let the guard take him back to his holding cell.

Ström was still hanging around. Obviously, he wanted to continue Kimmo's interrogation. I tried to adopt a friendlier posture as I walked over to talk to him.

"I've heard Hänninen's version of events now. Could you tell me your own? Why did you charge in like that?"

"What right do you have to ask?"

"Ström. We can make this whole thing very uncomfortable for each other. You can yell at me, and I can yell back and file complaints. But isn't it in both of our interests to catch the real perpetrator as fast as we can?"

"You don't think Hänninen is guilty?"

"How about instead you tell me why you think he is guilty."

"Well, first off, he was the last person who saw the victim alive. We're interviewing the neighbors right now. Who knows, maybe someone saw Hänninen leave and then saw the girl alive afterward. That wouldn't prevent Hänninen from having gone back, though. But if one of the neighbors did see someone else going there, and we find evidence on someone else that's just as good as what we have compiled on Hänninen, then we'll reconsider."

I stared Ström straight in the eye, even though I had to crane my neck to do so. With broad shoulders that rose toward slightly protruding ears, his heavy frame seemed tense. His washed-out brown eyes avoided my gaze as sweat began to emerge from the large pores in the skin of his face.

"And second, you know just as well as I do that these sorts of homicides are usually the work of someone close to the victim. And who was closer to her than her fiancé? Seems pretty straightforward to me."

"Each man kills the thing he loves," I muttered.

"What?"

"Oh, nothing." I didn't think Ström would know a line from an Oscar Wilde poem or have seen Fassbinder's *Querelle*. "But this is all circumstantial evidence."

"Whoever strangled Mäenpää was wearing rubber gloves. Hänninen was wearing rubber gloves when we showed up. They're in the lab right now. The rubber suit had Mäenpää's fingerprints on it. A piece ripped from it was under Mäenpää's leg on the lawn. Mäenpää fought against her attacker, and she had pretty long nails. Maybe she was able to rip a piece off of the suit with them."

"Are there scratches on Hänninen's thigh?"

"There was some kind of scrape."

"Have a doctor look at it."

"We just have to wait for the lab results on the gloves. If the gloves are a match, then this case is closed."

"I don't think rubber leaves a mark that easily," I countered.

"And besides, there was all the stuff Hänninen had in his room. Rubber clothing, chains, ropes. Handcuffs. A whip. And look at these magazines!" Ström slapped down a stack of English- and German-language magazines with names like *Skin Two*, «*O*», and *Bondage*. Each featured stylized pictures of beautiful women in rubber or leather clothing, with chains or without, bound or laid out for whipping. Looking at them with Ström so close was embarrassing, because for me many of the pictures were more than a little intriguing.

"He's clearly a pervert. This is the same as that Marquis de Sade stuff, and in those books, they hanged and strangled women all the time. The whole thing makes my stomach turn. Someone should put all these S&M freaks out of their misery. If you had seen what he was doing when we went in there, you would be just as convinced he's guilty."

"Why did you storm into the house?"

"Think about it. We're going to find a dead woman's partner, automatically a prime suspect. No one answers the door, but it's open and there are noises coming from upstairs. Who wouldn't think he might try to kill himself once he realized what he had done?"

"OK. So what was he really doing when you went in?"

"Well, he was covered head to toe in rubber, he'd put handcuffs on himself, he was looking at those magazines and…gratifying himself."

"Easy collar since he already had cuffs on," I said, but for some reason Ström wasn't amused.

"So there are materials in the lab, Armi's body is with the medical examiner, and your boys are interviewing the neighbors," I continued. "Have you notified Armi's parents?"

"What kind of idiots do you take us for? We had to call a damn doctor to calm down her mother. Some of the neighbors left for their summer cottages for the weekend, so their interviews will have to wait until Monday. So yeah, the wheels are turning even without your supervision."

"I don't doubt it. Do you still want to interview Hänninen? Because you're not questioning him without me present."

"I'm going to eat now and then go back to the crime scene. Come back at eight, and we'll continue then."

We talked for a minute more about practical matters: how long they were going to hold Kimmo, and what legal requirements had to be met. Ström was adamant that the evidence was sufficient to keep Kimmo in custody indefinitely. I disagreed. I decided to go to the Hänninens' house to check in with them. I'd call my boss from there.

As I walked along the familiar birch-lined lane, I considered why I didn't believe Kimmo was the murderer. It wasn't because I liked him—I had liked murderers before. Something just seemed off. And I intended to find out what.

3

A strange quiet hung over the Hänninen residence. The yard was spotless, as if a cleaning company had come with a giant vacuum to suck up all traces of the previous day's festivities. Risto answered the door wearing an expression of exhaustion and grief. The others were sitting in the large living room. Annamari Hänninen was drinking cognac, with Marita's arm wrapped around her. Antti stood next to the picture of Sanna on the mantle. He didn't even say hello.

Annamari lifted her eyes from her glass.

"Oh, Maria, how is my Kimmo holding up? When will they release him? I've been trying to call Eki Henttonen to ask him to help too, but..."

"Eki is out sailing and probably just isn't answering his phone. Don't worry; he'll be back by tomorrow night. Kimmo is doing just fine given the circumstances, and they can't hold him for more than forty-eight hours. Where are the kids?"

Marita explained, "My parents took them to Inkoo. They left about half an hour ago and took Einstein too. We thought it would be best if they left for a while. Sanna's death was such a terrible shock for the boys, and I don't know how they're going to take losing Armi now too."

Was wearing a long-sleeved black outfit on a hot summer day normal for her, or had she put it on out of respect for Armi? In her dress, Marita was a thin black line, drawn with a slightly trembling brush down the pale blue wall of the Hänninens' living room. Like Antti, Marita was naturally thin, but what on Antti was muscle, on Marita was only tendons.

I gave an abbreviated account of both my discovery of Armi's body and Kimmo's story. Talking about the rubber suit and S&M magazines was difficult, despite their essential role in the evidence the police had gathered so far. Apparently Annamari was not aware of her son's sexual tendencies—what parents ever are?—because she began to shake uncontrollably.

"Oh my God, what am I going to tell Henrik? I have to call Ecuador. What does this mean about Kimmo if he was doing that? Weren't things good for him with Armi?"

During my first year in high school, Annamari had been my French teacher. A frail, nervous type, she had never been able to control the class even by screaming. Usually I was the one to finally yell "Shut up!" for her and actually get results. I received an A in her class but was still relieved when she moved away a year later to follow her husband's new job. Her successor was a total wet blanket, but at least I didn't have to be embarrassed for my teacher anymore.

Now Annamari seemed to be losing all physical control. Her head bounced around restlessly; her body was in constant motion. Her brittle, shrieky voice rose.

"How can the police think that Kimmo would murder someone? My child…At least his own mother should be able to see him! Can I come with you, Maria?"

"Annamari, you should try to rest a little," Risto said firmly. The use of her first name grated in my ears, feeling disrespectful even though I knew that Annamari was only Risto's stepmother, not mother. "Let's go to the boys' room and you can lie down. It will be quiet in there."

His head bowed, Risto pressed almost affectionately against Annamari's shoulders as he guided her from the room.

"Hopefully Risto has the sense to give her a sedative," Marita observed dryly. "Do we have anything left or should we call Dr. Hellström to ask for a prescription?"

"Do gynecologists write prescriptions for tranquilizers?" I asked.

"He also does some family practice," Marita explained. "Not everyone likes him, of course. I guess mom got angry with him over something and changed doctors. He is a bit of a gossip, but when you need help, he just asks when and where." Marita swept back her hair in a familiar gesture; I realized that Antti did the same thing when he was nervous or upset. Under her hair, I caught a glimpse of a large, fresh-looking bruise on her neck.

"If Hellström is such a talker, I guess I should interview him too. I have to find grounds for Kimmo's release."

"So you still don't believe Kimmo did it?" Antti asked, uttering his first words since I arrived.

"No. I admit I'm basing that more on a feeling than anything I know for sure, but no, I don't believe it. Convincing the police of that is going to require facts. What did you know about Armi? What kind of person was she?"

Neither seemed interested in answering. As I waited, I mentally tallied what I knew about her: she was sweet, talkative, meddlesome, curious, determined.

"Armi was like an angel from heaven for Kimmo, even if Annamari didn't much care for her," Marita finally said. "And Armi was a bit...common, although of course in Annamari's mind no one was good enough for her children. Makke certainly got a taste of that medicine, as all of Sanna's boyfriends did."

"Are you trying to suggest that Annamari killed Armi?" Maria asked.

"No, oh God no! Armi just said what she thought, and that isn't the Hänninen way. At last Christmas dinner, for example, she asked why Henrik and Annamari don't get divorced, since for all intents and purposes Henrik doesn't have anything to do with his family. You don't ask questions like that if you want to be a Hänninen."

Outwardly immaculate, Marita had always seemed like just another Hänninen trying to maintain the façade, and finding out there was something more under the surface was comforting. Getting to know Antti's family had been exhausting, and the social scene that came along with our move to Espoo was oppressive. Now I was just becoming more and more tangled in the strange knots of their lives.

Sounds started coming from my stomach. I realized that it was almost seven o'clock, and all I'd had since vomiting into that ditch was a slice of bread and some salami.

"Is there anything around here I could eat?" I asked, feeling rude, though I knew I should try to feel more at home. "I need to get back to the police station, and my brain doesn't work well without food. I can make it myself if Antti shows me where everything is."

I wanted to be alone with Antti, even though he didn't seem in a terribly sociable mood.

In the kitchen, some of the chaos of the previous evening still showed. The dishwasher hung open, and the refrigerator was full of leftovers from the buffet table. Without a twinge of guilt, I finished off the shrimp salad and the last piece of caviar *smörgåstårta* cake, and then, with my coffee, had a cream puff that tasted like refrigerator.

Antti's silence irritated me. Sure, he knew Armi and Kimmo much better than I did, but this wasn't exactly a personal tragedy for him.

"Have a cognac, Antti. It will help. Have a double if you need to."

"How will that help? Why should I drown my emotions? Do you have to be so damn professional all the time? Is that how you stifle your feelings, or do you just not have any?"

"Yeah, that's right, what fucking feelings? You know me— not a day goes by without a murder and a look at a nice dead body! Asshole. Listen, right now I don't have time for feelings. Getting Kimmo out of that cell and finding out who killed Armi is going to take more than feelings."

Who knows how much worse that conversation would have ended up had Risto not entered the kitchen?

"Marita said there was coffee in here. I gave Annamari the last Valium in the house, and that put her out," Risto explained, turning to the coffeemaker and pouring himself a cup.

"Hey, would it be too much to ask for you to give me a ride to the police station?" I asked in a cautious tone. I knew Risto liked driving. I didn't even touch Antti as I left.

"What should we tell my dad?" Risto asked once we were in the car and on our way.

"Where is he now? Ecuador? Do you have to tell him right away?"

"Annamari is demanding it, and yes, it's important information. She wants him to come back and act like a father." Risto's voice was impassive.

I hadn't seen Henrik Hänninen in ten years. Once during that winter when the Hänninens lived in my hometown, my parents, who were also teachers, had invited their new colleague and her husband over for dinner. Horrible menstrual cramps had kept me home that night.

Annamari Hänninen had seemed a little scattered, but Henrik might as well not even have been present. He didn't seem the slightest bit interested in what was happening around him. Over the years, he became distant physically as well, taking one foreign posting after another for his company. Soon after Sanna's death, he left for Ecuador and wasn't due to come back from that assignment until the end of the year. His habit of interacting with his grandchildren, Matti and Mikko, only by sending them expensive gifts left Antti's parents—the boys' other grandparents—indignant.

"I don't think it's worth calling your father back yet. What could he do here? Getting in contact with Eki Henttonen is much more important—try the number for his boat a few more times. And keep Annamari away from the police station." I realized I was issuing orders again to people I had no authority over, but Risto didn't seem to mind.

"Listen, Risto, I wasn't at my most focused last night when Antti and I left the house. Do you remember who was still there? Most of the group had already left."

Risto didn't inquire why I was asking; he simply thought for a moment and then answered.

"I wasn't the most sober either. I'd knocked back a few too many glasses of cognac with Eki. So who was still here? Eki at least, and of course Kimmo and Armi and Mallu, Armi's sister. Makke was still around, over in the lawn swing, talking with Annamari. Which surprised me a little, since I had thought they weren't even on speaking terms. You know that Makke—"

"Yeah, I know. I thought it was nice of you to invite him to the party."

"Well, if we're being honest, Sanna was the instigator in their drinking, not Makke," Risto said darkly as he turned into the police station parking lot. "Sanna had been working on dying one way or another for so long that there's no one else we can blame."

I didn't know Risto very well, and this was the first personal conversation he had ever shared with me. The severity of his tone surprised me. For the first time, I saw a break in the façade of efficiency and congeniality he usually maintained. What had the relationship between the Hänninen siblings been like? I would have liked to continue what had become an interesting discussion, but my meeting time was quickly approaching, and being present to defend Kimmo was the best thing I could do now.

"If Antti is still at the house, tell him I might be home late. Really late." When the guard finally ushered me into the interrogation room, Kimmo looked somehow shrunken. I told him that his family sent love and support, but nothing I said seemed to register with him. Detective Sergeant Ström was getting nowhere either—as the interview began, it was as though Kimmo were in a trance.

"Wouldn't it be best to call a doctor?" I finally asked as Ström became increasingly agitated. "You can see yourself that he's in no shape for questioning."

"He's just playacting. He finally realized what deep shit he's in."

I didn't doubt that in the slightest. Kimmo wasn't stupid. And, of course, if he had killed Armi…

Ström told us that none of the neighbors the police had reached remembered noticing anything out of the ordinary the morning of the murder. The next-door neighbor had not been at home, and the only thing the neighbor two doors down saw was me riding up on my bicycle. I wondered why Ström was giving us so much information. Was it a strategy, trying to convince me that all the evidence pointed to Kimmo being the murderer?

After drinking a cup of coffee, Kimmo perked up enough to be able to go over the events of the morning again. He assured us that the disagreement they'd had over the rubber clothing hadn't prevented Armi from wanting to marry him in October.

"Why October? If you had decided to get married, why not do it earlier?" Ström asked.

"We bought an apartment in a new building in North Tapiola, and it won't be ready until early October."

"Where did you get enough money to buy an apartment? Aren't you a student?"

"Armi was stashing money away for a house for years; she had one of those government-subsidized down-payment savings accounts. And my dad is paying my part. I *am* working, by the way: I'm on full salary while I write my thesis."

To my great joy, I could see that Kimmo was starting to rise to his own defense.

"So who gets the apartment now that the bride-to-be is dead?" Ström continued cruelly.

Kimmo stared at him with glazed eyes, again as if he hadn't understood the question.

"Come off it, Ström," I said, interrupting the questioning. "How could Kimmo have thought about something like that yet?"

"Maybe the kid wanted to cut his mother's apron strings but wasn't quite ready to have a wife tie new ones on yet," Ström taunted. "Or maybe he didn't want to leave his mother yet after all."

Kimmo groaned and buried his face in his hands. I took a few deep breaths, suppressing my desire to rearrange Ström's previously broken nose. What would it help? Ström had decided that Kimmo was guilty, and I would need more than hunches to convince him otherwise. How had Ström made it so far up the ladder so quickly when he had such obvious biases?

Ström gave up sweating Kimmo at about nine thirty, and we arranged to continue at ten o'clock the next morning.

"Unless you want to go to church, Kallio," Ström tossed after me as I left.

I didn't want to think about what Kimmo's night at the police station would be like. How many other men were bunking in his cell? They would all know each other's crimes almost immediately, and if the police guard made even the slightest hint about Kimmo's rubber costume, the other men in custody would be like wolves at his throat.

Outside, the night air was just as warm as it had been the previous evening. I didn't have a clue about the bus schedule, so I decided to walk home. Luckily, I had put on comfortable shoes that morning, though a backpack would have been an improvement over my heavy shoulder bag.

Because I didn't have a map, I played it safe and stuck to the main road leading south toward Tapiola. After crossing the pedestrian bridge over the freeway, the surrounding neighborhoods were amazingly quiet—I suppose on Saturdays in the summer, most of the nightlife focuses around summer cottages and downtown Helsinki. Anyone left over was probably sitting on the couch watching the never-ending stream of police procedurals on TV.

As I walked, I mulled over my case. If Kimmo didn't kill Armi, then who did? What was the call Armi wanted to be left alone to make? Did Armi have something she wanted to tell me that could have been a threat to someone?

I hoped that Ström had the sense to check on all the usual suspects who had done time for rape or murder but were back on the street. Who knew? Maybe this was just some random recidivist. Or some neighbor who got sick of Kimmo and Armi's hanky-panky in the backyard and snapped.

Our law office was quiet at the moment. Eki had hired me at the beginning of the summer specifically so I could have time to acclimate, but I wasn't yet a full member of the bar. If this case were to go to trial, Eki would have to act as Kimmo's attorney. What was my title now? "Legal counsel," I guess. That sounded sufficiently official to justify continuing my investigation. I didn't know what Eki would say about it, but I wanted to do a little private detective work.

Plenty of people needed interviewing: Armi's parents, her sister, and her boss, whom I would try to get hold of the next day.

And all the others: Risto, Annamari, Marita. They would all have something to tell me. One of Ström's wiseass comments came back to me. What if Annamari really didn't want Kimmo to marry Armi? What if she was afraid of being left all alone in that big house? It seemed far-fetched, but then again, Annamari had always been unbalanced. How was I to know how Sanna's death might have affected her? Maybe she'd gone off the deep end.

Risto and, up to this point, Kimmo had struck me as surprisingly sane products of an absent father and hysterical mother, as if all the mental anguish in the family had accumulated exclusively in Sanna. Although, what did I really know about Risto and Kimmo? Was Kimmo a sadist or a masochist? Did that matter? We had to talk about his sexuality—the evidence necessitated it—but how do you ask a friend questions like that?

Upon reaching a large cross street, I turned left and walked until I reached a park where several groups of young people sat scattered around the grassy meadow drinking. From there, I proceeded past a school and church, following the path down to the bay. The lights of the occasional car shone from the West Highway bridges. A bustling hedgehog snuffled toward me on the shoreline path. I remembered that Einstein was in Inkoo and wouldn't be there to rub against my legs when I arrived home.

Home. Espoo wasn't *my* home. Hardly any of my belongings were here, since my beloved flea-market furniture was still in Antti's apartment in the city. Most of my books were in the city. Summer would be over soon, and where would I live then? Not in Antti's apartment—we wouldn't fit.

Antti was staring at music videos on TV when I entered the living room. In his hand was an empty whiskey glass; an empty bottle stood on the table. Antti rarely drank two nights in a row, but now he seemed to have taken my advice seriously. As he turned his head my way, I saw that the alcohol hadn't completely deadened his feelings. He had been crying.

"That took a long time," he said with apparent calm.

"I walked here from the police station, since it didn't look like any buses were coming."

"You walked? That's so you."

I didn't know whether that was meant to be positive or negative.

"How is Kimmo?" Antti took a sip of whiskey, as if to brace against my reply.

"Pretty messed up, but he's sticking to his original story even though he knows it looks pretty bad."

"Henttonen called half an hour ago. They'd made it all the way out to the tip of the Porkkala Peninsula before his hangover caught up with him. They docked on Stora Träskö and are heading back early tomorrow morning," Antti explained calmly with his eyes locked on the television screen, staring at a female singer gyrating in red leather shorts.

Immediately I dialed the number for Eki's boat. When my boss answered, the echo made his voice sound as though it were coming from much farther off than Porkkala.

"That Hänninen kid got himself in some goddamned hot water! It's a good thing you're there to look out for him. What the hell did he have to go and kill Armi for?"

A cold shiver went down my spine.

"Why do you think Kimmo killed Armi? Did Risto say so?"

"Those Hänninens are a weird bunch—I'm sorry, I know they're almost your relatives. If I were you, I wouldn't assume Kimmo is innocent, although of course, the client is always innocent and we never say any differently to the police," Eki said. "But we'll meet on this tomorrow. What time does the interrogation start?"

"Ten. Do you think you'll make it in time?"

Eki then explained something about the wind and how many knots they'd need to make, but I didn't have the patience to listen. After hanging up the phone, I didn't know what to think. Was I a naive idiot for believing Kimmo? Damn it, was Ström right after all? Maybe I *was* letting my relationship with Antti cloud my judgment about his friend.

I realized I didn't actually know Kimmo. I had seen him at the Hänninens' a few times over the winter, and we had been out for beers together once. Armi was supposed to come with us that night, but something got in the way—yes, that was it: her sister was sick. Had that been when Mallu had her miscarriage?

"Antti, could you help me clear up a few things?" I sat down next to him and touched him gingerly, afraid that he might shake off my hand.

"Yeah, like what?" he asked guardedly. I could feel his muscles tense.

"First, about Kimmo...Did you know about his S&M hobby?"

"It isn't like people go around broadcasting things like that! Once, I ran into him at the door of a hard-core sex shop in the city, and he looked really self-conscious, but I didn't think anything more about it."

So what were *you* doing there, I thought, but I didn't ask. I'd gone in the same shop too.

"Maybe that was Kimmo's way of exploring pain and death," Antti continued, a little more relaxed already. "Like Risto's constant hypochondria, and Sanna's cutting and drunk driving and drugs. Only finally Sanna succeeded in finding death."

"You think that was suicide?"

"That day, she left a copy of a Sylvia Plath's poem open on her desk. What more evidence do you need than that? She was always saying she wouldn't live to grow old. But I always thought the Hänninens' destructive tendencies focused only on themselves, not on outsiders. That's why it's hard for me to believe that Kimmo killed Armi."

Antti was now completely calm. I carefully stroked his back and then asked, "Well, who then? The killing looks so much like someone she knew did it. Or maybe the two juice glasses were meant for me and her, even though we would have been sewing inside."

"Am I supposed to start making lists of suspects from my own relatives?" Antti tore himself away from me and jumped up. "Fuck it; I can't stand going through all of this again! If you hadn't been with me the whole time, you'd probably even suspect me. You may call yourself a lawyer, but inside you're still a cop!"

Antti rushed down the stairs to his basement office. I stared after him silently for a moment, and then the tears I had been holding back all day began to flow. I cried for Armi and Kimmo, and for Sanna, but most of all for Antti and for me. We were going nowhere. I should just start looking for a new apartment and get it over with.

I drank a generous shot of whiskey, ate a banana, washed my swollen eyes, and tried to sleep. Antti hid out in his office, the faint sound of clicking computer keys telling me he was still awake. He wouldn't be crawling into bed beside me tonight.

Despite the whiskey and the long walk home, I didn't fall asleep until two.

4

My clock started beeping at eight thirty. When I looked out the window, I saw that the cherry blossoms had begun to fall. With a stop at the coffeemaker along the way, I dragged myself to the bathroom to look in horror at my swollen eyes. No time for an under-eye tea-bag treatment.

Makeup and coffee helped get me into tolerable shape, and after a moment's consideration, I left Antti a short note: "I'll be away most of the day. Could we try to have a talk tonight?"

Even pedaling at a relaxed pace, the journey to the police station took only twenty minutes. When I arrived, the place was dead, with no sign of Detective Sergeant Ström or my boss. I sat for a while and when nothing happened, I inquired with the duty officer at the front desk.

"Oh, yeah…Ström did call. He had to go to Kirkkonummi to check out a stabbing. He moved your interrogation to tonight."

A sappy-looking guy with a pimply face, the duty officer was straight out of one of those police jokes where they ask which of the cops knows how to read and which one knows how to write. This guy's partner would probably need to know how to do both.

Just as I had gotten the number to Ström's car and permission to use the desk phone, Eki dashed in.

"Why's it so quiet around here?" he brayed, startling the drunk man dozing on one of the benches in the waiting room. I called Ström, who said he doubted he would be back before seven. When I asked for permission to see Kimmo before then, he got difficult. For a good five minutes, we dickered over the intricacies of the Criminal Investigations Act before he finally acquiesced. However, he would allow only one of us to meet with Kimmo—either me or Eki, not both of us.

"Hmm, which of us should help Kimmo…" Eki wondered aloud when I explained the situation. "Perhaps it's better if you do, Maria. As legal counsel. It'll give you plenty of practice, and you probably know the routine of these police interrogations better than any of us. We'll see what happens if this makes it all the way to court."

"Should we meet to talk strategy once I've met with Kimmo? I'll come to the office as soon as I'm done here."

Eki stayed in the waiting room talking on his expensive new brick-sized cell phone while I asked the duty officer to let me in to see Kimmo. The young man scratched the pimples on his jaw for a little while before warily answering, "Well, I kind of think Hänninen is still sleeping. We had to call the doctor this morning around five, because he just kept screaming. The doctor sedated him pretty well. Wait a sec, and I'll call the jail."

The guard confirmed that Kimmo was sleeping, and I thought it best not to wake him. The duty officer's story was worrying, but there would be time to sort it all out later in the day.

Catching up with Eki in the parking lot, we loaded my bike into the back of his Volvo station wagon and started toward North Tapiola.

Our office adjoined Eki's home in a quiet residential area. When I had come here to interview for the job with the firm, I wondered how many clients would ever end up so far from downtown Helsinki, unless they were lost, but my misgivings were unfounded. With three practicing attorneys, Henttonen & Associates had its own established clientele for whom Eki and his staff drafted wills and estate inventories, handled divorces, and filed bankruptcies. Most of the clients were from Tapiola and other nearby areas of Espoo. They were used to Eki's personal way of handling their business and trusted him.

Henttonen & Associates had no time cards. In the few weeks I'd been on board, I'd already realized that most work occurred in spurts when it was available, and when things were quieter, most people stayed away from the office. When we were busy, government regulations on overtime had little meaning to the firm, but that was fine with me. As a police officer, I had become used to working without a set shift, and because Antti's research also went in fits and starts, slogging my guts out around the clock and then checking out for a few days meshed just fine with my personal life.

Eki Henttonen, Martti Jaatinen, and Albert Gripenberg were a team. The latter two each held five percent stakes in the company, while Eki held controlling ownership. During my interviews they told me straight out that they were specifically looking for a woman to join their team.

"Don't count on me being your barista or entertaining clients," I stated firmly, a comment that made the men snort with laughter.

"For coffee we have our secretary, Annikki, and we all take turns entertaining clients. We've just been thinking that since everybody keeps going on and on about the female perspective, maybe it's time we got some too."

This rationale was so amusing that I found myself genuinely interested in working for them. I also got the impression that they were excited about me as well, so I wasn't terribly surprised when the phone rang the next day and Eki asked when could I start.

Despite my grand speeches, I turned on the coffeemaker as soon as we walked into the conference room. Eki said he would pop over to his house to fetch some *pulla*—the ubiquitous Finnish coffee bread. I checked the answering machine and then started to hunt for the gynecologist's number in the phone book.

Eki came back with the *pulla*, and the smell of cardamom spread through the room. He had the biggest sweet tooth I had ever seen in a man and was constantly wolfing down pastries or chocolate. Despite this apparent weakness, the size of his belly remained within reasonable limits, and his bald spot rarely showed due to a skillful comb-over. However, Eki's appearance retained a fundamentally shabbiness: there was always a little dandruff dusting the shoulders of his suits; his face was always a little too flushed; his voice was always a little too loud and abrasive. Perhaps the fact that Eki lacked the usual slickness of most lawyers made people trust him more.

After the coffee was ready, we recapped the situation. Eki shoved his fourth sweet roll into his mouth and, through it, said, "At this point it's mostly up to the judge whether the evidence is sufficient to hold Kimmo. You don't think it is, I take it?"

"No, but that is influenced by my previous relationship with Kimmo. He isn't the murderer type."

"Believing in your client's innocence is a good thing. I'm not as sure, though. At this point, the Hänninens are almost your relatives, even if the priest hasn't yet said amen. But how well do you know them? Back before she died, I had to intervene in Sanna

Hänninen's life on several occasions. She had a couple of DUIs, I had to pick her up from the drunk tank a few times, and there was that charge for possession of marijuana. Keeping that girl out of prison was almost a full-time job. Then, when she died, the police almost charged that Ruosteenoja kid for her death. With Annamari Hänninen making hysterical accusations that Sanna's boyfriend murdered her, and him out of his mind with guilt because he was so drunk he didn't even realize she had gone into the water, it was a tough spot for everyone involved. Kimmo was one of the hardest hit by his sister's death, and without Armi, I doubt he would have come through it at all. Annamari had to take a medical leave for the whole rest of the spring semester."

"What does all that have to do with whether or not Kimmo did it?" I asked pointedly.

"I just mean to say that the Hänninens aren't the most balanced people you ever met. Who knows what someone like Kimmo might do in a..." Eki paused, clearly searching for the most roundabout expression he could find. "In a...state of sexual arousal. Maybe he didn't even realize he was strangling Armi until she collapsed."

"So you're suggesting that Kimmo denies killing her because he can't remember killing her?"

"Or doesn't want to remember. Should we request a psychiatric examination? What do you recommend?"

"If we want Kimmo to avoid prosecution, first we have to demonstrate that the evidence the police have fails *prima facie*, and then we have to find some evidence that suggests someone other than Kimmo could be the murderer," I answered like the model law school student.

We agreed that by the following day I would try to speak with as many people in Armi's close circle of acquaintances as possible. During that time, Eki would attempt to find any holes in the evidence against Kimmo.

"Let's call Erik and let him know you're coming," Eki said, dialing Dr. Hellström's number from memory. Someone answered on the other end, and Eki stated his business. I really liked his way of getting to the point and not dithering about things.

"Erik will be at home if you leave right now," Eki said after hanging up. "Do you want to take the Honda or ride your bike?"

I let the company car rest in the garage. The bike ride would give me time to think about what it was I wanted to ask Dr. Hellström.

When I arrived fifteen minutes later, Erik Hellström was waiting for me on the street-side balcony of his row house.

"The door is open," he announced in a trembling voice, seeming to expect that I would find my own way through the house to him. Hellström looked frightened. I had been mistaken in imagining that I would find him calm. I guess the uninitiated always expect calm, collected reactions to death from doctors, priests, and police officers, but from my own experience, I should have known how wrong that is.

I came through the dark entryway up the stairs, arriving at an enormous second-floor living room.

Lately I had seen a good number of handsomely decorated homes owned by the Espoo elite, but Hellström's living room put them all to shame. I don't know anything about antique furniture, but my instincts told me that the Gustavian-era relics I was seeing were extremely valuable. I glanced apprehensively at my pants, hoping they didn't have chain grease on them. I was relieved when Hellström invited me out onto the balcony.

"Perhaps we could chat out here. This lane has so little traffic that it shouldn't bother us. So, Maria—you don't mind me using your first name, do you?—what do you want to know?"

Dr. Hellström lit a cigarette. Nicotine stained the skin on the inner surfaces of the joints of the first and second fingers of his right hand. Perhaps the same yellow had once colored his teeth, but since that would have clashed with his image as a successful physician, he had apparently recently had them whitened. Overall, he had a rather elegant look about him. Moderately tall, his body retained some of the athleticism of his younger years. In different circumstances, his brown eyes might be quite alluring, but now anxiety predominated. Remembering where his gaze had traveled on me two nights before, I couldn't feel much sympathy toward him.

"First, give me your impression of Armi. What was she like as a person and as an employee?" I felt somehow stiff addressing Hellström. That he was my father's age wasn't what made it difficult. Nor was it the prestige he radiated or the dashing Don Juan silver at his temples. No, something else in him put me on edge. I knew that a large part of my antipathy derived from our run-in at the party, and I was irritated with myself for taking offense at something so trivial.

"Armi was a pleasant person and a good worker," Hellström said flatly as he rotated the cigarette between his fingers. Ash fell onto the white planks of the balcony, but he didn't notice.

"And where is your office located?"

"In the Heikintori Medical Center, near city hall. I share the building with several other medical specialists. We are all independent."

"Armi was a receptionist in your clinic?"

"Receptionist isn't quite the right word. Armi was a nurse with a specialty in gynecology. Of course, she did take care of making appointments for patients and other practical arrangements with the main reception desk."

"So she was quite involved with the patients?"

"Nowadays, we're calling them clients, not patients." Hellström picked a single strand of silver hair from the knee of his bottle-green slacks and dropped it over the balcony railing onto the grass. "Armi was happy and unreserved, and usually got along well with everyone. For some of my clients, her manner may have even been a little too informal."

"In what way?"

Hellström paused, seeming to consider the propriety of criticizing the dead, but then he continued anyway.

"Well, not every client wants to be called by her first name. Armi lacked the social grace that would have allowed more understanding of each client's preferences. And she may have kept a bit too well abreast of my client's ailments and other business."

"Do you mean that Armi was nosy?"

Hellström nodded.

"My clients include more than a few well-known women: actresses, business owners, politicians. I'm afraid Armi may have been in the habit of discussing their private matters somewhat too openly. Otherwise, she was a good worker, and I believe her interest in people came out of a genuine concern for them."

Hellström's last phrase could have served as an obituary. He lit another cigarette, which made me wonder whether he chain-smoked normally or this was just a reaction to Armi's death.

"What sorts of things does your practice handle?"

"A wide range of gynecological services, from checkups and contraceptive prescriptions to prenatal exams and cancer screenings. I have an adjunct professorship at Helsinki University

Hospital, so if my clients request it, I can also attend at cancer surgeries and births."

This all sounded rote; Hellström had presumably repeated it a hundred times in various languages at conferences and promotional events. Suddenly I remembered that I needed to renew my own birth control prescription, but I had no intention of going to Dr. Hellström's clinic. I patronize only female gynecologists. Besides, did I need the Pill at all anymore, since things with Antti seemed to be going down the toilet?

"I heard that you treated Armi's sister's for a miscarriage some time ago. What was the cause of the miscarriage?"

"That you'll have to ask Mallu Laaksonen herself—my clients' information is confidential," Hellström said firmly. Since he was right, I didn't argue.

"Did you notice anything out of the ordinary in Armi lately? Something she might have been concerned about—or especially happy about? New friends? More money than usual?"

Down the narrow lane came the rattling sound of a tricycle. A mother with a stroller followed the two-year-old cyclist, the contents of the stroller howling savagely. Hellström remained quiet for a long time before answering.

"This was about a month ago. Kimmo was visiting his father in Ecuador for a couple of weeks, and during that time Markku Ruosteenoja—I believe most people call him Makke—picked up Armi from work quite often. I asked Armi in jest whether she was thinking of swapping fiancés, but she claimed that her relationship with Markku wasn't like that."

Makke Ruosteenoja…What was it he said to me? Whenever he meets a nice girl, she's always taken…something like that. Had he meant Armi too? I added Makke to my mental list of people I'd have to interview.

"What if Kimmo was jealous of Markku?" Hellström asked. "Or Markku fell in love with Armi. Who knows what people are going to do, even people who seem nice enough."

Hellström was probably going to be more help for the prosecutor than for me. In order to change the subject, I asked, "You said Armi seemed overly interested in your clients' business. Do you suppose she could have misused any information?"

Hellström went strangely pale.

"What do you mean?" he asked, the cigarette trembling in his hand.

"Blackmail. You just said it yourself—who knows, even with people who seem nice enough. And your practice is full of perfect material for blackmail: abortions, sexually transmitted diseases—"

"No!" Hellström shouted, nearly jumping to his feet. "Armi wasn't like that!" He tried to compose himself. "Excuse me. This has been such a terrible shock. I'm just sick to death about Armi, and then you come here making accusations," he said, sitting back down. "Armi had a strong sense of justice and good medical ethics. Something as ugly as blackmail wouldn't have been in her nature."

"We have to investigate every possibility," I said, and then began to collect my things.

"So it isn't clear that Kimmo is guilty?" Hellström had noticed my intention to leave and was enough of a gentleman to rise.

"No, it isn't clear."

As I biked north along the small forested lane, I decided that on my way to Mallu Laaksonen's apartment I would stop and see whether Makke was home.

I didn't know his exact address, but I remembered him saying he lived behind the tennis center. I knew where he meant—a group of drab five-story apartment buildings on a little hill. Sure enough, the third stairwell directory I checked had a match to his name. I rang the doorbell five times and was just about to head back down the stairs when I heard plodding steps from inside the apartment.

Makke looked terrible. The previous evening must have involved more than two pints.

"Maria. Come in. Have you heard that Armi is dead?"

"I'm the one who found her. And it's Armi I came to talk about, if you're up to it."

"Yeah…Wait and let me brush my teeth." Makke slid past me into the bathroom, and I moved on to the living room. This was obviously the home of a dedicated fitness enthusiast. Apart from a TV and stereo, the only furnishings in the room were a stationary bike, rowing machine, and weight bench. Barbell plates and hand weights of various sizes lay scattered around. A narrow bed stood in an alcove, and the kitchenette offered only a small table and two chairs. Sitting down on the rowing machine, I adjusted the seat and pulled.

Makke pulled a hell of a lot of weight. Before he came back, I made it through ten reps, but I couldn't have managed many more. Based on the equipment he had at home, he must have visited the gym mainly for the social interaction and the sauna.

Makke marched straight to the refrigerator and pulled out a bottle of beer. He waved another toward me, but I shook my head. Pouring the beer into a glass, he added two effervescent tablets to the mix and threw a pill into his mouth before downing the bubbling liquid. The rest of the bottle he sucked down just as fast and then opened another.

"What was in that?" I asked in concern. Makke came and sat down next to me.

"Nothing dangerous. An antinausea pill, a vitamin C, and an aspirin. Taken with the finest Finnish pale lager. Markku's Miraculous Morning Cure."

"All that's missing is the raw egg," I said with a grin. "So I take it you've been drinking?"

Makke passed his hand through his wet hair. Apparently, when he went into the bathroom he had also put his upper body under the shower. His pectoral muscles glistened, and a small line of drops trickled straight along the centerline of his abs toward the fly of his well-worn jeans. He wore nothing else. Distracting.

"So it's true, is it? Shit," he groaned. "That's what the guys were saying yesterday. Stögö Brandt came into the store a little before three and said that Armi's street was full of cop cars. He was glancing out his window when he saw them wheeling a stretcher and a body bag away from Armi's place. So then we went to Hemingway's to see what the word was on the street and get a drink, and we just stayed. Who killed her?"

"They've arrested Kimmo. So you were at work yesterday?"

"Yeah. The store is closed on Saturdays in the summer, but I stopped in to finish up doing inventory, and Stögö came in, probably just looking for someone to tell. Why?" An apprehensive look crept onto his face.

"How often did you and Armi go out?"

"What the fuck? You aren't saying Kimmo killed her because he was jealous of me, are you? Armi didn't give a shit about me. I'm a drunk..." Makke took another generous swig of his second beer, then picked up a fifteen-pound weight in his left hand and started curling it mechanically. The muscles of his arm and shoulder bulged, and the color of the violet veins pulsing under his skin reminded me suddenly of Armi's swollen, purple face.

"My left delt is a little behind the right. A lot of reps with a little weight like this will help it catch up. By the way, we're going to have rowing machines like that coming on sale, if you need one. They're really handy—"

"Makke, listen!" I interrupted. "You and Armi had been going out together a lot lately? Did you see her yesterday? Did she call you?"

"You keep talking like we were dating or something. All I did was go over to her house sometimes to talk. She made me *pulla* and offered me a shoulder to cry on. I couldn't talk to anyone else about...about Sanna." Makke turned his face away from me, but I could see the muscles of his neck tense as he swallowed. "It's my fucking fault," he said to the poplars outside the window.

"Armi's death?" I asked, suddenly more alert.

"Armi's? No, Sanna's. Why didn't I see that she wasn't playing that time?" Makke turned and brought his face close to mine, not even trying to conceal his tears. "Even if I live a hundred years, I'm never going to forgive myself. Even though Armi said it wasn't my fault."

I could almost hear Armi's soothing voice, her blonde hair bobbing left and right. I could nearly smell the pungent cardamom aroma of the fresh-baked *pulla*. Dr. Hellström had talked about Armi having genuine concern for people. Perhaps I should take a lesson from her and not go around bullying the bereaved. No, figuring out who killed Armi was more important than people's feelings, I thought. I'd have to put off suppressing my malicious nature at least until tomorrow.

"You talked to Armi a lot about Sanna?" I said, continuing my line of questioning.

"Yeah, and about the Hänninens in general. She was nervous about marrying into their family and what kind of mother-in-law

Annamari was going to be. That bitch can't stand me. I was never good enough for Sanna—just a nobody with a degree in business administration from a second-rate school. She almost landed me in prison after Sanna's death. Armi was one of the only people who didn't blame me for anything. Just last Friday she said that I didn't have to be sorry anymore, that Sanna really did love me and that someone else entirely was responsible for her death. Like maybe her fucking mother! On Friday at the party, Annamari came up to me, all misty-eyed, talking some nonsense about reconciliation. But when her daughter was alive, she didn't give a damn about what was going on in Sanna's life."

"You weren't in love with Armi?"

Makke snorted. "Armi…Am I ever going to be able to love anyone but Sanna? And why are you asking all these questions anyway? Are you trying to be some kind of cop again?"

"Kimmo asked me to defend him. I'm collecting evidence to prove his innocence."

"I don't know anything about any evidence. I guess Kimmo could have been jealous of me. We weren't exactly best friends. By the way, how did Armi die? If somebody smothered her with a rubber hood, then Kimmo is your man. His biggest sex fantasy was to have someone do that to him."

Cold shivers again. One more point for the other side.

"You seem to be pretty well-informed about Kimmo's sexual preferences. Why would that be?"

"Sanna told me about it," Makke replied without looking at me. "Both of them were masochists. Sanna was just into more hard-core stuff. I was probably her first boyfriend who didn't hit her. I didn't, not even when she wanted me to…" Makke emptied his bottle. "And Kimmo was the same. He and Sanna even went to some sort of S&M club together. Sanna said Kimmo would end up peeling potatoes if 'the Army' ever found out. She was always making cheap digs like that."

Makke retrieved a third beer from the kitchen. I was growing tired of listening to him wallow in self-pity. Let him booze away his sorrows by himself—I needed to go talk to Mallu.

"Hey, don't go," Makke begged, as I climbed off the rowing machine.

"I have to work. And you should go to a bar to drink instead of moping around here alone. No, wait, that's not what I'm supposed to say. How about this: Haven't you had enough already?"

Another snort. "I'll be OK," Makke said with a wave of his bottle, his face distorting into something approaching a smile.

For some reason, I had a hard time believing him.

As I biked through the sports park toward Mallu's neighborhood, a pair of pheasants waddled across the bike path, and I suddenly had an urge to take off after them like Einstein, who two weeks before had chased a male pheasant right up a tree. The bird screeched in indignation from the branches for at least an hour, with Einstein circling down below. I could have sworn he was smiling.

Dandelions were blooming along the path of the underground heating pipes running back toward Makke's apartment complex. I wished I could forget work, ditch my bike, and go off wandering through the meadows looking for unusual plants in the vacant lots surrounding the park. That flower at least was stitchwort. Suddenly an image of my ex-boyfriend Harri flashed through my mind. He'd tried to teach me all the common birds and plants. These days, I could hardly remember that I had once dated people other than Antti.

I guess nine months is long enough together that you get used to having another person around. Imagining being alone felt difficult. Even though I liked being alone. Talking to anyone before my morning coffee was still a chore, and I despised having anyone tell me I needed to turn down my music. Antti usually understood, though, and he needed his space too.

The jungle of overgrown grasses ended at the indoor tennis center and a parking lot. If the hockey fans got their way, soon the meadow wouldn't exist anymore, and a new ice stadium, surrounded by a sea of asphalt, would rise in its place. I had heard that the city council hadn't had time to deal with anything other than this tug-of-war over the ice rink lately. Looming cuts to social services seemed incidental in comparison.

Mallu wasn't home. She was probably at her parents' place. I couldn't see a telephone booth anywhere close, and hunger gnawed at my stomach, despite Eki's *pulla*, so I pedaled back to the other side of the bay and home. Perhaps Antti would be in more of a talking mood now.

On the way, I rehearsed what I would say. Fortunately, I didn't have to interrupt Antti's work, because he was sitting in the backyard reading.

"Hi, Antti. I had a few minutes, so I thought I'd stop by home. Could we have a talk?"

"Hmm…" came the answer from behind the book.

"I know that Armi's death is a real shock for you, but this situation isn't my fault. I'm sorry to involve your relatives. Still, Kimmo asked me to help him, and he's in a really tough spot. If I'm going to help him, I have to do my job, and that might mean asking some uncomfortable questions."

The words I was hearing were smoother than I expected to come out of my own mouth. Kind of like a self-help magazine. Still, I forged ahead.

"I'd like to comfort you, but that would require you letting me get close to you. I'm sad too, even though I didn't know Armi."

I stopped when I noticed how Antti was shaking, laughing and crying at the same time. Gradually, the mixture of the two emotions gave way to uncontrollable laughter.

"Stop it!" When my shout had no effect, I poured the glass of water sitting next to Antti on his head. Fortunately, that worked, and I didn't have to resort to slapping him across the face.

"Oh man," Antti said, still chuckling as he shook his head and pulled me down next to him. "I was so sure you were pissed at me that I had my own speech ready too, and it would have sounded just as fake. Luckily, you beat me to it. How is Kimmo holding up?"

Relieved, I told him the latest news and mentioned that I was planning to do some private investigating.

"Can we talk a little about the people involved in this mess? You know them all so much better than I do."

"So I get to be Watson?"

"Watson is supposed to worship the ground Sherlock Holmes walks on, and that role doesn't fit you, even if you are a big enough dope otherwise. And we aren't Tommy and Tuppence either, just plain old Maria and Antti. Let's just go make lunch, and you can tell me about Sanna's death."

Antti had forgotten to go to the grocery store, but his parents' pantry still contained a box of pasta and a can of tomato sauce, so I was able to whip up a marinara. Throwing together pasta sauces out of random ingredients hidden in the back corners of my apartment cupboards could actually be considered my culinary specialty. My all-time triumph was a green-pepper–processed-cheese-spread–peanut-butter sauce. Which, believe it or not, wasn't disgusting. Now we settled for a more normal combination of crushed tomatoes, onions, cheese, black pepper, and dried basil.

"Well, for starters, I think you're right that you can't understand the Hänninen family without knowing about Sanna's suicide. What do you want me to tell you?" Antti asked as he grated three carrots for us to eat as a salad.

"Just tell me the story again, like you would tell someone who had never heard it before."

And Antti did. He started with Sanna, for whom the best descriptive adjective was clearly "self-destructive." Sanna, who theoretically had everything.

She had a good family. Her father was a successful engineer, her mother worked as a teacher, her older stepbrother was happily married, and her younger brother was following in their father's footsteps.

She was beautiful. She had large eyes the color of dried oak leaves and long, nearly coal-black hair. Her skin was pale, maybe a little sallow from her destructive lifestyle, but flawless otherwise, except of course in the places she had slashed or burned herself. She had a small nose and a large, sensual mouth that would have made even Nicole Kidman jealous. With her slender frame and large breasts, she was an irresistible combination of girlish insecurity and womanly eroticism.

She was gifted. Six perfect scores on her college entrance exams may not have meant all that much, even coming from a rural high school, but admission to the University of Helsinki in French and English did. She had planned to be a teacher; in the Hänninen family, girls followed the path of their mother. Just like in my family—if you didn't count me.

But Helsinki pulled Sanna away from her studying and dangerously toward darker pursuits. More and more alcohol, drugs, and violent men, some of them actual criminals. There were a couple of abortions, then a drunk-driving conviction that almost landed her in jail.

"After a while, Annamari and Henrik started acting as if Sanna didn't even exist," said Antti. "Their daughter was no longer presentable to their circle of friends. They still gave her money but lost interest otherwise. Not that they were great parents to begin with: Henrik has always been away a lot, and Annamari has those obsessive episodes of hers.

"Kimmo was doing his military service when Sanna attempted suicide the first time. It shook the Hänninens a bit, and that was probably what Sanna was looking for. After that, we all tried harder to include her, inviting her to parties and that sort of thing. But she always just got plastered and started making trouble as soon as you let her in the door. Once I had to climb up to pull her down from the Tapiola water tower. When she was sober, she would read and write a lot, and sometimes her grades were even good, but then she would always backslide again."

According to Antti, Makke's arrival on the scene that fall before she died cheered Sanna up for a while, as new boyfriends always did. Makke was practically a respectable gentleman compared to the types she usually went out with. I guess he was just starting his drinking career. But because Sanna believed she had found the love of her life, she started to treat every night as if it had to be a party.

On her thirtieth birthday, Sanna had wanted to go out to the Westend breakwater. The winter had been mild, and the seawater was free of ice. Makke and Sanna emptied a bottle of vodka. At some point, Makke passed out on the sand at the swimming beach, and Sanna went out wading. The shore was quiet even for a Wednesday night in March. Somebody taking his dog out for a pee found Makke on the sand and called the police. Makke later said he didn't even think about Sanna or what had happened to her until he started sobering up in the drunk tank; he was half-frozen to death himself.

Sanna's body washed up on shore the next day. On her writing desk at home, between a skull and a black candle, a book lay open to one of her favorite poems: "Lady Lazarus" by Sylvia Plath, underlined in several places. Antti and Kimmo considered two lines to be evidence of her intention to take her own life: "I am only thirty. And like a cat I have nine times to die." According to the autopsy, Sanna was intoxicated with alcohol and sedatives, so the police handled the case as an accidental drowning.

"There was nothing suspicious about it?" I asked.

"Annamari wanted Makke charged with criminal negligence, but Eki Henttonen and her husband brought her to her senses. How would that have helped anyone? Nobody, not Makke or anyone else, pushed her into the water. She went in herself. Of her own free will," Antti said, sopping up the last of his spaghetti sauce with a piece of bread.

"But somehow it feels like too much bad luck for one family," he went on. "First Sanna. Then Mallu's miscarriage after years of trying, and her separation from her husband. Now Armi and Kimmo..."

"Miscarriage and separation? What else can you tell me about Mallu?"

"I don't really know that much. She's Armi's sister. An unemployed architectural drafter. Married to a guy named Teemu Laaksonen, who's some sort of technician. According to Armi, they had infertility problems, but last November they finally managed to get pregnant. Then they lost the baby in March. Her husband moved out pretty soon afterward." Antti grimaced. "Sounds pretty bad, even if it is a pretty typical story. Life just goes wrong."

"No kidding," I said. "But I think you're right—it does seem like an awful lot of bad luck for one family."

Checking the clock, I decided I still had enough time to pay a visit to Armi's parents, if I picked up the Honda from the office. I called ahead, and after a moment's resistance, Armi's father agreed to see me. I would have preferred not to interrupt their grieving, but I had no choice. No one knew more about Armi than they did.

5

I parked our small black company car in the driveway of the weathered one-and-a-half-story house. The squealing of small children playing came from somewhere farther off. However, at this door, I was met with only silence. Fair-haired and sturdily built, the man who opened the door was obviously Armi's father. Instead of saying hello, he simply motioned for me to enter.

After all of the homes in Tapiola I had visited where the decorating was obviously the work of a fancy interior designer, the Mäenpääs' living room felt homey. Exactly the same busy wallpaper and faded plush sofa set as in innumerable other post–World War II–era one-and-a-half-story houses in Finland. On the bookcases, glass knickknacks, trophies, and souvenirs from long-ago trips were more prevalent than books, most of which were *Reader's Digest Favorites*. These were precisely the sort of people who could give their daughter a beautiful old Finnish name without realizing what a problem it would become once the schoolyard bullies started learning English.

Her face so swollen from crying that her eyes were barely visible, the woman perched on the corner of the sofa shattered the impression of normality. Her shabby black skirt and blouse, which was shiny at the seams, looked as though she had slept in them. She didn't seem to notice me at all; she simply stared past me.

"More police?" A young woman dressed in black and wearing an apron appeared in the doorway to the kitchen. It was Mallu, Armi's sister. We had chatted briefly at the Hänninens' party on Friday night, but she didn't seem to recognize me.

"A woman this time, is it?" Mallu continued testily. "Hopefully you're more respectful than the clods who came before. You're the third officer to show up here within the past twenty-four hours. I'll tell you exactly what I told the others: my parents were on an outing with their seniors' group all yesterday morning. If you want witnesses, at least twenty other people were on the same bus."

"I'm not with the police. We met the night before last at Risto and Marita Hänninens' house."

Mallu looked confused for a moment and then the lightbulb switched on.

"Oh, yeah, you're Antti's girlfriend! You just look so different now than you did that night. Why are you—what was your name—here?"

"Maria Kallio. I'm here from Henttonen & Associates. I'm Kimmo Hänninen's legal counsel," I said, sounding about as sympathetic as a gravestone peddler.

The mention of Kimmo's name seemed to smack into the woman hunched on the sofa. Tears began streaming down her frostbitten-apple-colored cheeks again, at which Mallu crossed the room to wrap her arms protectively around her mother.

"I'm very sorry about Armi's death," I said in the general direction of the couch. I couldn't handle looking at her frostbitten-apple cheeks and watering eyes.

"Is this the same Ms. Kallio who found our girl?" Paavo Mäenpää, Armi's father, asked in his loud, nasty-sounding smoker's croak.

"How can you be Kimmo's legal counsel, when you found Armi? Aren't you almost like a suspect yourself?" Mallu asked with surprising perspicacity.

The question was a good one. No one had questioned my position so far, and no law prohibited me from acting as Kimmo's legal advisor. However, morally speaking, my situation was definitely awkward. I had wondered a bit why Ström let me off so easily, but perhaps he was just so sure of Kimmo's guilt that he didn't feel like wasting his energy on me.

"The police told us so little. Armi was strangled...Was she... Had anything else been done to her?" Armi's father asked. No doubt he meant to ask if she'd been sexually assaulted, which is what fathers always ask about when their daughters turn up dead.

"Armi was strangled, but nothing else was done to her."

Nothing else. As though strangulation weren't enough.

"Um...Did she...Did she suffer much?" he asked, his voice faltering. I thought of Armi's blue-black face, her tongue lolling out. I thought of the patch of lawn gouged by her pink toenails as she fought for her life.

"It was over quickly. She probably went unconscious within less than a minute." That sounded like a short amount of time, one minute, although for Armi and her murderer it likely felt like an eternity.

Following these words, a thick fog of silence enveloped us. The sounds of the outside world were muffled, unreal. A clock on the bookcase ticked, as if in a reminder that time at least meant to soldier on.

"Armi was never any trouble to anyone," her mother suddenly said. "Why did she have to die? She was supposed to be getting married. I always thought Kimmo was such a nice boy…"

Mallu patted her mother comfortingly.

"And you still intend to defend him? You must have come here to ask whether Armi had any other boyfriends, just like the police yesterday. Our Armi was a decent girl—one boyfriend was enough for her. What on earth got into Kimmo?" Armi's father said in obvious anguish.

The questions I had planned to ask felt unnecessary, even cruel. And presenting them to Armi's parents made no sense. At least not yet.

"I imagine we could revisit this a little later, at the end of next week, perhaps. I'm sorry," I said. I meant sorry for everything: Armi's death, my own intrusion, representing Kimmo. I started my retreat toward the front door, but Mallu stopped me and asked for a ride home.

"Listen, Dad, I need to stop by my place to switch the laundry I started yesterday, so the clothes don't mildew. I'll be back as soon as I can. You and Mom will be alright without me for that long."

Mallu's departure resembled a getaway. As we turned onto the old Turku Highway, she began making excuses for herself.

"I really did have laundry in the machine when my father called me over to their house. Thanks for the ride; I don't have a car. Teemu got it."

"Teemu who?"

"Teemu Laaksonen. My future ex-husband," Mallu said darkly. "Mind if I smoke?"

"Yes. This isn't my car." Whereas my prospective sister-in-law, Marita, was naturally slender, in comparison, Mallu

Laaksonen looked diminished by worry and care. Now two sizes too large, her dark clothing hung off her, the lines on her face were too deep for a thirtysomething, and her hair already contained strands of gray. The expression of her face was more bitter than sad. I wondered how a person could survive a miscarriage, a divorce, and a sister's death all within six months.

"What do you want to know about Armi?" Mallu asked and then shoved a piece of nicotine gum in her mouth. She was probably in full-on withdrawal, since she seemed to be one of those women who even as adults still don't dare smoke in front of their parents.

"Anything. Biographical information, friends, other previous love interests. You don't have any other siblings, right?"

"Right. That's the great tragedy of our family, if you ask my father. Two girls, no boys. Dad had a little delivery company with a couple of trucks and a van. His greatest dream was that someday the sign on the side of each would read 'P. Mäenpää and Sons.' When I was five and Armi was one, Dad came down with meningitis as a complication of the mumps, and that apparently damaged him, making it impossible to have any more children. After that, he sold his company and started driving a taxi.

"Then they started dreaming about grandchildren. Teemu and I tried for five years. Then came the miscarriage, and my uterus ended up so scarred that there's a ninety percent chance no egg will ever be able to implant in it. They still had Armi, though. But now she's gone too."

Mallu spoke in an even, expressionless tone, but every word still sounded like a shout.

My hands trembled on the steering wheel. "We only have us three girls too," I said. "I'm the oldest. My middle sister is pregnant now, and the whole family is hoping for a boy."

"I don't know if I ever even wanted kids," Mallu continued, as though she hadn't heard me. "I was so tired of trying, and all the tests. Teemu has a low sperm count, and I had endometriosis, which I got surgery for. We tried and tried, and in the end, we didn't have anything left but trying to have a baby."

"So you're divorcing?"

"It's for the best. Let him test out his weak sperm on some other woman," Mallu said bitterly and then continued giving driving directions. As I brought the car to a stop in front of a shabby apartment building, she burst out, "All I've done is talk about myself. If you have time to come inside, I can try to tell you about Armi too. I'm in no hurry to get back to my parents' place. I might go crazy if I don't get a little breathing room." Mallu was lighting a cigarette before she even got both feet out of the car.

I still had a while until Kimmo's interrogation, so I followed her through the building entrance to a rather dark first-floor apartment. Besides the lack of natural light, the other first impression the place gave was that it had been strangely ripped in half. There was barely any furniture or decoration. Only two chairs stood next to the kitchen table, which should have been able to seat four, and the sofa set in the living room was missing a coffee table and a second armchair. At least the stereo still had two speakers. Mallu watched my eyes as they surveyed the scene.

"Teemu got the car and VCR, and I got the rest of the appliances. Damn it, the laundry!" she said, rushing into the bathroom.

A cigarette still dangling from her lip, Mallu bent down to empty the washing machine, which smelled like my uncle's root cellar. Mallu sniffed the clothing for a moment and then decided washing them again would be best. She added detergent, started the machine, and then said she was calling her parents to tell them she would be a little longer than expected.

We ended up sitting on the two lonely chairs in the kitchen, sipping cups of coffee.

"OK, so about Armi. You heard what my mom said, that Armi was never any trouble to anyone. In a way that was true. She was a nice little sister. You know, the smiling girl with a bow in her hair. When she was little, she walked the neighbors' dogs, and when she was a teenager, she babysat their children. She always wanted to take care of people, and I guess that's what led her to nursing school. But even as a little kid, she also had an amazing knack for finding things out about other people's lives. 'Mom, why do the Kervinens have so many empty liquor bottles?' she asked once after she had been babysitting at the neighbors' house."

"Caring for others can create a kind of power," I observed, not really knowing exactly what I meant.

"You said it. I've always thought Armi specialized in gynecology because of my issues, and I don't think purely out of a desire to help. Maybe it was a way to get control somehow."

"What does your mother do for work?"

"She used to work for the Elanto food co-op, but now she's on disability. Naturally, my family was never good enough for that Hänninen witch. If the police hadn't arrested Kimmo, my first guess would have been that she strangled Armi to keep her from contaminating their bloodline. It wouldn't surprise me if one of them was mixed up in Sanna's death too. They couldn't stand what a disgrace she was."

Mallu sensed my shocked stare and raised her eyes from her coffee cup.

"You don't believe me either." She took a sarcastic tone. "Yeah, I just say whatever pops into my empty head. Everybody knows I'm unstable. Because of the miscarriage—I even go to therapy! And I'm out of work, so I have plenty of time to sit around and dream up crazy stories, right?" Mallu clearly meant her icy tone to echo someone else's idea of her. I wondered who. And why was Sanna's ghost constantly looming in the background whenever the subject of Armi's murder came up?

"Were you and Armi close?"

"Close...If you have sisters, then you know how it is. Hate, jealousy, and love all rolled up into one—but probably that last one least of all. We did a lot together, especially lately. Armi seemed to think it was her duty to cheer me up, so she dragged me all over the place with her. Like to the Hänninens' party the other night. Armi even took me to my appointments with my psychiatrist."

Caring is power, I thought again and then wondered what kind of power Armi would have liked to try to use on me. I was surer than ever that she wanted to talk to me about something more than sewing needles and wedding gossip.

"How long were Armi and Kimmo dating?"

"About four years. There was a party thrown by the nursing school and Helsinki Tech—they were assuming that nurses are all women and engineers are all men. Of course, they met there! Before Kimmo, Armi only ever had one boyfriend, and he lives in Lapland now, in Rovaniemi."

"Was there anything between Armi and Makke Ruosteenoja?"

"I doubt there was anything on Makke's side—I always thought he liked his women in a more intense flavor, like Sanna. Armi pitied Makke, so of course she wanted to take care of him. Makke is kind of like a lost puppy dog. Teemu and Makke were in the same class, which is why I know him."

Switching gears, I bluntly asked Mallu, "Did they figure out what caused your miscarriage?" Unfazed by my question, she simply lit another cigarette. "There wasn't anything to figure out. One Saturday, Teemu and I were coming back from Kimmo and Armi's. It was March, and the roads were slick. Teemu was a little drunk too, since he and Kimmo had been doing shots after their squash match. We were crossing the street in the middle of a block. Suddenly this car came speeding out of nowhere. I jumped out of the way and tripped and fell."

"Did the car stop?"

"I'll give you one guess. We didn't think anything happened to me, that I'd only torn my tights and bruised my knees, so we just hobbled the rest of the way home. The bleeding started during the night. Early the next morning, Teemu called Dr. Hellström, and he made us call an ambulance. But there was nothing anyone could do. When I came to from the anesthetic, Dr. Hellström's red eyes were the first thing I saw. At first I thought he had been crying for me, but he was just getting over the flu."

"My God." I wished I had something else to say, but I couldn't find the words.

"You know what the strangest thing was? It happened so fast and it was dark—we couldn't even tell the color of the car, let alone the make or license plate number, but Teemu swore up and down that Armi was the one driving it."

My breath caught. Did Mallu realize she was offering me a motive for Armi's murder? A motive both for herself and for Teemu?

"But it couldn't have been Armi. She didn't even have a driver's license, let alone a car. And she and Kimmo were going to bed right after we left. I still can't understand why Teemu would say something so stupid. Armi was floored when I told her."

A clicking sound came from the bathroom as the washing machine began the first rinse cycle. I was baffled. What if Armi had been behind the wheel of that car?

"Where does your husband live now?"

"With his parents, in Kirkkonummi. You'll find the number in the phone book under Taisto Laaksonen. Hold on, let me check to make sure I remembered to put the washing machine hose in the tub so it doesn't just drain onto the floor."

As I poured myself more coffee, I wondered how much I could trust Mallu. Perhaps I should look up Teemu Laaksonen and hear his version of the accident. High speed, Saturday night, and fleeing the scene. Sounded suspiciously like drunk driving.

Mallu returned with a photo album.

"I have some pictures of Armi when we were younger, if you want to see." Mallu laid the album in front of me and began turning pages. "This is Armi when she was six, with our dog."

A slightly plump, owlish-looking little girl with braids hugged a decidedly nasty-looking German shepherd. On the facing page, the same little girl with braids and Mallu, much huskier than now, posed next to their bicycles. Unceremoniously skipping past whole pages, Mallu showed me Armi's confirmation, high school graduation, and college commencement portraits. In a more recent-looking picture on the final page, Mallu weighed at least twenty pounds more than she did now and smiled happily under the arm of some man. A Christmas tree stood in the background. I heard Mallu's breathing speed up. Without saying a word, she tore the picture from the album, crumpled it into a ball, and hurled it into the trash.

"That was at Armi and Kimmo's engagement party. Last Christmas," Mallu said, pointing to another photograph.

This picture had the same Christmas tree as the previous photo, with Kimmo and Armi hand-in-hand, showing off their engagement rings. I remembered Antti's words: "Last November they finally managed to get a bun in the oven." Last Christmas Mallu was also probably celebrating her pregnancy.

"Do you know how soon we'll be able to bury Armi?" Mallu asked, her breathing now steady again.

"Two weeks from now, at the earliest. The final autopsy can take up to a week, and that's once they actually start."

"I just want to get it over with as soon as possible. That's the best kind of burial. I would have liked to see my baby too, but they didn't bring it to me. They said it came apart because they had to scrape me out. They just threw her in the trash or something. Maybe they have some place they bury discarded children. I didn't ask."

Mallu slapped the photo album shut, knocking over her empty coffee cup. It banged to the floor but didn't break.

"God, I just keep talking about myself. You wanted to know about Armi, not me," Mallu said as she straightened up from retrieving the cup. "Did you still have something to ask? If that machine would just finish, I could get back to my parents' house," Mallu said tensely. Since this sounded like an invitation to leave, I did.

When I reached the car, I realized that I hadn't asked Mallu what she had been up to the previous morning. I would need to pose the same question to Risto, Marita, and Annamari. Makke had been partly at his store and partly at home. It was only a short trip from his apartment to Armi's neighborhood, and he would pass there on his way to work.

I decided to drive back to Armi's house myself. As I could
have guessed, blue-and-white police tape and yellow velcro clo-
sures blocked off Armi's backyard, and the front door was sealed.
However, no one was on guard.

Standing outside the vine-covered fence, I looked toward the
neighboring residences. To the east were a couple of apartment
buildings, the windows of which almost certainly had views
into Armi's backyard. Hopefully Ström's boys had realized this
as well and were making the rounds questioning the residents.
Although you would hope that if someone saw a strangling in
progress, a call to the police would have been forthcoming. But
you never know—as a police officer, I had picked up plenty of
people passed out in the middle of the street, and even dealt with
a few dead bodies, where someone had keeled over from a medical emergency and passersby just walked around them for hours
without stopping to help.

My conversation with Mallu had depressed me and made
my conflict with Antti seem petty in comparison. After dropping off the car at the office, I headed toward the police station
on my bike. Riding like a bat out of hell, I nearly got run down
twice—both times while I was in a crosswalk. Perhaps the urge
for self-annihilation was catching. I hadn't done anything but
talk to miserable people for the past two days.

Ström wasn't at the station yet, but Kimmo was finally
awake. If I had been more on the ball, I would have brought
a change of clothing with me. The jeans and shirt Kimmo was
wearing looked grubby, and he could have used a shave and a
shower. How could a blond man's stubble be so dark?

"Hard night?" I asked cautiously.

"Yeah." Kimmo shook his head groggily. "During the night
it just sort of hit me all at once, knowing that Armi is really

gone. And that I'm in jail. And they think I killed her. I never thought these things really happened, at least not in Finland, and definitely not to me. But during the night, I suddenly realized this *was* happening to me, just like in the movies." Such helpless terror filled Kimmo's eyes that I had to look away.

"We can't save Armi," I said cruelly. We would all just have to live with her death. "But if you didn't do it, we have to save you. We can get you free, probably as early as tomorrow."

"Oh, so he'll be a free man by tomorrow, will he?" Detective Sergeant Ström said in a nasty tone as he entered the room. "Don't count on it; I have new evidence. Hänninen, you claimed that you and your fiancée didn't have a fight. Well, I just talked to one of the neighbors, who says differently. You claim you left the house at noon, but this neighbor heard you fighting at one fifteen. How do you explain a witness placing you there more than an hour after you told me you left?"

I swallowed. This sounded bad. What reason did Kimmo have to lie? He looked utterly petrified.

"But I know I left then. I had already been home for a while before I heard the one o'clock news on the radio."

"Do you have any witnesses? Was your mother home?" Ström asked dubiously.

"Mom left a note on the table about going into the city with Matti and Mikko."

"Did you meet anyone you know along the way, a neighbor maybe?" I asked before Ström could continue his attack. I hoped to God that someone could verify Kimmo's movements. Did Ström really have a reliable witness who could nail Kimmo to the wall like this, or was he just trying to bluff and make Kimmo contradict himself?

Kimmo thought for a moment. "I don't remember seeing anyone," he said, sounding depressed.

"You should probably send your boys around to interview the Hänninens' neighbors in case any of them noticed Kimmo," I suggested to Ström.

That was a mistake.

"Goddamn it, Maria, don't you tell me how to do my job! I went to the same goddamn police academy you did. Keep your opinions to yourself, or I'll have your ass thrown out of here!"

I had been kind and empathetic enough for one day already.

"No, you watch yourself, Detective Sergeant Pertti Ström, or you're going to be up to your ears in shit. Is your closure rate down on your cases? Is that why you're in such a hurry to pin this murder on Kimmo? Worried about hitting your numbers for that next promotion, are we?"

Both on our feet now and clenching our fists, Ström and I stared at each other like two fighting cocks. If Ström said one more irritating word, he was going to get the *Legal Code of Finland Volume III* across the forehead. Kimmo and the officer recording the interview gaped at us in surprise.

"Let's get on with it," Ström finally said.

I tried to calm down, even though what I really wanted was to challenge him to duel. I knew I couldn't best him at pistols, but what about swords? Our bad dynamic had been the same at the academy; we were constantly getting on each other's nerves.

Perhaps asking Eki to represent Kimmo would be a better idea after all.

"I want to know what grounds this witness has for saying I was still at Armi's place at one fifteen," Kimmo demanded, surprisingly clearheadedly.

"I don't have to tell you that! And you keep quiet, Kallio! You know I'm right."

The recording officer grimaced at me apologetically behind Ström's back. I felt better. Maybe we were three against one here.

Ström went through Kimmo's account repeatedly until we were all growing impatient. Finally, he changed the subject.

"If your bride-to-be didn't like this pervert stuff you were into, then why did you have the rubber suit with you at her house?"

I had wondered the same thing. This one detail didn't line up with Kimmo's otherwise sensible story.

"When I picked up Armi on Friday to take her to Risto's house, I was coming from the city. I had the suit with me because I was looking for the right kind of product for it. You have to condition rubber, and I didn't want to use silicone because it makes the surface so sticky. I was looking for something more like a furniture wax. When we left to go to Risto's, I left my stuff at Armi's because I was supposed to stay the night."

"Ah, so. Rubber suit polish…" I stalled. Christ, this guy was not helping me out. "Where did you buy it?"

"Stockmann, in the home furnishings department."

"You went in there, asking for rubber-sex-suit polish?"

"I didn't ask anyone anything. I just discreetly tried a few on the suit and then paid for it at the register."

"Do you still have the bottle and receipt?" I asked quickly.

"The bottle is probably in a bag in my room, and the receipt should be there too."

Ström mumbled something like, "We'll check on that," and changed the subject.

"OK, so since you're one of these perverts who gets off on wearing rubber, tell me: Are you a sadist or a masochist? What is it you want to do to women?"

The recording officer grimaced at me again, and Kimmo blushed.

"Ström, really? Kimmo, you can answer the first question and ignore the second," I said.

"Masochist," Kimmo said quietly. "And I don't want to do anything to anyone," he continued, ignoring me. "I want things to be done…"

"Such as…?" The curiosity in Ström's voice was poorly concealed. Sexually repressed as he was, of course the tawdry aspects of the case would interest him. A lot of people consider police officers sadists; perhaps in Ström's case, they were right.

"Is this really relevant? We've already established that he's a masochist," I grumbled.

Ström gave in surprisingly easily.

"Can anyone confirm that you're specifically a masochist? Some old girlfriend, a whore, whatever?"

"Ström!" I yelled.

"Well, I've talked a lot with people at my club, my S&M club," Kimmo continued. "They could probably tell you."

"They who? We need specifics."

Kimmo was silent for a moment, then said, "I don't want to get them mixed up with the police, especially if you'd treat them with as little respect as you have me."

Kimmo wouldn't give names or say anything else about the club. I tried to express to him that gallantry was pointless, but Kimmo kept his mouth stubbornly shut.

"If you don't give me any names, I'm not going to believe a word you say about this masochism thing. I'm going to work from the assumption that whipping and strangling women is your thing, and that's exactly what you did to your girlfriend," Ström said.

Here I broke in again. "Markku Ruosteenoja. Makke. There's your witness. Address Hakarinne 6, stairwell B. He can tell you that Kimmo is a masochist."

"And who is this Ruosteenoja? Hänninen's boyfriend or something?"

"No—his dead sister's boyfriend."

"So was your sister the sadist then?" Ström asked Kimmo, and had the door not opened at that moment, Ström definitely would have gotten that book in the face. The person at the door was the duty officer, coming to tell Ström about a call he needed to take. After being gone for less than thirty seconds, Ström returned and declared the interview over, ordered Kimmo taken back to his cell, and left the room. I stuck my tongue out at Ström's back, which made the other officer smirk. He looked like a grown-up Dennis the Menace.

"Kimmo, tell me the name of at least one person from the club. I promise to treat them right."

"Elina Kataja, but she goes by 'Angel.' She's one of the club's organizers. I don't remember her number, but it's in the phone book."

"Let's go, Hänninen," Dennis the Menace said gently, throwing me a farewell smile. He nodded toward the table, where, for some reason, he had left his interview notes. As soon as the two men left, I flipped back a few pages, to a page from the day before, and there it was: the name and address of Ström's key witness, which I quickly wrote down. Apparently, Ström's methods had begun to aggravate more than just me.

6

When I arrived home, Antti's parents' car was in the driveway. Completely exhausted, I didn't feel the slightest bit like socializing, but I had to go inside.

"Hi, Maria," Marjatta Sarkela yelled from the kitchen. "Is Kimmo out yet?"

"No, unfortunately not. We'll see tomorrow what the judge decides. I think he'll get out," I said as I entered the kitchen, where Antti sat with his parents over tea.

"We brought Matti and Mikko home and thought we'd stay over tonight so we can run some errands tomorrow morning," Tauno Sarkela explained. "Hopefully we won't be in the way."

"No, no, of course not. This is your house." I tried not to sound grumpy, even though these were precisely the sorts of situations that had made me think twice about moving to Espoo. And the Sarkelas had chosen the perfect time for their surprise visit: the whole house was a disaster, and the cupboards were bare. But, damn it, I'd spent the whole weekend running myself ragged trying to help *their* relatives, so when would I have had time for housekeeping? Besides, the state of the house was just as much Antti's responsibility as mine.

What irked me the most, though, was that I cared at all. Why did I consider the cleanliness of my house and the frequency with which I baked fresh *pulla* a measure of my value as a woman?

"Sit down; pour yourself some tea," Marjatta said. We were clearly in *her* kitchen, not mine. Einstein came to rub against my legs as I peered hopefully into the cupboard, looking for something to nibble with my tea. I was glad the cat was back; he could keep Antti company during the lonely nights to come.

And, wait, the refrigerator looked surprisingly full. Wagging a wedge of cheese at him, I gave Antti an inquiring look.

"I stopped at the store under the train station on my way in from the city."

I laughed in relief, although of course Antti knew how to take care of the shopping—he had lived alone just as long as I had. After making myself a heaping ham-and-cheese sandwich, I sat down at the table. The tea tasted of citrus and vodka. I should have guessed. The Sarkelas went in for hard tea, and Antti had inherited the habit from his parents.

"What's in this?" I asked politely.

"Lemon vodka," Antti's mother replied. "Do you like it? Tauno and I needed a little restorative after taking care of the boys. The poor dears were frightened, of course, with Sanna's death so fresh in their minds, and now Armi. Mikko insisted on calling Marita last night before going to bed to make sure his mother was still safe."

"Einstein needs a restorative too, now that he's escaped the little dudes' clutches," Antti said. He fished around in the freezer, pulling out a frozen lump and putting it in the microwave to thaw. As the smell of the shrimp spread through the room, the cat went wild, purring like an electric generator, head-butting

Leena Lehtolainen

each of us in turn, and meowing insistently. The purring rose a few decibels when Antti put the food down.

I remembered I was supposed to call Elina Kataja, Kimmo's S&M witness. Since I didn't really feel like talking to an S&M expert with my pseudo in-laws listening, I snuck away to the phone in Antti's office.

"Thus spake the angel from heaven: I'm partying now, and I don't know for how long. Leave a message and I'll call you when I recover," said Elina Kataja's answering machine. Apparently, everyone knew her by the name Angel.

I remained sitting and rested my head on Antti's desk for a moment. My shoulders hurt, and my calves were sore from the previous day's walk. For a second I had an intense yearning for the solitude of my old apartment and its large bathtub. The Sarkelas' row house had no tub, and it was already too late to heat the sauna.

I returned to the kitchen to finish my tea and then let Marjatta pour me another cup as well. I suddenly remembered Risto Hänninen's wife mentioning her mother's dissatisfaction with Dr. Hellström.

"Listen, Marjatta, when you left Dr. Hellström's clinic, did your decision have anything to do with Armi?"

Antti's mother looked confused.

"Armi had nothing to do with it. She was a pleasant, no-nonsense nurse. It was Erik I was upset with." She snorted. "As you know, I had a hysterectomy the winter before last. I'm not ashamed of it by any means, but hearing that Erik had been blabbing to some of his other patients that I was 'back in good working order' now that my uterus was out was repulsive," Marjatta explained indignantly.

"Also, I prefer a more natural approach to healing," she continued. "I felt Erik was always pushing the drugs and hormones a little too much. Some say he's his own best patient in that regard...but those are just rumors. The last straw was when I saw Erik kissing one of his patients in his office. I know the Hellströms' marriage is on the rocks, and we're all grown-ups, but a doctor should have some discretion when it comes to his patients."

I was stunned. "So he's quite the ladies' man, is he?" I managed to mutter sympathetically.

"He thinks he's quite the catch. I guess some women might go for a handsome doctor like that. Erik's wife has had enough, though. She's an artist who lives half the year somewhere on the French Riviera near Nice. I imagine it was a hard thing for Erik to hear that Doris has some pretty young sculptor on the side..." Marjatta smiled maliciously, and I grinned back, liking both her and Doris Hellström a little bit more, even though the latter was a complete stranger.

Erik Hellström kissing a patient...and writing himself prescriptions? Could Armi have had dirt on Hellström himself, not one of his patients?

I was still thinking about what Armi might have known as I rode to work the next morning. With the familiar wobble of my old green bicycle under me and the warmth of the morning sun making the mist rise from the vegetation, I had no particular interest in going indoors. I knew full well that Hellström was the person I most wanted to be guilty—I didn't like him, and he wasn't related to Antti. I chided myself: Was my own attitude any better than Detective Sergeant Ström's?

After our normal Monday morning meeting, Eki and I sat down to discuss the Kimmo Affair. Eki seemed even more concerned than before.

"Are you sure of the Hänninen boy's innocence?"

"Ninety-five percent."

"But if the police have a witness who heard Kimmo and Armi fighting after one o'clock, then..."

"I have a date with that witness in half an hour. Want to come along?"

"No, you go ahead. I'll go to court with Kimmo if I can just get a summary from you beforehand."

I didn't know whether I should be relieved or disappointed. I had already imagined the arraignment, with me as the heroic defense attorney striking Ström's pathetic theories to the ground with a few trenchant rejoinders. But that was only in my mind. In reality I would lose my cool, as would Ström, and the ensuing display would help Kimmo not one whit.

So, instead of trying to convince Eki I could handle the hearing, I set off to meet Armi's neighbor, the widow Kerttu Mannila, Ström's key witness. She lived at the other end of Armi's row of houses and had stopped by to visit Armi on the morning of the murder.

At least six inches shorter than me, stooped, and wrinkled, the old woman nevertheless still had plenty of pep. "I popped by that morning because I'd just made rice pudding and dough for my Karelian pies. Armi had asked me to teach her how we made them properly back in my village in the old days. I tried to tell her the night before that I would be making them, but she wasn't home. So I went to ring her doorbell around nine o'clock, but she said she didn't have time for baking. 'Is that boy of yours visiting?' I asked, to which she said she had all sorts of things going on. I promised to bring her some to taste later, and we agreed she would bake with me next time."

"And at one o'clock you took her some of the pies?" I asked. If Kimmo was lying, I was going to hang him from a tree by his balls.

"My sister called just as I was taking the last batch out of the oven, and I forgot all about Armi. Then at around five minutes to one, I set out with the pies to go through Armi's backyard, but when I came to the gate, I heard Armi speaking crossly to someone. I'd never even heard her raise her voice before. She was always such a sweet girl." The old woman's eyes twinkled amusingly—she was clearly conscious of her significance as a witness.

"Are you sure the person Armi was fighting with was Kimmo Hänninen? What were they saying?"

"Well, I only really heard Armi's voice. When I came to the gate, Armi was saying something like, 'I can't look the other way anymore; it just isn't right.'"

"And what did the other person say?"

"Well, you see, my hearing is not as good as it was when I was younger. Low voices are harder to make out. Armi's was loud and shrill. But the other one, he just mumbled. I couldn't make anything out. Then Armi said that she was going to call the police. At that point, I realized this conversation was none of my business, and I went home. I thought I would call first next time, before taking the pies over, but when I called at one thirty, no one answered."

"Luckily, you didn't go back and have to find the body," I said comfortingly.

"Oh, I'm not afraid of the dead, girlie. I was a nurse on the front lines during the war and saw more dead bodies than you ever will. They aren't any stranger than the living," Mannila said pointedly. "I just wish I'd had more pluck and just gone on in with my pies. Then maybe Armi would still be alive."

Responding to that was difficult, because in a way it was true. She was the only one so far with any direct knowledge of the moments preceding Armi's death. If the murderer were to hear about her testimony, Kerttu Mannila might herself be in danger. Had Ström's boys realized that?

When I brought up the issue, the old woman laughed.

"But what do I know? I didn't hear the murderer at all. I can't even say for certain whether it was a man or a woman. Whoever it was spoke quietly, as if they were afraid someone would hear. Of course I thought it was Kimmo at first, that they were having a lovers' quarrel, but now I don't know..."

If Ström was going to hold Kimmo and file charges based on Mannila's testimony, he was on shaky ground. If only I could find someone who could confirm that Kimmo had been back at his house by one o'clock. I guess I'd have to go drum up the witnesses myself, since the police seemed to be sitting on their hands.

After arriving back at the office, the first thing I had to do was rush to reach the phone ringing in my office.

"Hello, this is Elina Kataja. You left a message for me to call you."

"Yes. Thanks for returning my call. I wanted to chat a bit about Club Bizarre and Kimmo Hänninen. You do know Kimmo?"

"Kimmo? Of course. Why? What's it to you? Are you Kimmo's girlfriend he's always going on and on about?" Elina's low voice was irritated and suspicious.

I explained what had happened and that I needed to come up with some basis for my argument that sadomasochistic sexuality didn't automatically make Kimmo a murderer.

"Kimmo told you to talk to me?" Elina asked. "Dear Jesus. Will I have to go to court?"

"No. Not yet, at least. If the prosecutor's office decides to go to trial, that might be a different matter. Are you willing to confirm that Kimmo is a...masochist?"

"No doubt about it," Elina said with a laugh. "That was his problem. He wanted to do S&M with a dominant woman, but he didn't want to cheat on his girlfriend because he loved her so much. When you called, I freaked out. I thought Kimmo's girlfriend was calling to tell me to keep my hands off him."

"Why would she have done that? Was there something between you two?" I asked.

"No! We did this one performance at a club party where I tortured Kimmo, but it was just foreplay. Letting people watch us have sex would have been against the law—and Kimmo's morals. We'd have the cops down on us the second we started screwing in public...And like I said, Kimmo didn't want to cheat on his girlfriend. He keeps this side of his life strictly walled off from everything else. He's a prisoner of his sexuality and of Armi's love at the same time. I doubt he talks about this stuff with anyone in his normal life, at least not since Sanna died. Kimmo's sister, I mean."

"I knew Sanna. Was she a member of your club too?"

"Kimmo got into the club through her. Sanna knew this guy, Otso. I think he's still in jail. Anyway, Sanna was dating him for a while, and Otso brought Sanna to the club, and Sanna told Kimmo. But Sanna was different. For her this was all real. It was exciting but frightening at the same time."

"What do you mean by real?" I asked, remembering the slash marks on Sanna's arms.

"She wanted someone to hit her. I mean *really* hit, not just a little slapping for show. Not like...Ugh, I hate talking about this on the phone! Listen, we have a club party tomorrow night in this old warehouse downtown. Maybe if Kimmo gets out, you could come see firsthand what we do."

I am rarely at a loss for words, but that did it. My memories of the magazine images Ström had waved in front of my face were simultaneously intriguing and alarming.

"You don't have to dress up in leather or bring a whip," she said, a bit tauntingly. "Come in jeans if you want. I'll be easy to find—just look for the longest hair," Elina said. I was puzzled that she was telling me about the club's party so openly. I would have assumed outsiders weren't exactly welcome. We agreed that I would call Elina back once I knew whether the court would decide to hold Kimmo and file charges, or release him.

I hung up the receiver and did a mental inventory of my wardrobe. I did have that black leather skirt. Surely Antti's sister had a sewing machine. The leather jacket from my punk days was still hanging in my closet. I could do up my hair and maybe put on some real makeup. The thought of attending an S&M party was sounding more stimulating by the minute.

Eki interrupted my ruminations. Telling him about my last phone conversation without getting flustered was difficult. Taking notes, Eki kept his composure like the long-time divorce lawyer he was. I suppose life held few surprises for him anymore.

After Eki left, I tried to do a little work on some of my other cases. Forcing my brain to focus on a libel suit was difficult, though, when I had sex and murder running around in my head. Especially when this particular defamation case was a farce starring two home appliance salesmen. The recession was getting the better of their businesses, and their solution was to try to sink each other in a ruthless war of words and imagined affronts. The roles of plaintiff and defendant were just a matter of who had happened to file the paperwork fastest.

I forced myself to wade through the long list of complaints and then walked over to the grocery store to buy lunch. I dropped in at Makke's sporting goods store to see if he had recovered from his weekend of bingeing yet. At our first meeting, Makke had claimed he drank only a couple of pints in the evening, but that standard seemed to have gone out the window.

The store was summer boredom incarnate: the only customers were two little boys comparing baseball bats, while the radio softly burbled "Love Me Tender." Leaning against the counter and looking in serious need of a beer, Makke responded to my greeting with only a dip of his head.

"How do you feel?" I asked, though I could smell the answer from ten feet away.

"Terrible. After you left, I went to Hemingway's and sat on the patio until they closed, and then after that I don't remember much. Have they let Kimmo out yet?" Makke turned the King up as if to prevent the boys from overhearing our conversation, although they were clearly interested only in the baseball equipment.

"The court is considering that as we speak. What was the name of that friend of yours who came and told you about Armi's death?"

"Stögö. I mean Steffan Brandt. Why? Oh, I bet you want to hear how I reacted to the news, right? Is a defense lawyer's job to find someone else to blame?" Makke's cheek muscles tensed, his expression taking on a strange hardness. "What time was Armi killed? I don't have much of an alibi. I came here to the shop at about one thirty, and I rode my bike right by Armi's neighborhood. I stopped at the pizzeria around the corner to pick up a calzone to go. You can go ask the pizza dude whether I looked like I was out for blood."

"Your answers seem pretty well thought out," I replied just as aggressively.

"I'm sorry. I'm just worried some genius cop is going to decide I killed Sanna and now Armi. You never know what pigs will dream up."

Makke almost jumped into the air when the radio suddenly started blaring a heavy-metal song. He twisted the volume down because two middle-aged men were just entering the store.

"I'm not accusing you of anything," I hissed and then left, back to the office. However, what he had said bothered me: "I killed Sanna and now Armi." After all, it could be true.

I was just finishing an avocado when the phone rang again.

"Hi, it's Eki. Bad news. They're going to keep Kimmo in custody. He's asking for you. Take the Honda and get down here."

"What the hell?" I was so surprised I could have swallowed the avocado pit out of sheer consternation.

"Some new evidence came to light. We'll talk when you get here."

My hands were shaking as I started the car. I tried to keep my speed in check on the empty residential connector street that led downtown from our office. Where was the notorious cross-city traffic that meant we had to throw millions into building the Ring II beltway?

The familiar duty officer led me to the interview room where Eki and Kimmo sat. Eki looked irritated. When he saw me, Kimmo jumped out of his seat as though he wanted to throw himself into my arms. I was wrong—when I hugged him, his body was stiff and he didn't move to put his arms around me.

"Why didn't those damned idiots let Kimmo go?" I asked Eki as I sat down at the table and dug through my bag.

His shoulders hunched and his feet dragging as if he were obviously guilty, Kimmo walked to the window. Had he succeeded in pulling the wool over my eyes after all?

"The prosecutor wanted to continue conducting interviews and said they would likely file charges against Kimmo for Armi's murder. The motive they're proposing is an argument over sex, and they're basing that on the conversation the neighbor overheard, Kimmo's quote-unquote sexual perversion, and the forensic findings that Armi was likely strangled with gloves similar to the ones that go with Kimmo's suit. The rubber suit also had fibers from Armi's clothing and dirt from the lawn on it."

"But we have perfectly good explanations for the fibers and the dirt! And what the neighbor heard didn't have anything directly to do with Kimmo. Why would Armi have said she was going to the police over a disagreement with her fiancé about their sex life? And Kimmo said he didn't have the gloves with him. What if they were Armi's own dishwashing gloves? Have they even checked the house for a pair of those?"

"And apparently one of the neighbors was sure that Kimmo didn't come home until one thirty," Eki said, interrupting me. I could see in his eyes that he believed Kimmo was guilty.

"What neighbor? I want to talk to them right now!"

Eki shook his head, perhaps to say that he didn't know the name of the neighbor, perhaps to say there wasn't any point in trying.

"Goddamn it! Kimmo, I'm only going to ask you one more time: Did you kill Armi?"

When all he did was stare out the window, I marched over, grabbed him by the shoulders, and made him look me in the eyes. Kimmo's skin looked terrible—greasy, sweaty, with pitted acne scars studding his cheeks. His voice had a tone of resignation when he replied.

"No, I didn't kill her. But no one is going to believe that. Not the police, not Eki...and now not even you..."

I felt like Brutus. Ignoring Eki, I began explaining my telephone conversation with Elina Kataja. When he heard that I intended to investigate leads at the Club Bizarre event the next night, a slight smile crept onto his face.

"You'd better take Antti with you."

"Why? I know how to take care of myself."

"I'm sure you do, but within half an hour you're going to be sick of all the men panting and circling around you. And it won't be just men—a lot of people there are going to be interested in a new girl."

"I don't know what Antti would say. Or wear. Would you have something for him if he goes? Or has Ström emptied your stash?"

Kimmo forced a grin.

"My stuff is in a locked cabinet in my room. The spare key is on the bookshelf in my copy of *Seven Brothers* from freshman literature class. I figured it was a good bet no one would ever pick that up to read it."

"I'd also like to talk to some of Armi's friends. Any suggestions on who might be the most helpful?" I asked.

Kimmo gave me a few names and phone numbers of Armi's closest girlfriends, and then the guard escorted him back to his cell.

Eki and I caravanned back to the office. As I drove, I tried to get my thoughts organized, making lists in my mind. Lists of things I had to do. Lists of people I had to interview. Lists of suspects: Makke, Mallu, Mallu's husband, Armi's parents, Risto and Marita, Dr. Hellström. Wait, even Eki had been at Risto's party. What if Eki had killed Armi and thought the best way to get away with it was shifting the blame onto Kimmo? But what would be the motive there? I stared ahead at the thick neck and bald head of my employer, driving ahead of me. I didn't really know Eki. The few weeks I'd been working for him weren't much to go by. Perhaps Armi wanted to tell me something about him.

I'm going completely paranoid, I thought as I parked the Honda in the office driveway. Eki climbed out of his own car and said we needed to have a talk. The office was quiet, the only sound a muffled conversation coming from behind Martti's door.

"Just so you know, and this is to be kept between us: I do not believe Kimmo Hänninen is innocent." Eki sat down in the most comfortable chair in our conference room and grabbed the last piece of chocolate out of the bowl on the table. "That seems clear enough now. At this point, pleading down to manslaughter is our best bet, and we should probably request a psychiatric evaluation as well. All of the Hänninens are messed up, at least Annamari and her children," Eki added, as if afraid of insulting my almost-relatives.

"I disagree. I think Kimmo is innocent."

Eki's eyebrows went up. "On what basis?"

"Ström's...Detective Sergeant Ström's evidence is shaky. And then just my general impression. My instincts tell me that Kimmo didn't murder Armi."

"But the law doesn't operate based on women's intuition," Eki said sternly. "In any case, we need to concentrate on defending Kimmo the best way we can. You can go to that club if you want, if you think it will help somehow. Kimmo trusts you. But perhaps it would be best if you try to get him to confess and we'll move forward with a plea bargain."

I stared at Eki. I felt terrible—how was I going to be a lawyer when I couldn't even convince my own boss that our own client was innocent?

"I understand that as a former police officer, you naturally want to investigate the case more broadly. It's in your blood. By all means investigate, but not on office time."

I counted slowly to ten. Losing my cool wasn't going to help. Eki had chosen his side, and I would have to adapt to that. The police considered the case closed as well. Only one doubter remained: yours truly.

Concentrating on my other cases, I was a good girl for the rest of the day. Although I did try to reach Elina Kataja—Angel—as well as some of Armi's girlfriends. After work, I headed to the gym. I hoped that wrestling with some weights would improve my mood.

In the women's dressing-room mirror, I witnessed my transformation, morphing from no-nonsense legal counselor to serious weight trainer. I wiped my makeup off and pulled my hair up into a high ponytail. My lightweight dress got shoved into my gym bag, and I donned a sleeveless top and green stretch pants in its place. Leather sandals went into the locker and cross-trainers on. Lifting gloves velcroed at the wrist. Another Maria Kallio stared back at me now. Just how many of me were there?

Apparently, nobody felt like being indoors on a beautiful summer evening, so the gym was a ghost town. As I worked my way systematically through my routine—first legs, then upper body—for an hour and a half, I tried once more to sort everything in my mind. I wondered where Marita might have come by her bruise and whether the vitamins accompanying Makke's morning cocktail were as innocent as he claimed they were. Did performance-enhancing drugs and hormones change hands here, in this gym? Did Makke use them? He was not muscle-bound by any means, but the way he drank must have made maintaining his physique a challenge. Maybe steroids were his trick. And if he had the connections to get those, perhaps he had scored drugs for Sanna.

When I left the gym, I had a whole list of questions in need of answers. At the very least, I was sure that this case was nowhere near as straightforward as it looked to Detective Sergeant Pertti Ström.

Antti was in his office. In order to let him know I was home, I banged around a bit in the kitchen. Chomping on a piece of bread, I called Marita, since she was the only person close I thought might own a sewing machine. In addition to the help with my leather skirt alterations, perhaps I could also get some information.

"Why don't you come over right now? And how is Kimmo holding up?" Relaying the bad news was difficult. I almost felt like Marita was starting to believe her brother-in-law was guilty. I promised to come by as soon as I could. I also called one of Armi's friends whom Kimmo had suggested I contact, a class-mate from nursing school named Minna.

I explained who I was and that I hoped to help find out what had happened to Armi.

"Yes, I heard. Sari Rannikko, another girl we know from school, called me. Sari is actually on her way over here now. This is just so terrible," Minna said, bursting into tears.

"Would it be possible for all three of us to meet up? I was just going to call Sari too," I said. "Would tonight at seven thirty at Café Socis downtown work?"

Minna agreed, and I started feeling better. I knew that my close friends, though there were only a few, knew a lot more about me than my parents did—Sari and Minna were bound to be able to tell me something new about Armi.

Finally, Antti came ambling up from downstairs.

"How did it go?" he asked, and then saw the answer written on my face.

"Oh shit...Is he guilty?"

I went over the evidence again and told him where each of the parties stood, ending with some choice words about the stupidity of both my own boss and the police. Antti, however, appeared pensive.

"I know Kimmo a lot better than you do," he said once my tirade ended. "And I don't know...Maybe he could have killed Armi. Anyone can kill if they're angry enough."

"I'm betting you didn't say that to the review board when you applied for your conscientious objector's exemption from military service," I said belligerently. "Will you go with me to that party tomorrow?"

"Uh. Here's the thing: I don't think I'm really the voyeuristic type. And I'm not Kimmo's lawyer. Are you sure your old grudge against this Ström guy isn't affecting your judgment? You are an ex-cop. You have to know they don't put people in jail without the proper evidence."

"Oh, so you know all about cops now because you've been sleeping with one? Let me tell you about cops—they just want an easy ride! What do you want me to do, sit on my thumbs while Kimmo goes to prison for twenty years because of one lazy, prejudiced prick?"

"You aren't a cop anymore."

"No, I'm not, but I have no intention of just letting things run their course! As far as I'm concerned, you can go right ahead and hide your head in the sand, just like you did during Tommi's case."

That hurt. First Antti went red, then white. His eyes narrowed as like an angry cat's. For a moment, I thought he might hit me, but then he just turned on his heels and stormed back down to his office, slamming the door as he went. I knew I had attacked Antti in the most tender spot he had. He still felt guilty for his friend's death and the whole mess surrounding it.

Jackass, I thought, not really knowing which of us I meant. Would it just be better for us to split up, since we couldn't seem to stop fighting? Still, I wasn't in the habit of giving up easily, not in my work or in my personal relationships.

7

A few hours later, I was looking out of a bus window at the clouds wandering across the sky, still thinking about Antti. As if by common consent, neither of us had spoken about Tommi's death since last summer. Guilt about what had happened still ate away at both of us. Antti had failed to reveal vital information, and I had rushed the arrest. The perpetrator—another of Antti's friends—remained confined to a psychiatric hospital.

However, Antti was more sensitive and withdrawn than I was on the subject. When things got hard, he usually retreated to the sanctum of his office to sulk. I, on the other hand, was more likely to yell for half an hour and then try to extend an olive branch. Antti wanted to mull problems over, to study them from every angle like a good mathematician. I was hastier, jumping to rash conclusions and never wanting to dwell on anything.

Just like every other teenage girl, I used to dream of finding a tall, dark, melancholy lover. Antti definitely fit the criteria of my adolescent daydreams, but it turns out that actually living with the moody leading man wasn't always easy. Maybe Jessica Rabbit was right to want a man who could make her laugh.

However, as I stepped off the bus in downtown Helsinki, I realized that Antti did make me laugh. It was just the pressure of his dissertation that had been sapping his sense of humor lately. And, of course, getting mixed up in a murder investigation for the second time was bound to traumatize him. I had always wondered about the heroes I saw on detective shows who just went on with their lives as person after person dropped dead around them every episode. In real life, every violent death left an indelible mark on the people involved. Without the flimsy wall of protection provided by my professional role, I might have been on the verge of coming unhinged too.

With the descriptions Minna had given over the phone, I easily found Armi's girlfriends sitting at a window table talking over cups of tea beneath the chandeliers of the ornate café. Minna had a low, nervous voice; Sari startled me with her loud, piercing tones.

I was already grumpy, and hearing Sari's voice didn't do much to raise my spirits. I've always despised people with ugly voices. Tall and thin with sharp features and short-cropped hair, Sari's jagged looks fit her voice. Nearsighted eyes darted restlessly behind stylish glasses.

"Is it true that Kimmo murdered Armi?" Sari practically yelled as I joined them at their table.

"The police believe so," I replied quietly and then rehearsed my increasingly tiresome account of events so far. "I was hoping you two might be able to suggest other possibilities. What was your impression of Armi and Kimmo's relationship? Did Armi say anything out of the ordinary recently? I'm going to get a cup of tea, and then we can talk. Can I offer you anything?"

"I could really use some ice cream, but I don't know if I can right now since Armi..." Sari said, her voice now a whine.

"Armi wouldn't mind," Minna said. She was short, with soft curves and dark curls. Under normal circumstances, she probably looked like a Lappish doll with those round eyes and red cheeks, but shock had sucked all of the joy out of her.

Sari was still at the counter dithering over what flavor of ice cream to choose when I returned to the window table. Minna blew her nose into a handkerchief and then quickly said, "I don't get Sari. Armi and Sari were in the same classes all through elementary school. But it's almost like she's enjoying this."

Sari returned to the table. "I got vanilla and rum raisin," she announced. "Armi liked rum raisin with strawberry. Strange combination, don't you think? The last time I saw Armi was a week ago when she was over at my place. I live just north of the sports park in those new buildings. But I called her on Saturday. I've wondered whether I should tell the police."

"You called on Saturday? What time?" I didn't bother to conceal my enthusiasm, although the reaction of pleasure I saw in Sari's face nauseated me.

"Around twelve thirty. I was going to invite her to go into the city, but she said she had visitors coming and—"

"Did she say what visitors?" I said, interrupting unapologetically.

"Some Maria. Did she mean you? And then she had to call her sister."

I made a mental note to ask Mallu about that call. Did it ever take place?

"How did Armi sound? Angry? Frightened?"

"Perfectly normal. I guess she and Kimmo had been fighting, but it wasn't anything serious. Kimmo had just gone home."

I guess my expression gave away how important that last sentence was.

"I wondered about that too," Sari continued. "Did Kimmo come back?"

"You need to tell the police about this call. It could mean a lot for Kimmo." I couldn't help breathing a sigh of relief. At least for Kimmo.

"Minna, when did you last see Armi?"

Minna looked uncertain. "A couple of weeks ago, I guess. I worked the night shift last week, and I don't think we even talked on the phone the whole week. When I had seen her, we went to the movies and then had a glass of wine. Armi was obviously worried about something. She was quizzing me about pharmacology, asking me about different benzodiazepines."

"What are those?"

"Sedatives, pretty mild. She said someone she knew was popping them like they were candy."

Perhaps I needed to make the rounds of everyone's medicine cabinets. Although drug abuse didn't make anyone a murderer. Armi had worked in a private physician's office, though. Was it possible she had been dealing prescription drugs?

"She talked to me about Sanna recently," Sari said, butting in. "Kimmo's sister, the one who drowned last spring. She was totally nuts, and she used drugs too. A couple of weeks ago, Armi came over for coffee and said she had had a fight with Kimmo about Sanna. Armi didn't believe Sanna committed suicide."

Sari was speaking so loudly that the people at the neighboring tables turned to look at us. Great—a confidential conversation about sex, murder, and drugs, with only half of one of the busiest cafés in the city listening in.

"Armi thought Sanna was murdered!" Sari yelled, even more emphatically. Minna looked scared.

"So who killed her?" I asked, more aggressively than necessary.

"Her boyfriend. That's what Armi said. That Sanna's lover murdered her."

"Makke? Why? Did Armi say that to Kimmo?"

"She just said she and Kimmo had a fight because Kimmo thought Sanna committed suicide, but Armi was convinced she was murdered."

I emptied my teacup, wishing something stronger had been in there. Armi believed that Makke killed Sanna. Why? Makke told me himself he talked with Armi a lot about Sanna. Did he let something slip? Did he just feel responsible, or was he confessing to killing her? I thought back to the bits of conversation Armi's elderly neighbor had heard coming through the garden gate. What if Armi had been talking to Makke? I remembered the harried eyes juxtaposed with his boyish face, the bulging, veined muscles of his arms. Strangling Armi would have been easy for him.

Or did Armi mean she was going to call the police on someone else? Forensic analysis had shown liquor and drugs in Sanna's bloodstream. What if Armi meant that Makke gave Sanna an overdose? Or could Armi have been talking about her own boyfriend, Kimmo?

"Armi was talking about Sanna's boyfriend, not her own, right?"

Sari looked confused and then her brow wrinkled. "I don't think she was talking about Kimmo. Why would she have been fighting with him?"

Oh, you have no idea, I felt like saying, but I left it alone. Sari's story certainly opened up new possibilities—I would have to give Makke a closer look and ask Kimmo about this fight.

As a tram trundled by, the wind picked up, blowing a yellow plastic bag under the wheels. Women's skirts tried to make for the sky, where blue-black clouds were gathering in promise of rain. Soon nothing would be left of the cherry blossoms in the yard.

"You were Armi's best friends. I only met her once. Can you help me understand: What kind of person was she, really?"

Again, Sari took the initiative.

"We were in the same classes all through school. Back then, she was always nice and a little quiet. No offense, Minna, but she was exactly the type who grows up to be a nurse. Always did her homework and came to school with her clothes neatly pressed. I've always been a chatterbox, as you can tell." Sari smiled with apparent self-satisfaction. "And I guess Armi needed someone to stick up for her at school."

"She didn't seem at all shy to me," I interjected. "Quite the opposite."

"I was just getting to that. In junior high, she started to change. Yes, she was still meticulous, but she started to have a little more spirit. We ended up fighting a lot then and spent less time together—typical preteen girl stuff. We didn't really become friends again until our senior year in high school. She still would get on my nerves sometimes; she could be really stubborn. And although I don't like speaking ill of the dead, she was nosy too."

"Was Armi a gossip?"

"She wasn't a busybody at all," Minna said quickly, as if fearing that Sari would interrupt. "She did always want to know about people and what made them tick, but she never talked behind their backs."

"Armi definitely knew how to get people to talk. She knew everything there was to know about me," Sari said.

I didn't doubt that one bit. Sari struck me as the sort of person whose favorite hobby was talking about herself.

"Armi may have been a little tactless to be a nurse. She was a little too direct. She didn't dress things up," Minna explained. "That was why she did better working in an outpatient clinic like she did, where you only ever deal with one patient for a little while. She could never understand how I worked in a hospice surrounded by people who were all going to die. Armi wanted to heal people. That was why she had such a hard time with Mallu's situation, that she couldn't have children no matter how much she and her husband tried. Armi spent a lot of time studying medical journals and talking with Dr. Hellström about how to help her sister."

"Did she talk to you about Mallu's accident?"

"Several times," Minna replied. "Armi blamed the driver of that car that almost hit Mallu for causing her miscarriage. In fact, she even mentioned it to me the last time we met. She said something strange like, 'If only I could make it up to Mallu.'" Minna's brow wrinkled. "She really did say 'make it up.' But the accident wasn't her fault."

A chill went through me as I recalled Mallu's husband's thinking that he saw Armi behind the wheel of the car that nearly ran them down. What if one of them really believed Armi was responsible for the loss of their baby?

"There is no way Kimmo killed Armi. Armi liked helping people, but she knew how to set her feelings aside when she needed to. If she had known something dangerous about someone, she would have gone straight to the police," Sari said, still speaking too loudly.

More chills. Was Armi's death my fault? Armi wanted to tell me something that someone else didn't want me to know. Was it about the hit-and-run driver or Sanna's murderer? Had that person been among us at the Hänninens' party? I thought back to that pleasant late-spring evening, trying to figure out which of the partygoers could be a wolf in sheep's clothing.

"Well, if we're going to think about other possible suspects for the murder, then I guess I should ask about your alibis too," I said, trying to sound playful. "Where were each of you between one and two last Saturday afternoon?"

"At work," Minna said quietly.

"Between one and two? I guess I was in Tapiola shopping," Sari said angrily. "Is that a good enough alibi for you? I saw at least a dozen people I know, including Mallu. I guess I could have slipped away to strangle Armi at some point, but why would I have?"

"Was Mallu in Tapiola?" I remembered her claiming she was home the whole morning.

"Yeah, I saw her at the outdoor market looking at wild mushrooms. I remember because she said she couldn't afford them living on unemployment."

"What time did this happen?"

"I couldn't say exactly. Maybe around one thirty."

Mallu in Tapiola at one thirty looking at mushrooms? Would a person who had just murdered her little sister then calmly go off to do her grocery shopping? Who knew? I was starting to feel as though I couldn't be sure of anything anymore.

When we parted, I made Sari promise to contact the police with her side of the story. It was already nine o'clock at night— too late to go see Mallu again. The thought of returning home terrified me, though; I knew I had treated Antti unfairly, but I wasn't in the mood to apologize quite yet.

The house was quiet, with no sign of Antti even in his office. Two flashes drew me to the answering machine. The first message was a direct recording from Antti, not a phone call: "Hi. I'm going for a walk."

The second message was from Annamari Hänninen, her hysterical voice asking me to call back no matter what the hour. She wanted to talk about Kimmo. After considering for a moment whether I was really still up to calling her back today, I realized this would give me an opportunity to ask some questions I had about Sanna.

At first, Annamari seemed as though she wasn't going to answer. Seven rings later, however, she picked up and whispered a frightened hello.

"Maria! Could you come over here right now? We have to talk. I know it's late, but this is important."

"I'll be there in fifteen minutes." Throwing on my denim jacket, I jumped on my bike and set off pedaling.

The beauty of the evening seemed to demand a slower pace. Seagulls and ducks swam along the shore of Otsolahti Bay, and the dog walkers were out in force, their pets sniffing each other, tails of various sizes and lengths wagging excitedly. As I rode over Westend Bridge to the road that hugged the far shore, I admired the pillar of light made by the setting sun. A blackbird trilled, competing with the song of a finch, with doves and nightingales providing accompaniment in the background. The tiny yellow blossoms of the cloverlike bird's-foot trefoil had already burst into flower along the shore.

For a moment, I thought about biking by the breakwater to see whether Antti was sitting in his favorite spot, but in order to save time I kept focused and stayed on the larger streets.

I had only once visited the house where Annamari and Kimmo lived, and then only downstairs in the sauna facilities. The location where the house stood was beautiful, opposite the water with a wide street separating it from the seashore. If this family had nothing else, they had plenty of money. I had always appreciated how unspoiled and down-to-earth Antti was, and now I realized I could probably say the same for Kimmo. Neither of them had that self-assuredness that often accompanies growing up with lots of money, and in fact, just a pinch more of that might actually have done them both good. Insecurity and whining seem particularly unattractive in men, and this case I was working on seemed to have an overabundance of that type, especially if I counted Makke's constant self-pity.

Coming to answer the door, which was arched by climbing roses, Annamari didn't seem particularly self-confident either. Her usually perfect makeup now ran in smeared little streams into the wrinkles around her eyes. Her hands were in constant motion, flitting up to her hair, touching her shoulders and forearms, and then moving back to her hair as the tone of her voice oscillated almost as erratically.

"So lovely you could come! Tell me everything about Kimmo! Are they treating him properly? Why do they insist on keeping him in jail? My little Kimmo is no murderer."

"Didn't Eki Henttonen call you?"

"Yes, he did, but he wouldn't really tell me anything. Men are like that. They don't understand a mother's feelings. Would you like a little cognac? I know I need some at least."

Based on her breath, I could tell she had a good head start on me. No wonder. I hoped it would make her feel better.

"He was talking as if Kimmo is guilty," Annamari said as she handed me a snifter nearly filled to the brim with cognac. At first, the contents burned the roof of my mouth and throat, but then they moved pleasantly down to my stomach in a warm stream. The finish was heavenly—I guess there really were differences in cognacs. Up to this point, I had never had the wherewithal to sample anything much above cheap one-star cut brandy.

"The police have found a lot of evidence against Kimmo. None of it will necessarily hold up in court though."

"The police came today and rummaged through Kimmo's things. They took a lot with them when they left."

"What did the officers look like? Did they have a search warrant?" Apparently, Ström had beat me here. Irritating.

"One was big and rude, and the other one was smaller with red hair. They waved some piece of paper at me, and asked me all sorts of questions about Kimmo. Had I noticed anything out of the ordinary in his personality? Was he violent as a child? Did he have many girlfriends? Did I beat him?" Annamari shook her head, with good reason. That kind of questioning sounded just about right for Ström's primitive grasp of psychology. Ström had decided that Kimmo was a deviant sex murderer, and now he was grasping for ways to support that hypothesis wherever he could.

"They also wanted to know where I was on Saturday. Was I able to prove when Kimmo came home? But I left for Stockmann in Tapiola at eleven and then went for my massage. I went to get the twins after their lunch so we could go into the city. I wasn't home at all. If only I had known."

"Exactly what time did you go to Risto and Marita's house to get the boys?" I asked.

"One fifteen, maybe one thirty. I don't remember exactly. The boys weren't ready yet, so we had to wait for the two o'clock bus."

The walk home from Armi's house would have taken Kimmo only fifteen or twenty minutes. Why the hell had every person I talked to spent Saturday running around downtown Tapiola? The only people home in town seemed to be Antti and me, home nursing our hangovers.

"What do you and Henttonen intend to do to get Kimmo out?" Annamari demanded.

"Well, my intention is to gather evidence showing that someone else murdered Armi. Now, I know you may not want to talk about this, Annamari, but I've heard rumors that Armi suspected Sanna's suicide was really a homicide."

I knew this wasn't going to be a pleasant subject, but I hadn't expected quite as strong a reaction as I now received. Turning bright red, Annamari's breathing sped up and she began to shake uncontrollably.

"Murdered!" Annamari's voice was piercing. "No one murdered Sanna! It was an accident! Sanna was just celebrating... too much. She drank, she must have been tired, she fell in the water. That's all. A horrible accident! I don't care what people say. Why would Sanna have committed suicide? And why would you think anyone killed her?" With trembling hands, Annamari poured herself more cognac.

I wondered whether she could have become this worked up in a conversation with Armi and rapped those skittish hands around the neck of her future daughter-in-law. Would a mother murder his son's fiancée and let him take the blame, though? My notions of motherhood were still idealistic, even though none of the mothers I knew seemed to live up to them.

"Did Sanna leave anything personal behind? Letters, diaries, notebooks?" I thought the best way I could get a handle on Sanna's death was by getting into her thoughts. Maybe I would learn she was planning to commit suicide and could put the idea of a second murder to rest.

"Sanna filled dozens of diaries," Annamari said proudly. "But Henrik and Kimmo burned them all after she died. They claimed she would have wanted it that way. And we think her last one went into the sea with her. I do still have some of her old schoolwork and papers in a closet upstairs. Would you like to come look at them?"

Climbing the stairs to the second floor, Annamari led me into a walk-in closet filled with miscellaneous stuff. A couple of shoeboxes of Sanna's papers stood stacked in one corner. As I carefully leafed through the topmost box, a photograph fell out of a stack of what looked like lecture notes. A very innocent-looking Sanna kissing an ugly man with a black beard.

"Who is this man?" I asked Annamari.

She wrung her hands as if not wanting to answer. "That's that horrible Otso Hakala. Thank God he went to jail for selling drugs."

"Was Sanna dating him?"

"No! She didn't even like him. He just controlled her using all those drugs."

"Could I take these with me? I might be able to find something new in them."

"How is dredging up the past going to get Kimmo out of jail?" Annamari asked dubiously. I didn't have an answer, but Annamari relented anyway.

While Annamari went downstairs to get me a bag to pack all of Sanna's things into, I pocketed the photograph. After banging around on the main floor for a while, Annamari yelled up that she was going out to the shed. Suddenly I had a vivid memory of Sanna. It was a night about this same time of year—late May or early June, a couple of days before school was set to end and Sanna would graduate. After band practice, the boys and I went to the only park in town to drink. Then other people started showing up, including Sanna. One year had been plenty of time for her to gain a terrible reputation in our small town.

Most people couldn't understand how a loser like her could get six perfect scores on her college entrance exams. Having only admired her from afar, I didn't really know Sanna, but I envied the intense color of her brown eyes and the diffident beauty of her manner.

At some point, Sanna and I were the only girls left. That always happened, since most small-town girls felt they had to keep up appearances and go home to sleep like good little dollies. Sanna sat on a rock rolling a cigarette. That was a sign of degeneracy as well, since a girl who smoked should at least buy packs of proper "light" cigarettes.

Even though I didn't smoke, I asked Sanna for one. In retrospect, I realize this was an attempt to get closer to her. Even at that age, I longed for other women to relate to.

Sanna rolled me a cigarette, licked the glue surface with her kitten-pink tongue, lit the result in her mouth, and handed it to me. Then followed my miserable attempt to act like I did this every day while simultaneously trying not to vomit. The evening was hot, but Sanna was wearing tight black jeans and a worn brown leather jacket. She held her beer bottle close, with both hands wrapped around it. I tried to think of some great conversation starter, but my mind felt completely blank. Then the boys started raising a racket about going to some bar, and Sanna left with them.

At Sanna's graduation, we had all stared at her scars. I remember how she stared back at us, at once defiant and ashamed, how I tried to smile in reply to the challenge of her drunken eyes, how she offered me a drink from her bottle as if in thanks.

Then Sanna moved, disappearing into Helsinki. We bumped into each other a couple of times in the city and said hi. Two girls from the sticks. She stayed the same, just as thin and girlish. Only the skin of her face paled, like a death mask. I didn't dare tell Sanna I went to the police academy; I just said I worked various jobs before getting into law school.

I would see her at the university behind a glass of beer back when you could still get that in the café, and sometimes she would be in the courtyard of the Porthania Building smoking with that same old brown leather jacket slung over her shoulder. She said she was doing her thesis on the metaphorical language of Sylvia Plath's poetry. Did she ever complete that thesis?

Annamari returned with a large Stockmann shopping bag, pulling me back into the present moment.

"Could I maybe come get the papers later? I'll bring a backpack so carrying them is easier," I suggested. I didn't want to leave the papers at the Hänninens' for a single moment longer than I had to, but transporting them now would be a pain.

"Henrik is calling again tomorrow. What will I say to him?" Annamari asked, wringing her hands like the heroine in a gothic novel.

"Tell him the truth." I remembered Henrik Hänninen's strangely diabolical dark eyebrows.

"I can't stand to listen to his shouting. Isn't there any hope of Kimmo's release?"

"There is always hope" was my banal attempt at comfort. Annamari's company was depressing, and when I opened the front door to leave and smelled the climbing roses, I felt as though I were escaping from somewhere suffocating.

Once on my bike, I pointed my wheels toward the breakwater, wanting to see the place where Sanna died. On that dark March night, the breakwater would have been a lonely place, strangely far from the homey lights glimmering on the shore. How did Sanna feel when she fell into the water? I thought about the frigid grip of the sea at only one or two degrees above freezing as I rode far too fast along the narrow strip of gravel leading out to the breakwater. Suddenly my front wheel slammed into a rock. I turned the handlebars violently—and then it happened.

The handlebars separated from the frame of the bicycle. I madly squeezed the brake levers to no avail. The world turned upside down, the water and sky trading places, and suddenly I was in the water, under the water, scraping the gravelly seafloor and drawing my lungs full of something cold and salty, fighting hopelessly toward the surface.

Fortunately, the water was less than a meter deep so near the shore. Fortunately, I had injured only one wrist and my left knee.

"Damn it!" Sitting in the seawater, I watched my handlebars floating a little farther off. They *had* felt a little strange on the way to the Hänninens'.

Slowly, how damn cold the water was and how badly my knee hurt sank in. I fished the handlebars out of the water. My poor bicycle was a couple of meters farther on down the shore, so I waded over to it and carried it over my shoulder back to land. The brake lines had snapped with the force of the collision, so the bike was nearly useless, and I was wet through.

With more cursing, I rammed the handlebars back into place, tightened the bolt as well as I could by hand, and started riding carefully back around the bay. I couldn't figure out how the handlebars had managed to come loose. I had just done my spring tune-up and checked all of the components, especially the brakes. I felt lucky, though; even though I ended up in the water, the handlebars could have come off in a much worse place. For example, I could have been riding at my usual clip around a steep curve—there were two on my way to work—turned the handlebars quickly, and…

Was this the work of some idiot passerby? Vandals had knocked my bike around before. They had the air let out of my tires more than once, and once someone had even slashed them. Painted bright green, my old men's bike had its own personality—in the whole world there wasn't another one like it, and I had no intention of giving it up. Perhaps my easily recognizable bicycle irritated someone. Or—did I irritate someone?

I like to think my teeth were chattering only from the cold when I finally dumped my bike at our front door. I walked in, tearing my clothes off and dropping them in a wet heap on the dressing room floor, followed by ten minutes under a burning hot shower.

When I finally stepped into the living room wrapped in a thick bathrobe, Antti looked at me in concern.

"What on earth happened to you?"

"I fell into the bay on my bike. Do you want some tea?" I tried to sound calm, even though I was afraid. Despite our earlier fight, being with Antti felt wonderful.

"How did you end up in the bay? Where?"

"My handlebars came off just as I was on the path out to the breakwater."

"They came off? But we just did a tune-up on both bikes less than a month ago."

"I'm thinking someone wanted to play a nice little practical joke on me." The forced nonchalance in my tone did not fool Antti.

"That must have been scary."

I let Antti take me in his arms.

"Your nose is still freezing. Put on some wool socks so you don't catch cold. I'll get the vitamin C."

Antti's concern brought tears to my eyes. The day had been far too long, and I was afraid. Who had sabotaged my bike? Antti stroked my hair, and Einstein rubbed his head sympathetically against my shins. Even though there might be a murderer on the loose, I still had my tall, dark, and handsome man, and a big, ferocious cat to come home to.

8

I was sitting on the breakwater looking out to sea. Suddenly slimy, algae-covered hands stretched out of the water and began pulling me into the depths. Under the water, I saw Sanna's green face. Her hair swirled around her, moving with the water current, and her body was covered in scales, all the way down to a mermaid tail. Sanna had come to take me away.

I woke up to Einstein, agitated by my kicking, jumping off the foot of the bed and knocking over the radio sitting on the floor. The clock said five o'clock in the morning, and the birds were already making a racket outside. Pulling my pillow over my ears, I curled up closer to Antti and fell back into a fitful sleep for another two hours.

After our morning coffee, we gave my bicycle a thorough going-over. There was nothing wrong with it—the handlebars just should not have come loose like that. Now Antti seemed perplexed by the incident as well.

"Maybe that hideous green paint is getting on someone's nerves. Although I have a hard time imagining someone just walking around with an Allen wrench loosening handlebars. Do you have any secret enemies?" Antti asked, only half kidding.

I was starting to get unnerved again. Who would have wanted to hurt me? I remembered Annamari going outside while I was in the house. But would she even have known how to sabotage my bike?

Then I went through all the places where I had left my bike in the last few days, still ending up none the wiser.

"Are you sure this bike accident has something to do with Armi's death?" Antti asked, as I was standing in the yard ready to leave for work. I didn't know how to answer, and pedaled away.

With fog rolling in off the water, the day was cooler than the previous few had been, and most of the dog walkers I normally saw seemed to have decided to stay home instead of taking their usual loop around the bay. I found myself riding slower than usual because my knee still hurt a little. Hopefully I would be able to go for a run later. That would help calm me down.

After lunch, I went to see Kimmo and nearly blew my top when I heard that Ström had questioned him for at least two hours already that morning without any legal representation. If Ström had still been at the station, I would have given him an earful. Instead, I suggested to Kimmo that we file a complaint and refuse any further interviews, but he just shook his head in resignation.

"What will that help? They've already decided I'm guilty. I'm going to prison either way. And what does that matter anyway, since Armi is dead," Kimmo said, slumped in his uncomfortable chair, his eyes bloodshot. I felt like kicking him in the head.

"Kimmo, stand up for yourself! This isn't some Kafka book—this is real life. They can't put you in prison if you're innocent. Why the hell didn't you tell them about Armi's theory that Sanna was murdered?"

"Armi's theory that what? I didn't," Kimmo muttered, so wormlike that I felt like marching right out the door. "I don't know how Armi got that idea into her head. I thought she was just trying to offer my parents some comfort. But I'm one hundred percent sure that Sanna committed suicide." Kimmo looked past me at somewhere only he could see.

I remembered the green-faced Sanna from my nightmare and wondered whether Kimmo dreamed about his sister.

"Sanna did talk about how she meant to have a fresh start, a new life, after she turned thirty and how she was happy with Makke, but she was pretty hooked on the booze and the pills at that point. Armi didn't know Sanna like we did, so she could believe her stories. Maybe Sanna killed herself because she felt like she would never be able to change her life. You should read the poem she left on her desk. Even Antti thought it was intended as a suicide note."

"Why would Armi start bringing up this theory and talking so much about Sanna being murdered now? It's been more than a year since it happened."

"She said she never understood the whole context of the poem until now, that she'd never read the Finnish translation before. She claimed it was a story about rebirth, not just death. I don't know—I'm not a literary scholar! Read it yourself."

Kimmo's last comment bothered me though. Armi didn't seem like much of a student of literature either. I tried to remember whether her bookshelves contained any poetry beyond the standard *Collected Works of Eino Leino*. Analyzing Sylvia Plath really didn't seem in character for Armi.

I left Kimmo with a couple of books Antti had sent, hoping they would make his time in jail pass more easily. Then after work, I went to Marita's to alter my leather skirt. To my disappointment, she didn't have any time to talk because one of her friends from work was visiting, sitting in her living room. "Gossiping," Marita said darkly, as she led me to the kitchen and set up the sewing machine. I hadn't realized what a stir Armi's murder was causing in Tapiola. Maybe instead of investigating the hard way, I should be sitting downtown, in the square, listening to rumors and chatting up winos.

As Marita bent down to show me how to thread the bobbin, I again noticed the bruise under her ear, which was starting to turn yellow around the edges.

Just as I was backstitching the seam, the twins came bouncing into the kitchen and attacked the juice pitcher. Only after it was empty did they have time for me.

"Maria, was it you who arrested Kimmo, since you're a policeman?" Matti asked.

"No, not me. It was other policemen. And I'm not a police officer anymore," I said as I snipped the last thread end.

"Are they bad policemen like sometimes on TV?"

I didn't feel up to doing my bit to instill in the rising generation a deep and abiding faith in the Finnish justice system, so instead I just nodded.

"Some bad policemen took Otso too, and Sanna cried," Mikko explained.

Otso, Otso Hakala. The one Angel and Annamari had mentioned. The man who beat Sanna and was serving out a drug sentence.

"Is Kimmo a murderer? Why doesn't anyone ever tell us anything?" Mikko asked pointedly, but before I could answer, the boys were already tumbling out of the room as if they didn't want to know the truth after all. I knew that Marita couldn't wait for school to end on Friday. She meant to send the boys to their Sarkela-side grandparents in Inkoo until the situation here resolved itself.

As soon as I reached home, I hurried out for a jog. My knee was holding up really well, but a stabbing pain shot through my left shoulder whenever my left shoe struck the ground at too severe an angle. I ran south, crossing under the highway to Karhusaari Island to admire the old Sinebrychoff Mansion; a construction crew had just freed it from its tarps after a renovation of the exterior.

The shore of the island was deserted as I jogged into the shade of the forest, dodging the protruding roots of the trees. The noise of the West Highway was on the far side of the island now, and birdsong was all I could hear. Once back on the shore, I did a few stretches and then ran leisurely back along the forest path.

Then from behind I heard loud, thudding steps and heavy panting. Someone was coming up on me, running like he thought he was Carl Lewis.

Instinctively I sped up. I hate it when someone tries to overtake me. I attempted a look over my shoulder, but all I saw was a dark tracksuit disappearing into the trees as my Olympic pursuer turned onto the trail leading to the interior of the island. Perhaps he would cut across and be waiting for me farther along the shore, ready to push me into the sea like Sanna.

Almost tripping on the root of a pine tree snapped me back to my senses. Why did I think someone was stalking me? I was making far too big a deal out of my bike accident. Still, getting back into the mix of other people and dogs on the pedestrian path along the highway was a relief.

At around nine o'clock, I started getting dolled up for Club Bizarre. First, I pulled out a shiny black leotard I sometimes wore at the gym. Over that came fishnets and the leather skirt, followed by four-inch stilettos, which I might someday learn to walk in if I wore them enough. Fifteen minutes and half a can of super-hold hair spray later, my hair was in a messy, edgy style. The lower stratum of my makeup arsenal yielded white face powder, black eyeliner, and fire engine–red lipstick. Occasionally, I cursed myself for not bothering to throw out my old stuff. Apparently keeping some had been a good idea after all.

When I was ready, I swayed into the entryway and pulled on my old leather jacket. Teenage Maria stared back at me from the full-length mirror—tasteless punk makeup, that mane a small animal could nest in, and the same leather-jacket security blanket. But I wasn't the same person I had been back in high school. Although I may not have looked that much older, I was different all the same. My eyes radiated more self-assurance, and I was less afraid. I wouldn't go back to being that age for love or money.

Click-clacking down the stairs, I knocked on Antti's office door.

"Mind if I come show off?"

The way Antti's eyes went wide made me laugh.

"Wow. You should dress like that more often. Turn around a little. Yeah, that's what I'm talkin' about. What do you have on under that leather jacket? Maybe I should go with you after all," Antti said with a grin. "You're going to get into trouble dressed like that."

"I think I can take care of myself," I said with a smile. "We'll just have to hope none of my office's clients are on the bus." I hesitated. "I thought I'd have a pick-me-up before I leave. Want to come up?"

"Yeah, I can take a break, but I still need to work tonight."

At this rate, Antti would have his dissertation done before the end of the year, despite the occasional bouts of despondency that made him fling his notes across the room, asking me whether I'd still like him even if he never amounted to anything—"anything" being a brilliant, PhD-anointed mathematician. He still had three years of fellowship funding remaining, but he had been talking about going abroad immediately after graduation the next spring. He would probably go to the United States. Where I would have nothing to do. Or could the FBI use a Finn for something?

I poured myself a generous shot of the lemon vodka Antti's parents had brought and then added some Sprite. I shouldn't have been drinking, since I was going to work, but I felt like I needed some liquid courage.

"If you were a murder suspect, would you want me to rip open your whole life, exposing everything if it meant proving your innocence?" Antti asked suddenly.

"I don't have any deep, dark secrets, Antti. Do you have a problem with what I'm doing for Kimmo?"

"I don't know. Maybe I'm just a little jealous. Why are you going to so much trouble for him?"

I almost burst out laughing. At most, the feeling I had toward Kimmo was the fondness of an older sister. "I would go to fifteen times more trouble for you. And part of it is that I just really want to know the truth. You can bet your ass there's more to this case than meets the eye." I thought of what Sari had said about Sanna's death, that Armi thought Sanna's boyfriend—whoever she meant—was responsible. However, I didn't want to discuss that, even with Antti.

Antti walked me to the bus stop. I had to pay with cash because I couldn't find my bus pass anywhere. It must have fallen out into the water during my bike crash the day before. Damnation!—there were still nearly two weeks left on it. The bus carried me across the series of bridges and islands between Espoo and Helsinki, depositing me across the highway from the Finnish Orthodox cemetery. Although I met only a few people on my short walk through the wall of new glass office buildings to the older, grittier part of the neighborhood, I had the distinct feeling that there were eyes watching me closely.

Finding the right warehouse required several minutes of tottering around the deserted industrial area in my high heels. The warehouses wouldn't be there much longer; soon the crews would be arriving with their explosives and heavy equipment to raze these buildings too, to make way for a new upscale condo project.

Techno music pulsed past the shaved-headed young man in leather overalls standing at the door, turning my trepidation into a rapidly intensifying anticipation—I hadn't been to a serious party in ages.

The place looked like something from another world: two old warehouses connected to each other, lit by only a few lights and dozens of candles. There were a couple of tall tables, hardly any chairs, and, farther toward the back, a bar. I could also see a stage, which was set up with all sorts of strange apparatuses. The song switched to ABBA's "Gimme! Gimme! Gimme!" As I paid to get in, I asked a girl dressed in a glittering wig and black velvet whether Angel had arrived yet.

"Over by the bar, the one with the long hair."

In the front room, two screens had videos going: one a wobbly amateur sex tape and the other Madonna music videos. I swayed farther into the room, finally starting to feel more comfortable in my shoes. A surprising number of men were dressed in street clothes, and I could feel their leering gazes on me. Never before had I felt so vividly like a sex object.

Angel was right when she said she would be the one with the longest hair. Seeing it now, I realized I had frequently seen the same hair and its owner at the university and had even watched it bouncing around in front of me at my aerobics class. It would be hard to miss that hair: golden blonde with subtle waves, it streamed in a thick mass over Angel's rear end, all the way down to her thighs.

She was equal to her name in other respects as well. Her face was like something out of a Renaissance painting. Her clothing, which consisted of an extremely tight black rubber dress that widened at the knees into a floor-length skirt, was a fascinating contrast to her natural, not overly made-up face. The bodice had long sleeves and an open neckline revealing glowing white skin. Yes, she was an angel—and certainly the fulfillment of many a fantasy.

"You must be Angel...Elina. I'm Maria, the one who called about Kimmo Hänninen."

"Oh, hi. Grab a drink, and then we can find somewhere to talk."

Since I didn't have the patience to fiddle with a glass, I drank straight from the mouth of the half bottle of wine once the bartender opened it.

As we walked to the edge of the room, I asked Angel for permission to record our conversation with my miniature voice recorder that always made me feel like Dale Cooper from *Twin Peaks*. I tried not to stare at the implausible creations that kept entering the room. The fog belching from the smoke machine at irregular intervals added to the surreal feeling, as did the music, now something that sounded like Klaus Nomi.

I asked Angel about the club's activities. Other than the hobby itself happening to be a little eccentric, it seemed like any other normal association of people with a common interest.

"But isn't this also sort of a pickup joint? How many men come here looking for sex partners? Why are some of the men dressed in regular clothes?" I had already made it halfway through my bottle of white wine, and the worst of my inhibitions were starting to fall away.

"I don't know about calling it a pickup joint per se. As you can see, the ratio of women to men is about one to three and at least half of the women are lesbians too. Of the other half, most of the club members come with a steady partner. So you see, there aren't many potential targets to hit on. You should watch yourself," Angel said with a disconcerting grin.

"What was Kimmo looking for here?"

"The same thing as most people. The knowledge that they aren't the only person in the world who gets turned on by S&M. A place to show off their new outfits and see what others are doing. Kimmo wasn't looking for sex. As I said on the phone, he was far too stuck on his girlfriend. As I understood it, he kept this part of his life completely separate from her. But he was really active in the group. He even helped organize parties and did the member newsletter with Joke," Angel said, pronouncing the nickname like the English word. "Joke should be coming tonight. I'll introduce you."

"What were your 'performances' like?"

"Well, as you know, Kimmo is a masochist. I'm whatever anyone needs though, submissive or dominant, and I like men and women." Now there was a challenge in Angel's smile. "With Kimmo I did these scenes where I would torture him in different ways: binding, whipping, breath control. Kimmo was always really aroused, but he would never allow himself anything more. He's a completely different man up there on the stage, not at all shy and reserved like usual. Sorry, hold on a sec—I'm being waved to the door."

Feeling orphaned when Angel left me, I pressed myself closer to the wall and sucked down some more wine. I stared at the partygoers. A woman about my size, dressed in a low-cut rubber dress and jingling chains, danced passionately in the middle of the floor with a tall man wearing a rubber Nazi uniform and sporting a hedgehog flattop. Based on what Angel had told me, I could now presume this was a steady couple out for an evening of entertainment. How did they manage to get dressed like that without the babysitter seeing?

As people frankly sized each other up, the mood was somehow expectant, hungry. One of the men in street clothes locked eyes with me, looking like he wanted to make a move on me. I turned away. Two leather-clad escapees from a Tom of Finland drawing kissed feverishly in a corner, while a man who looked like an employee of the tax administration stared on lasciviously. The guy who had been eyeing me across the floor approached, but gave up when Angel swept back up alongside me.

"Some mix-up with the comp list," Angel explained. "But back to our performances. You should know that Kimmo planned them. He knew exactly what he wanted. I was just an actor taking directions. Given all that, I have a hard time imagining him enjoying playing dominant. He's a pure-blooded masochist who wanted to be under someone else's control."

"I've noticed," I mumbled petulantly and then explained to Angel how I lost my temper with Kimmo earlier in the day over his sniveling. Angel again laughed that dangerous laugh of hers.

"That's why I can't imagine Kimmo murdering anyone," Angel said. "He's just so passive. Maybe not all sadomasochism fetishists are the most upstanding members of society, but they usually don't dare play out their fantasies in real life. And strangling his girlfriend wasn't ever Kimmo's fantasy, anyway."

"You said something about how this was all 'real' for Kimmo's sister, Sanna. Tell me about her."

"Sanna got involved with this guy named Otso Hakala. Otso was pretty dangerous—he sold drugs, he used drugs, and now he's sitting in prison. Sometimes we'd have to intervene when he and Sanna started making a scene here at the club. For them, the beating and dominating was an everyday thing, not just a fun ritual. It seemed negative. The rest of us had several conversations about whether we really wanted their kind here. Did you ever meet Sanna?"

When I nodded, Angel continued. "Then you understand. People could forgive Sanna for almost anything. Yeah, she was a druggie and an alcoholic and a complete mess in every other way too, but she was still sweet and wonderful. When the police arrested Otso and he wasn't near her any more, Sanna's life started looking up. We even attended some lectures together at the college. Her lack of interest in women was a shame. The last time I saw her was at the university, two days before she died. She was as sober as a judge and said she had found a boyfriend she could start a new life with. I almost believed her. Then, a few days later, Kimmo called and said she was dead. I wasn't even surprised. I'd always known that call was coming sooner or later."

I imagined Sanna in this cement warehouse, the sleeves of her leather jacket rolled up, scars on her arms, a submissive look in her eyes. Hoping for trouble.

"Did Sanna visit Otso in jail?" I asked.

Angel didn't know. If I were still a police officer, I easily could have checked on Hakala's movements around the time of Sanna's and Armi's deaths. Otso was my ideal murderer: criminal record, violent tendencies, and, best of all, I didn't know him.

"By the way, that guy's a cop," Angel said, pointing at a man with long blond sideburns, who was wearing jeans.

As he turned away from the bar holding his drink, I thought the jeans-wearing cop looked vaguely familiar. He was probably on the force seven years previously, after I had graduated and then worked briefly on the vice squad. I hoped he wouldn't recognize me.

"Maybe he's here because of Kimmo."

Unless Ström was a complete ape, he would have his team checking these connections too.

"That may be, but then he'll have to blow his cover. The poor thing thinks he's undercover, but he looks like a cop from a mile away. It's strange that they always send the same guy to safeguard our virtue. I would have expected them to fight over who gets to come to our parties, since half of them would probably like to get involved."

"What half do I belong to then?" I blurted out. "I went to the police academy before I went to law school. Cops aren't all bad." I couldn't help how much the stereotyping irritated me. However, Angel simply grinned in a way that put me so off balance that I emptied my wine bottle and then excused myself to the restroom.

Of course, there was no restroom in the warehouse itself, just some portable toilets at the back of the parking lot. The summer night was surprisingly dark, and on my way I discovered that my liberal vodka bracer and the small bottle of wine already had gone to my head. I would have to lay off for a while if I wanted to get anywhere with my work. The dark Angel both enthralled and annoyed me. Why was she flirting with me? Couldn't she tell I was just a shy hetero doing my job too, just like the cop?

I clambered into the surprisingly clean porta-potty. As I was pulling my skirt back over my thighs, I heard steps approaching outside. Although the other units were empty, no one entered them. As if someone were waiting for me outside.

My heart pounded.

Probably one of the gawking men from inside who had followed me and now wanted who-knew-what. I considered for a moment what to do, but then I remembered that I was a woman, not a worm, and that I had a small knife in my purse like I always did. So I just opened the door.

Outside, a woman with a shaved head was stamping a cigarette on the ground and then stepped in past me. She laughed and said, "My mistress won't let me smoke at home, so now I can't even imagine smoking in an outhouse."

As I returned to the party, an imposing apparition happened to walk through the door with me. About Antti's height, the man had long black curls any heavy-metal rocker would have envied. His boots and well-broken-in brown leather costume fit him like a second skin. For a moment, I wondered whether I still had what it took to pick up a hot guy. Then I tweaked myself by the mental ear—I wasn't here for carousing.

During my absence, something had started to happen on the stage. A fat man with tattoos covering his entire body sat in lotus position in the middle of the stage pushing long acupuncture needles through his skin after a whip-thin woman, just as tattooed, sterilized them first. An antiseptic hospital smell reached my nose over the emissions of the smoke machine. A young man in high heels danced with abandon in the middle of the floor. I felt adrift and, despite my good intentions, marched to the bar for another demibottle. The wine tasted better this time. I moved closer to the stage to see the ritualistic needle performance, trying to force myself to watch as the needles penetrated the man's skin, going in and coming out through his thigh, his arm, and, finally, his neck. Did he feel anything? Was he like a yogi who could pass his spirit outside his own body and feel no physical pain?

"Does that turn you on?" a male voice asked. I looked up involuntarily and saw a perfectly normal, pleasant-looking young man in the classic rebel's outfit: jeans, white T-shirt, and the same sort of black leather jacket I was wearing.

"No, not really."

"Want to dance instead?"

Why not? I thought, joining him to dance to the frantic commotion of synthesizers and drums until we were weak at the knees. Suddenly I was eighteen years old again, at a bar legally for the first time, looking for that one "right" person. When Pelle Miljoona's "I Wanna Make Love to You" started to come over the speakers, the song took my mind to an even more distant memory, to a high-school party with Sanna dancing next to me to the same song.

Sanna. I wasn't here to dance. After the song ended, I walked off the dance floor with my chevalier trailing after me.

"Have you had enough dancing?" The way he looked me up and down now was too similar to what I'd seen in Dr. Hellström's eyes. "I like that skirt on you. If piercing isn't your thing, then what is? Are you a domina?"

"I can be…whatever—I'm a Pisces: fluid, changing, mixed," I answered, striving for the challenging tone of Angel's voice.

"You can be...whatever? Sounds interesting. I'm Sebastian," the man said, extending his hand. I took it.

"Maria."

"Not the virgin though, right?"

I pulled my hand away.

"Bad joke, and old to boot."

"My apologies, m'lady. I vow to do better." Sebastian bowed as a suitor might in a movie from the 1940s, at which point I realized I had unwittingly set in motion a role-play I now desperately wanted to escape. All I could think of to do was lop him off at the knees with as much hauteur as I could manage without breaking character.

"I do not care for men who tell old jokes!" I snarled, then marched back into the first room and scanned for Angel, whom I found talking to the man with the devastating black curls. When I caught her eye, she beckoned me over.

"This is Joke," Angel said.

Immediately Joke started asking about Kimmo. The concern in his voice was at odds with his outward appearance. Down to the riding crop hanging from his waist, he was the epitome of the twisted gothic hero. True, he would whip the heroine with his crop, but then he would enclose her in his tender embrace and explain that the chastening he gave was only out of love.

"Do you think you could be ready to testify in Kimmo's defense?" I asked him. "To say that he isn't violent? To say that— Oh hell!"

Next to the girl collecting entrance fees stood Detective Sergeant Pertti Ström, arrogantly waving his badge. After talking his way in without paying, he turned to examine those present with the same expression my mother might wear upon finding a colony of silverfish in a bag of flour.

"There's the man who arrested Kimmo. The arch-ass-hole himself," I explained to Angel and Joke. Ström hadn't overlooked this avenue of investigation after all. Maybe I was underestimating him, or maybe he wasn't as sure of Kimmo's guilt as I thought. I remembered my own experience as a police officer, meticulously combing through details and checking every possible lead. Surely Ström had needed more than sharp elbows to rise through the ranks. He must have been good at his job.

The nascent respect I had managed to feel for Ström for two whole minutes disappeared in the blink of an eye when he marched over to us and the first words out his mouth were: "I should have guessed you were defending that pervert because you're just like him!"

"Watch out—it's catching," I said icily. "Although, I have a hard time believing there's anything left for you to learn about sadism."

Ström couldn't get his eyes off my leather skirt.

"If I had known you were into this rubber stuff, I would have arrested you for Mäenpää's murder, not Hänninen. You wanted Mäenpää out of the way so you could play your own lit-tle games with him."

This idea was so absurd that I burst out laughing right in his face. "Why haven't I killed my own boyfriend then?" I asked and then emptied the rest of my second bottle of wine down my throat so I wouldn't dump it on Ström. Ström didn't answer; instead he asked Angel and Joke the same sorts of questions I had, albeit in a much less civil tone. Even though I knew it was a punishable offense to tape people without their permission, I dis-creetly switched on my miniature voice recorder. The wine was moving pleasantly through my body. Now that I was too drunk to do anything sensible, I decided to spend the rest of the night observing and acting as though I was just there to have fun.

Despite my buzz, I realized that Ström was presenting his questions with more skill than I expected. Not that he got anything more out of Joke or Angel than I did, since they took such a dim view of the police in general. Joke was repeating word for word something Kimmo had written for the club newsletter, when I suddenly needed to use the restroom again and headed outside.

Inside the portable toilet, I kind of came to my senses. What was I really doing here? Going home would be the best course of action. I decided to stop inside to say good-bye to Angel and then leave.

As I stepped out, a figure in a leather jacket stepped out of the shadows and grabbed me firmly by the wrist.

"You aren't going to get away from me that easily, Maria," Sebastian said, putting an unpleasant emphasis on my name.

Anger flashed in his eyes, with something else I didn't care to name thinly veiled beneath.

"Hands off!" I jerked my wrist back the way I learned in my self-defense course, but his grip held. However, he wasn't prepared for the sudden kick of my high-heeled shoe to his ribs, and he doubled over and fell to his knees on the asphalt, gasping in pain.

"Be more careful about who you try molesting next time," I hissed and then ran back inside. Sebastian wasn't really injured—the pain would pass soon enough—and I didn't know what he would do next. Disappearing back into the crowd was my best option.

Inside, Ström still seemed to be bullying Joke, who looked like he needed some help. I was in no shape to play the Good

Samaritan tonight, so I continued on to the back hall where Angel was talking to a small group of attractive-looking lesbians clad head to toe in leather. Onstage, a slender man in a white halter dress was doing a drag imitation of Marilyn Monroe. I joined Angel to listen to the women's conversation, since they were talking about Kimmo and the police, and I didn't object when a bald girl with sharp eyes offered me some whiskey from a flask.

"Everyone is certainly dressed to the nines," I stuttered to her, and then smiled at a transsexual dressed in the guise of a 1960s housewife who danced past. People had strange fantasies—there really were people who wanted that old-fashioned life. Did he want his partner to dress up in a shocking-orange flowery dress with an electric-green scarf over his (or her) hair as well?

"Hopefully you'll see Kimmo done up in full garb someday," Angel said. "He's always one of the best-dressed men here."

"Speaking of the men here, do you know a guy named Sebastian? He got a little too enthusiastic outside, and I had to bring him back to earth."

Angel shook her head. "I don't; he must not be a regular. Ah, Joke escaped from the police!"

Joke danced over to us, and there was no sign of Ström or Sebastian anywhere, so I joined the general revelry, recording a comment about Kimmo every now and then. Everyone thought he was a nice, sweet guy, and no one believed he would actually hurt someone. Awash in a sea of black clothing, red lips, and gleaming chains, Joke and I danced wildly, oblivious to anything else. At some point, I got thirsty and had a beer.

I realized it was two thirty in the morning, and I was completely drunk.

The lousy warehouse even lacked a phone. No one knew where the nearest taxi stand was, so I decided to try to flag down a cab on the West Highway.

My steps clacking against the worn asphalt as I walked toward civilization, the old cop in me said bad things could happen to a drunk woman walking alone at night dressed this way. The old feminist in me said a drunk woman walking alone at night dressed this way had the same rights as anyone else. I tried desperately to walk without swaying my hips—or listing to one side.

"Mariaaa! Maaariiaaa!" A male voice echoed over the asphalt. The shout had something familiar about it, but the echo made it strange and frightening. Sebastian? I didn't want to hang around to find out, so I ran toward the lights and people on the highway as fast as I could in my high heels. The shouts continued behind me for a while. When I reached the stop where I had gotten off the bus earlier, I stopped to wait for a taxi, but all of the cabs that whizzed by were occupied.

Then a dark blue Saab pulled over in front of me.

"Kallio. Why didn't you stop and wait for me? I was yelling for you. C'mon, jump in!" A familiar voice, gruff and commanding.

"You couldn't pay me to get in the same car with you right now, Ström."

"Do I have to arrest you first?"

"On what grounds?"

"Public intoxication and general indecency. Where are you headed? You live in Tapiola, right?"

Ström's unmarked police Saab did look inviting. Only ten minutes separated me from a shower and my bed. I swallowed my pride and climbed into the front seat, trying to tell myself it was OK to take advantage of dickheads. Avoiding a taxi ride would save me a fair amount of cash anyway.

"Why did you leave the force?" Ström asked, sounding surprisingly docile as we crossed the first bridge on the way from Helsinki back to Espoo.

"It wasn't a good fit for me."

"And being a lawyer is a better fit? What you were doing tonight looked more like playing private detective."

"What wouldn't a self-sacrificing attorney do for her client? Ström, I heard you interrogated Kimmo without me. Let that be the last time, or I'm reporting you!"

"He didn't ask for his lawyer to be present. And are you absolutely sure this little excursion isn't a waste of your resources?"

"You mean tonight, or defending Kimmo Hänninen?"

"I mean the whole lawyer thing. Do you really want to sit in front of a desk for thirty years, shuffling paper, flipping through law books, and then going off to boring trials where you have to pretend to think exactly the opposite of what you really know? How is that a good fit for someone like you? You need action—that was obvious enough tonight. And besides, trying to make a murderer look innocent is immoral."

"Immoral? If you ask me, it's a hell of a lot more immoral that you're trying to put an innocent person in jail because you're obsessed with what kind of sex he likes, instead of trying to catch the real murderer. Jesus. You haven't checked into half of the other possibilities!"

Despite my intoxication, I realized I was running at the mouth—I was supposed to be solving Kimmo's case, not dropping hints to Ström.

"What other possibilities? Kallio, if you're concealing information, you're going to find yourself joining Hänninen in a cell."

"I'm not hiding anything, and enough with the bullying already. Let me out right now!"

Ström slammed on the brakes without saying a word and illegally pulled off to the side of the highway. We were already back on the mainland at an intersection not far from my house— even walking I would be home in a matter of minutes, but I didn't need to tell Ström that. Taking off my shoes, I ran the rest of the way in stocking feet. I knew that if I'd used different tactics and been drinking less, I could have gotten more out of my trip to Club Bizarre. I was irritated with myself, but maybe once I sobered up and listened to the tape I would find some useful information. And at least some of the night had been fun.

9

"I might be remembering some of the details wrong, but you can't accuse me of any wrongdoing," Mallu said angrily to me on the telephone. It was Thursday morning, and I had finally reached her again to ask about where she had been on the day of Armi's murder.

"I've told the police every single thing I did that day, and, as far as I understand, you aren't even a police officer anymore anyway."

"Mallu, come on. Please, can we just sit down and talk?" I knew Mallu was right: I didn't have any right to interrogate her.

My hangover had rendered Wednesday a complete loss. I barely managed to get a little routine work done and spent the evening in front of the TV with a carton of Double Crème & Meringues Mövenpick. Thursday morning began with the euphoria familiar to anyone who has ever suffered a hangover—waking up and realizing I was myself again felt amazing.

Eventually, I talked Mallu into coming to the office later that afternoon and then headed out to downtown Tapiola to get a little lunch before another client meeting.

"How's your bike been working?" Makke asked, standing at the door of his store, having a cigarette.

I flinched. Was that irony in his tone—or a warning?

"What do you mean by that?" I asked. "Did you have something to do with this?" I showed him the broken brake wires Antti and I had managed to get back in working order, but only just.

"Were you in an accident?" Makke sounded genuinely surprised.

"Oh, my handlebars just came off when I was riding out to the breakwater, and I got dumped in the water. I think somebody fiddled with it."

"Your handlebars, that's weird. Usually thieves just take the back wheel. And I can't believe anyone would want to steal that old rattletrap anyway. Some kids probably just thought they were being funny."

"Maybe. Listen, how long did you and Sanna date before... you know?"

The sudden change of topic elicited a confused glance.

"You mean, before she died? Well, not very long, really... Sanna...Sanna died in March, and we met just before Christmas at the bar around the corner there."

Despite Makke's attempt to maintain his relaxed front, this was no longer a casual conversation.

"Four months of dating. That doesn't sound like a very long time. But you still seem to be in mourning more than a year later."

Makke ground the butt of his cigarette under the ball of his foot as he replied.

"You can't understand what it feels like, when you love someone, and your love just isn't enough. When the person you care about most in all the world kills herself, despite how much you love her. And you're even there when it happens but you were too fucked up to stop it."

"But Makke, no one can really redeem anyone else. Everyone has to save themselves," I said, sounding like a preacher and hoping I would be able to remember these wise words the next time Antti slid into one of his dissertation-writing funks.

"Sanna was so amazing. She was a lot smarter than me, always talking about books and poetry and philosophy. Maybe she was a little too smart for this world," Makke said pathetically.

"What did you know about Sanna's previous boyfriends? Who was she dating before you?"

"She was with this shithead who beat her. He got sent to prison for dealing drugs just before we met. His name was Hakanen or Hakala or something like that."

"Otso Hakala," I said.

"Yeah, that was him. Sanna showed me some pictures— black hair, really nasty-looking guy. Sanna went to see him a couple of times in jail, and I remember being a little jealous. Why do you keep asking me about Sanna?"

"I'm curious. And I'm sorry I didn't keep in better touch with her. Maybe I'm carrying a little guilt around too."

Makke's face brightened.

"Ah, now I get it...You were the one Sanna was talking about—she said that back in that mining town she used to live in, there was only one girl who understood her. You two are a lot alike. Maybe that's why..." He trailed off.

"Maybe that's why what?" I asked, although I could guess the answer.

"Well, when we met, I hoped you were single," Makke said, blushing slightly and then walking back into the store.

Downtown Tapiola was bustling with people. Schoolchildren roaming in raucous or sullen packs, families shopping for supplies for the upcoming vacation season, book-buyers searching for graduation gifts and surveying the summer crop of mystery novels. I was so used to having no vacation during the summer that the whole commotion felt foreign. Of course my parents—both teachers—were always champing at the bit for school year to end. Some weekend soon, I would have to drag myself back to my hometown for a visit, at the very latest when my sister had her baby. Crazy—me, an aunt. What was carrying another person inside you like? How did that feel, those kicks and wiggles of that other being, pressing against your own body? And giving birth?

I passed a woman pushing a stroller. Her toddler was forcefully repeating the words "mommy" and "poop" as he banged on the frame of the stroller with a toy shovel for effect. I thought of Mallu's dead baby. Did I want a child? The idea almost frightened me. A child? Me? With Antti? Just imagine what an egotistical curmudgeon it would be, even from birth.

Although, having a baby didn't feel completely impossible either. I imagine it was perfectly natural: I was coming up on thirty—that clock was ticking—and I had a mostly functional relationship with a decent man for the first time in ages. "Functional relationship"—how was that for nauseating. Like a piece of furniture, a new couch.

Even though I knew I shouldn't, I went for a hamburger and fries, and, after returning to the office, I still had time before my client meeting to make a call to my very own spy in the police archives. As luck would have it, my old partner, Pekka Koivu, happened to be in his office.

"Hi, it's Maria. There's a beer in it for you if you'll check a couple of rap sheets for me. Hakala, Otso—I don't know the birth date, but he can't be much older than thirty—with at least one strike for distributing. And Hänninen, Sanna, born March 2,

1962. If Hakala is still inside, please check to see whether he might have been out of jail for some reason last year on the second of March or Saturday last week. That's it."

"I think I can manage that."

"How are things at the old Helsinki PD?"

"Same old, same old. Kinnunen showed up to work drunk yesterday, and the captain is still just as pompous as ever. Sometimes I think about just giving up and leaving since you aren't even here anymore," Koivu said.

I snorted. I had no desire to return to my old job in the Helsinki Violent Crime Unit. Ström was wrong—I did better as a lawyer than as a police officer.

I had a whole slew of questions planned out to ask Mallu. However, once she was standing at the door of my office, looking so thin and dressed in black, I didn't even know where to start. As I offered her coffee, I remembered the Agatha Christie novel in which the sculptor Henrietta Savernake is planning to create a female figure representing Sorrow. With her too-large black dress and face marked by lines that drew downward at the corners of her eyes and mouth, Mallu would have been the perfect model. Just since Sunday, she seemed to have lost several pounds.

"Have you had any contact with Teemu since we talked? I've been trying to get in touch with him, but no one answers."

"I haven't heard anything about him," Mallu said, growing angry.

"Haven't you tried to inform him of your sister's death? It's been in the papers too—hasn't Teemu tried to contact you about this, to offer any condolences at least?"

Mallu's expression was withdrawn, almost dreamy when she answered.

"What does it matter to Teemu? We don't have anything to say to each other anymore."

Not even three months had passed since the accident and miscarriage in March. How could those months have cankered their relationship so thoroughly? How could years of shared life now mean absolutely nothing? Had other issues besides their childlessness come between them?

"Why did you lie to me about last Saturday? You weren't home all day. You went shopping in Tapiola."

"Maria! Someone murdered my sister. I must have been in shock or something, and I took a couple of tranquilizers on Sunday morning to keep myself together. I didn't lie; I just remembered wrong. When the police asked, I told them about it. I bought frozen fish, even though what I wanted was wild mushrooms."

"Armi was supposed to call before two o'clock. Did she manage to before her death?"

"To call?" Mallu sounded genuinely confused. "Armi didn't call me. Who said that? I mean, she could have called, but I was at the store."

"When we talked on Saturday about Sanna Hänninen, you said that you wouldn't be surprised if one of them was mixed up in Sanna's death, meaning one of the Hänninens. Armi was convinced Sanna's death was a homicide. Did you know that?"

Mallu buried her face in her hands. Rather than a gush of tears, the gesture seemed more like a fierce attempt at concentration. The sun flooding through the window landed on the thick silver streaks on her bowed head, which glittered in the light like Christmas tinsel.

"You mean that Armi was murdered because she knew that Sanna..." Mallu muttered through her hands.

"That is one possibility. Does it seem plausible to you?"

"Yes, actually, it does." Mallu raised her eyes and looked straight at me. "I can imagine exactly how Armi could slap Sanna's murderer in the face with the truth, not having the slightest clue how much danger she was in. And I don't mean blackmail or anything. Armi just enjoyed having the upper hand."

"Who could you imagine murdering Sanna?"

"I guess her father is the one I always thought of. He's just so strange."

"Strange how? I've only ever met him once."

I remembered the tall, slender, slightly stooped frame and the dark Leonid Brezhnev eyebrows. Henrik Hänninen's mouth was wide like Sanna's, but there was something cruel about it.

"It's like Henrik lives in some other world," Mallu continued. "He's sort of cold and frightening. Maybe it's just the eyebrows, but he reminds me of the hit men in those old gangster movies. But he couldn't have killed Armi—he's in South America. But maybe he killed Sanna and then someone else killed Armi to cover that up. Like maybe Kimmo."

Or Annamari. Or Risto. Oh, how I hoped the solution would turn out to be Otso Hakala.

"By the way, when you were coming in, did you notice whether my bike was still standing up against the wall?" I asked as Mallu was leaving. "I left it leaning there a little precariously."

"Your bike? I only saw one bike, a bright-green one, and it was still standing." The mention of the bicycle seemed to have no effect on Mallu, so apparently she wasn't the one who had sabotaged my handlebars.

A phone call back from Pekka Koivu destroyed my wonderful Otso Hakala theory. Otso was currently sitting in his prison cell and would be there for at least another year. Over the past year and a half, no extenuating circumstances had warranted him leaving prison. Sanna's and Otso's criminal records were long enough that my old friend and I decided we'd go through them more carefully on Sunday over beers. Despite the knockout blow to my theory, seeing him would be nice, since we hadn't done anything together since my law school graduation party. Koivu's passionate congratulatory kiss had aroused some mild yet entirely unjustified jealousy in Antti.

My phone rang again.

"Is this Maria Kallio?" the quavering voice of an elderly man inquired. When I confirmed that I was Maria, he continued by asking whether I had misplaced my bus pass.

"Yes, on Monday night on the beach in Toppelund by the breakwater."

"That is exactly where I found it. I have it here with me."

"Excellent!" So 150 marks hadn't gone to waste after all. Fortunately, I hadn't yet had time to get a new one. I arranged to pick up my bus card that evening. Perhaps this meant things were taking a turn for the better. Perhaps I would find some hint about her murderer in Sanna's papers. Her father and brothers burning her diaries was a shame, though.

Wait...Eki was Sanna's lawyer before she died. That meant our office had files on her. I went into the firm's records room—that is, the Henttonens' rec room—which had boxes and shelves piled high with folders and papers from past clients. Dust particles danced in the light filtering through the windows high up on one wall. Apparently, no one had been in to vacuum in ages. In appropriate alphabetical order, I found a red binder with HÄNNINEN, SANNA typed neatly on the label. Would anyone notice if I borrowed it for the weekend? I was just pulling the binder off the shelf when I heard the doorknob rattle.

I don't really know why I crouched down out of sight behind the bookcase, but when I peered through the gap on the lowest shelf, I saw a familiar pair of light-gray, thick-soled shoes. Eki.

I knew I should have come out and claimed to have dropped an earring or something, but I didn't—I eased myself farther back behind the shelving. Eki was doing something with the cabinet where he kept his boating gear. I was sure he would hear my breathing. When he started walking straight toward me, I stopped inhaling altogether.

Eki stopped right at the H's, snatching a binder off the shelf and leafing through it furiously. Dust particles danced toward my nose. Oh hell—I felt a sneeze coming on. I listened as Eki ripped a page out of the binder and then, a moment later, crumpled it up. Then he shoved it into his pocket, replaced the binder, and left the room.

After another two minutes, I finally dared to leave my hiding place. My heart pounding, I returned to Sanna's binder and saw immediately that it had been moved: the shelf in front of it was free of dust. Why would Eki remove a page from Sanna's records? I was irritated at not having come five minutes earlier, and seeing myself in a mirror increased my irritation. One more set of clothes headed for the washing machine.

As I pedaled around the bay that evening, I was still in a bad mood. A message from my mother hadn't helped, and after I called her back, I had to listen to her "You should come visit" griping and "I'm so worried about Eeva's pregnancy" hand-wringing for fifteen minutes. Then my youngest sister called.

"Isn't the house you and Antti live in pretty big?" she asked right off. When I said yes, Helena informed me that she and her boyfriend and Eeva and her husband needed somewhere to stay on Monday night. They were leaving on a cruise to Stockholm together, and wouldn't it be so nice to see each other?

Of course I had to agree to this, even though I had plans to go to the movies with a friend from school that night. There was nothing I could do but cancel. Actually, I was a little curious to see Eeva's big belly. What irked me was that they only ever condescended to come see me when they had some other reason to be in Helsinki—it was never just to visit me. I had become used to being little more than some sort of Helsinki rest stop for my parents and siblings, a convenient bed close to the harbor and the airport. I was also the one they called and sent to buy things at the main Stockmann store in the city when they saw sale ads in the national media.

Although a trip to Stockholm with my sisters and their boring men would have been pure torture, I was still put out that they hadn't even bothered to invite Antti and me. Of course, Eeva and Helena were much closer to each other than to me. The difference in ages between them was only a little over a year, and between me and Eeva was a gap of more than two. Our mother must have had quite a time of things after Helena's birth, what with two in diapers and me a defiant three-year-old. And all three, unfortunately, girls.

As the oldest and most spirited, I took on the role of the boy of the family. Living hundreds of miles away from the rest of the family and only seeing them infrequently, I had such a habit of telling them only the most superficial things about myself that I felt like no one in the family really knew me. But did I know them? What did I know about, say, what Eeva thought about her pregnancy?

Maybe I lacked the ability to get close to people. Even Antti needed a vacation from me. After coming home from work, he had announced his intention of taking the morning bus to Inkoo because he wanted some time alone in the woods.

"I thought I'd take a tent and row out to this one island I know for the night..."

"Oh. Well, I was planning to go out and party a bit on Friday, because last weekend I was working the whole time."

Antti suggested that I come to Inkoo on Saturday so we could go out for the second night together. When he assured me Einstein could get along just fine by himself for one night, I agreed out of pure curiosity. Years had passed since I had spent any serious time camping. Still, I was irritated by the way Antti had announced his plans—"I'm doing this, and you can do whatever you want"—even though I knew we had an agreement that we wouldn't get in the way of each other's pursuits.

I snapped out of my thoughts, but my vexation increased as I came upon a dog running back and forth on a retractable leash in the middle of the bike path. It looked like a crocheted potholder someone had washed in too-hot water. The cord stretching from dog to master blocked the entire trail. I rang my bell testily, and when the dog owner turned to look, I recognized him as Doctor Hellström, Armi's boss. I didn't remember seeing a dog when I had visited him.

"Oh, hello, Ms. Kallio. How do you do?" He seemed like he was in the mood to talk. "I hear Kimmo Hänninen is in jail for killing Armi. Is that right?" Hellström lit a cigarette and tried unsuccessfully to curb the dog, now yapping at a crow perched in a tree. The crow cawed back, flapping on a branch and raining last year's dried pine needles down on us. The dog strained at his leash. "I'm really no good with this animal; it's my sister's dog, and I told her I'd watch him for a couple of days," the gynecologist complained.

With a thick jacket and a scarf pulled up almost to his ears, Hellström looked overdressed for the rather warm late evening. Suddenly he sneezed violently. Obviously, a cold. Physician, heal thyself, I thought, and then replied, "Yes, it looks that way. The prosecutor plans to charge Kimmo with murder."

"Such an unfortunate incident. One feels sorry for Annamari. First Sanna's death and now this. Annamari isn't a terribly well balanced person to begin with."

"Was Armi on good terms with her?"

Hellström laughed.

"Armi was generally on good terms with everyone. Although Annamari may not have been on equally good terms with Armi, if you catch my drift. I doubt any daughter-in-law would have lived up to Annamari's expectations. She doted over Kimmo too much, and let Sanna walk all over her, doing whatever she wanted."

"Was Sanna Hänninen your patient as well?" I remembered Eki mentioning an abortion and thought that Hellström might know something interesting.

"My client. Yes, she was."

I wasn't able to talk to Hellström about Sanna's sex life after all. Suddenly the dog started a row with an approaching greyhound just at that moment, and instead of waiting for things to calm down, I pedaled off.

When I arrived, Annamari was flitting around at home like a moth caught in a light fixture. She was dressed in a flowing yellow dress with big sleeves that rippled with each of her abrupt, nervous motions. The police had allowed her in to see Kimmo the previous day, which seemed only to have addled her even more.

"I don't really know about your seeing Sanna's papers," Annamari said. "Perhaps destroying them would be best, like we did with the diaries. Wouldn't it be best to let poor Sanna rest in peace? She had a hard life—why would we want to dwell on that anymore?"

"Is that stack of paper all that's left of Sanna's belongings? Is there anything else remaining in her room? Keepsakes, clothing, books?"

"We turned Sanna's room into a guest bedroom; Matti and Mikko sleep there sometimes. Henrik took Sanna's clothing and donated all of it. None of us would have worn rags like that. I suppose Kimmo kept some of Sanna's books and music. I don't remember what is whose anymore. Look in Kimmo's room."

"Let's get those papers out as well, though," I coaxed. I had with me a large backpack and my bicycle saddlebags to transport the whole lot home. As it turned out, my decision to leave the papers at the Hänninens' Monday night had been a godsend. A bath in seawater would have rendered most of them illegible. Would Annamari have wanted that?

"Maria, you don't understand how difficult being a mother is. And alone, like I am, with Henrik always traveling. To raise Henrik's child and two of my own. To be in constant fear of what will happen to your children. What if they get run over by a car or fall in with a bad crowd and start getting into trouble? And then you realize you can't save them if they do. The worst can happen no matter what you do, no matter how much you love them, just like with Sanna. Yes, I do want to forget that." Annamari stayed at the base of the stairs while I fetched the stack of papers from the closet.

Then I opened the door into Kimmo's room. No one had cleaned it since the police had visited. The bed covers were a tangled mess, the clothes closet was turned inside out, and here and there lay strange objects, which, upon closer inspection, turned out to be various S&M paraphernalia: a riding crop, a small rubber sheet, locks. Apparently Ström's investigators had dumped the sex-toy section of Kimmo's closets onto the floor.

"Did the police say not to touch anything in here?" I asked Annamari, who was now behind me, peeking over my shoulder.

"No. I just didn't want to go in there. I don't want to find out what horrible things Kimmo keeps there."

Except for the sex-toy section, Kimmo's room was just like that of any young male college student. A computer on the desk and a printer, a couple of posters, and a giant picture of a smiling Armi wearing a flowery sundress. In one corner there was a TV and a VCR, and most of the books on the shelves were technical manuals and textbooks, along with a few best sellers. Sanna's books were easy to pick out: *Collected Works of Sylvia Plath*, some Virginia Woolf, and some older English poetry. The margins of the Plath books were full of notes, so I added them to my bag. Next to the books sat a grinning skull.

"Where is this from?" I asked Annamari, who stood hunched in the doorway.

"Sanna bought it somewhere—she always kept it on her desk. Kimmo wouldn't let me sell it. Ugh, it's repulsive. Take it away!"

Since she told me to, I shoved the skull into my backpack. I had the urge to start cleaning Kimmo's room properly, but I couldn't very well do that with Annamari watching.

When I promised to return the papers, Annamari waved her hand dismissively.

"No need—just burn them. We don't want them. It's just more of Sanna's scribbling. Sanna was gifted, yes, but why couldn't she have just studied normal things like everyone else? Why did she have to drink and do all those other horrible things and be with all those horrible men? Sometimes she was like a complete stranger, and once I even said to Henrik that maybe the nurses switched her by accident at birth in the hospital. She looked exactly like Henrik, though."

"When is Henrik coming back to Finland?"

Annamari began shaking again. "Maybe next week. He shouted so much on the phone. He told me…" She stopped, as if to steel herself. "He told me…that this was all my fault, that I didn't know how to raise our children. But maybe he will be able to get Kimmo out of prison."

I realized that Annamari feared her husband, which brought me back to Mallu's suspicions that Henrik Hänninen might have had something to do with Sanna's death. The Hänninen patriarch was interesting me more by the minute, his shadow constantly lurking in the background behind the rest of the family.

My backpack was heavy as I biked over to retrieve my bus pass from Mr. Herman Lindgren, who lived south of Annamari Hänninen right next to the swimming beach and breakwater. When I rang the doorbell, a dog started barking with a sound like a bass drum with a loose head, but nearly a full minute passed before someone came to the door.

The man looked to be about a hundred, and the graying Labrador retriever next to him should have been in a doggy retirement home. Still, the dog sniffed me curiously, probably smelling Einstein and Hellström's loaner dog on my legs. The old man got straight to the point, handing me my bus card after first glancing with a smile at the picture and then me.

"Yep, it's the same girl."

"You must have gone to a lot of trouble tracking me down, since the number for me in the phone book is old."

"I got your number from the phone company. And it was no bother—I have plenty of time for tracking down pretty young girls. I found your pass over there on the beach. It was almost in the water," the man stated with a question in his tone that made me feel as though he deserved an explanation.

"Monday night I was riding a little too fast and flew off the walking bridge into the water. The card probably fell out of my pocket during the fall."

"Into the water? Well, thank goodness you weren't hurt. Thank goodness you didn't drown like that other girl."

"What girl?" I asked, feeling my heart rate suddenly accelerate.

"The girl who drowned the winter before last out on the breakwater. I will always remember—it was the second of March. My wife died the same night."

The elderly man seemed to withdraw backward in time, into his memories.

"It was a rainy night, as gray as autumn, no snow anywhere and no ice on the sea. I took Karlsson out here at around seven o'clock, and he ran off to the beach to sniff at something. I went to see what he was up to, and there on the beach lay a boy with blond hair. I was startled, worrying that he might be dead or sick, but his snoring and the smell of him told me he was just drunk. I couldn't leave him there, as cold as it was, but an old man like me couldn't do anything for him alone. Out on the breakwater I could see two people, and I shouted to them that a man was lying there and asked them to help.

"One of them—the woman—ran a little closer and shouted back that the man was her friend and she would take care of him; I could leave. When I arrived home, I found my wife on the kitchen floor. Her heart had given out, the doctor said later, and she didn't suffer. But I still wouldn't have wanted her to die alone."

The dog whined as if chiming in. The old man bent over to pat his companion.

"I ended up in the hospital myself then for a while, since my own pump was acting up too, and then I spent the following month living with my son. I didn't hear from a neighbor until several months later that a girl drowned that same night. They said it was suicide. It was the same girl who ran toward me on the breakwater."

"I knew that girl," I said, unable to restrain my impatience any longer. "I didn't know someone else was out there on the breakwater with her in addition to her boyfriend. Who was he? Or was it a woman? What did he look like?"

The old man simply shook his head apologetically.

"I couldn't see very well in the fog, and it's been such a long time. I do remember that the other one had an umbrella and a long, black coat. Maybe a man, maybe a woman. How should I know, when women are so tall nowadays."

Suddenly the old man looked directly in my eyes as though searching for something small and valuable there and then said pointedly, "Besides, I'm not sure it was human at all. I think it was Death. He had come to take my wife and now he was coming to take that girl. Maybe you'll say these are just the ramblings of an old man. I may be three times older than you are, but I'm not senile yet. Someone was out on the breakwater with that dead girl."

"I believe you," I said reassuringly. "But you didn't tell the police what you saw. You didn't tell them about the other person."

"What difference would it have made two months after the fact? The neighbors said the police ruled it a suicide and closed the case. Didn't she even leave a note?"

"Would you still be willing to come and tell this to the police if the need arose? Information has recently come to light that calls into question whether it was a suicide after all. You might be a key witness..."

"A key witness. That sounds like something from one of those strange American miniseries on television. But what do I have these days other than time? What do you say, Karlsson?" The man patted his dog again, obviously very much back in the present.

Thanking Mr. Lindgren sufficiently was difficult, and I decided to send him a bouquet of flowers the next morning. I was sure he was right: the figure he saw out on the breakwater was Death. But not the imaginary scythe-wielding phantom— Herman Lindgren had seen Sanna and Armi's murderer.

10

On Friday night, I was sitting comfortably ensconced in an arm-chair in our living room reading snippets from a draft of Sanna's thesis on Sylvia Plath. Abundant notations filled the margins of the pages, but they all kept strictly to the topic of the paper. The working title of the thesis was "Body Language and Images of Self-Destruction in the Work of Sylvia Plath." At the very least, Sanna had chosen an appropriate subject for herself.

I was tearing through Sanna's papers with a defiant determination after having words with Eki earlier in the day about my investigation into Armi's murder. Eki told me flat out that I was wasting my time.

"In this job you have to learn to make judgments about what's worth doing and what isn't. Our job is to get the Hänninen boy, if not released, then sentenced as lightly as possible. Rummaging around in his sister's unfortunate life isn't going to help you in that task one bit."

Since I disagreed, Eki thought I was losing perspective. Even so, I announced my intention to take Sanna's file home with me. I assumed that if Eki didn't trust my judgment, the chances he would continue my contract after my three-month probationary period were slim. On the other hand—if he didn't trust me, I wouldn't want to work for Henttonen & Associates anyway. When I entered law school, my intention was to train for the bench, but I had put my court internship on indefinite hold. Placements in the Helsinki area district courts were few and far between, and I had no intention of going somewhere out in the sticks. I didn't want to admit to myself that one of the most important things preventing my departure was Antti, now that our relationship had subsided from the initial giddiness to a fumbling process of working out a life together. Despite my weekly questioning of "whether this is really going anywhere," we still wanted to be together. I just hated feeling dependent.

I decided to read the thesis more closely after inspecting the rest of the material. I had just finished sorting the papers and was starting in on the binder of files from our office when the phone rang. I rushed into the entryway, thinking that it might be Antti wanting to clarify something about our plans for the next day.

"Sarkela residence, Maria Kallio speaking."

Complete silence. Then a strangely disembodied, husky voice: "Don't go digging around in things that don't concern you. Otherwise, you might be next..." The voice disappeared into the ether, and then came a click as the speaker hung up.

My old police instincts failed me this time, because I lowered the receiver before realizing that I could have tried to trace the call. When I returned to the living room, I was angry. Someone wanted to intimidate me. I knew in my heart that the person who sabotaged my bike wasn't just a kid playing a prank—he was a double murderer.

People had threatened me before, and I'd had some close scrapes. But usually the threat had a face—when you were arresting someone, you knew what you were up against.

I watched as a motorboat docked in Otsolahti Marina. The rocks along the shore glistened from the recent rain. The living room's large picture window no longer looked like a charming way to view the scenery—it was part of the threat. How easy it would be for anyone to come right in through the window.

I shook myself mentally. Sneaking up on me wasn't easy, as Sebastian had learned at the Club Bizarre party. This murderer was an idiot if he thought he could get rid of me as easily as Sanna and Armi. Having thus laughed down my fear, I opened the binder and worked my way toward the end of Sanna's life.

Hänninen family drama had kept Henttonen's team busy, and Eki personally had done a considerable amount of work keeping Sanna out of jail. Two DUIs, both squeaking in below the standard for aggravated drunk driving, one charge for possession of marijuana, and a long list of citations for public intoxication.

The first drunk-driving arrest occurred at a sobriety checkpoint during Sanna's second year in college. The car was full of drunk students, but Sanna claimed to have consumed only a single beer.

"Performed well in court. Dressed nicely. Schoolgirl," Eki had written in his notes. I could imagine Sanna standing before the judge looking sweet, her big brown eyes scared, her voice even more childlike than normal. That was an easy case.

However, by the time of Sanna's next DUI arrest, she had spent several nights in the drunk tank. One of these detentions was a result of a run-in with her boyfriend, whom Sanna threatened with a large folding knife. When Sanna ran her dad's car into a lamppost, her with a blood alcohol level of 0.14, getting her off was a bit more difficult. Eki's argument centered on Sanna's grief over her boyfriend leaving her and the stress of school. Her broken leg was sufficient punishment. The result was just more fines and a suspended license.

"Works hard to save her own skin. Knows how to play innocent better than anyone I've seen. Criminal material?" Eki had written in the margins. I was starting to understand why he doubted Kimmo's protestations of innocence.

Sanna's marijuana possession charge came at the same time as Otso Hakala's arrest for distribution. Eki managed to convince the judges that Sanna had been completely under Hakala's influence, and the court dismissed the count against her of distributing a controlled substance due to lack of evidence. For possession, Sanna still took home a three-month suspended sentence.

This case lacked any notes. Was that what Eki had removed? Why? Would Martti or Albert remember what had been in the file? I was leafing through copies of the trial transcripts and Sanna's deposition when the phone rang a second time.

Probably the same person trying to scare me again. This time I would leave the line open.

"Hi, it's Angel. How was your head on Wednesday morning?"

"Not the best." I didn't know whether or not to be pleased by Angel's call.

"Listen, I just remembered that our old member newsletters have some of Kimmo's drawings in them. Would they be of any use? I was thinking they could be, since they all show women dominating men."

"Maybe. Go ahead and put them in the mail."

"You don't want to come pick them up?"

"No time, not until early next week." Why I didn't really want to see Angel again was unclear even to me. What reason did I have to fear her?

"That policeman friend of yours asked Joke how long you've been involved in the club and didn't seem to believe him when

Joke said you weren't. He kept demanding to know whether you were a sadist or a masochist. Joke told him he was sorry he hadn't had the chance to find out." Angel's voice had the same irritating tone of amusement as before.

"What category would you put me in?" I asked, to my own surprise.

"I don't know. Dangerous, in any case. Is there any news on Kimmo's case?"

I was almost disappointed at Angel's change of topic, and, after our conversation ended, concentrating on Sanna again was difficult. I had never flirted with a woman before. People had called me a lesbian plenty of times—you have to get used to that as a policewoman. It never bothered me much, since the word "lesbian" was hard for me to take negatively. But Angel's obvious interest bothered me almost as much as it flattered me.

Einstein came padding into the living room and began cleaning his fur. He started with his face: first, he wet his left paw with his tongue, then rubbed his face, followed by more licking and then rubbing behind the ears. Inspired by this feline orderliness, I returned to Sanna's papers.

Essays, research papers, lecture notes. Most of Sanna's papers related to school. Photographs: Sanna and Annamari in matching dresses, Sanna horseback riding, Sanna and Kimmo on a carousel. Then a family portrait: Kimmo as a baby in Annamari's lap, Sanna as a toddler in an acne-faced Risto's arms, Henrik Hänninen behind his wife, looming dark and shadowlike. Strange family. Henrik's first wife, Risto's mother, had died of cancer. Annamari was not Matti and Mikko's real grandmother, although she gave Marjatta Sarkela a run for her money in spoiling the twins. Did it matter? To love a child, did you have to see your own features in them? Did you have to see them as your own flesh and blood?

The most interesting thing I found was a half-finished letter to Kimmo from a few years back while he was in the army. Why did Sanna keep it? It read:

> Maybe you were right when you told me to get away from Otso. I don't think I'm addicted to the drugs or the medicine yet, but you may have been right when you were home last time and yelled at me that I would be soon. But I'm afraid of Otso. Thanks for offering to help, but neither you nor Risto will be able to do anything about it if he decides to kill me. But I guess there are good men too. You don't hit Armi.
>
> Maybe I should see a shrink like Eki Henttonen suggested. Sometimes I wonder what that man wants from me. It's probably like you said, that he's just worried about me.
>
> You're right about Dad at least. He doesn't care about us, or about anybody. Sometimes I wonder what Leila was like, since we're more like our own mother and Risto is more like Dad. Be happy that you don't have a father complex like I do. Maybe we, you and I, want pain because we don't think we deserve love. But is it that simple? I still feel bad for you. It doesn't seem right that you have to give up part of who you are, your sexuality, because of Armi.

The letter was dated a couple of weeks prior to Otso and Sanna's arrest. Sanna's second drunk-driving case had been the preceding spring. Apparently, Eki and Sanna had contact during the intervening time as well. Well, everyone knew everyone else in Tapiola. Maybe Sanna was just asking Eki for advice, about what she should do with Otso. Or was there more to it? What was Eki hiding from me?

I returned to Sanna's thesis draft. After reading a few pages, I retrieved Antti's English dictionary from his office. I found the subject of the thesis intensely interesting, largely because Sanna's writing was so insightful and compelling. I wondered how long Sanna had been working on it.

Around the midpoint of the thesis was a detailed analysis of one of Plath's best-known poems, "Lady Lazarus." This was the poem on Sanna's desk the night of her death, the one everyone took as her suicide note.

Sanna's analysis of the poem suggested something else entirely:

> "Lady Lazarus" has been analyzed from many perspectives, with claims for the object of the poem ranging from the Jewish Holocaust to the general subjugation of women to, of course, Plath's own life, particularly her relationship with her father. Sound bases exist for all of these interpretations. However, these researchers have neglected the most important theme of the poem, the relationship between self-destruction and corporeality.
>
> The title of the poem, "Lady Lazarus," makes clear that resurrection is the intended meaning. The woman rises from the grave, removes her graveclothes, dissolves into ashes, and is born again. The imagery of the poem reeks of death and decomposition, while still remaining vivid and full of life.

Reading the poem, one wonders what killed
Lady Lazarus. The previous deaths presented in
the poem match up with those in *The Bell Jar* and
Plath's own life history. But who is or are Herr
Doktor, Herr Enemy, Herr God, and Herr Lucifer,
whom the speaker addresses in the poem? Plath
often used German terms of address in her poems
in describing her relationship with her father; in
the poem "Daddy," she compares her father with
the Nazis. In the end, she compares the faithless father and faithless husband. One might thus
assume that "Lady Lazarus" was written to a faithless, yet beloved man, whom the speaker in the
poem finally conquers.

Next to this section, Sanna had scratched something nearly
illegible. I stared at it for a moment, unable to make anything of
the content or the associations it aroused. "Like me and E," the
marginal note seemed to say.

Herr Enemy? Eki? Was he the Death Mr. Lindgren saw on
the breakwater? No, it couldn't be. But it would all be so logical:
Eki's lack of enthusiasm for defending Kimmo, trying to bully
me into giving up on the case. What did Sanna say about a father
complex? Perhaps she saw Eki as a protector, the omnipotent
defender who helped her out of all her run-ins with the law.

The third resurrection is clearly a turning point
for Lady Lazarus. She controls the situation, even
though she is returning from the dead. The poem
burns with defiant self-confidence, with courage to leave the old and take a stand against one's

enemies. The body of Lady Lazarus is attractive
to this enemy, an enemy we may clearly interpret
as male due to the term of address "Herr." In the
final statement of the poem, "And I eat men like
air," the word "men" means men specifically, not
people in general.

I read the poem "Lady Lazarus" again, and found that I
agreed with Sanna. When she left this poem out, it had nothing to do with her wanting to die. Sanna was reading it on her
birthday as a psalm of resurrection. But she wasn't able to swallow Herr Enemy after all. Instead, he killed her.

I couldn't sit still anymore, so I sprang up, knocking my
backpack onto the floor. Sanna's beloved skull rolled out across
the parquet floor, and Einstein rushed over to sniff it. My stomach churned. What could Armi have known about Eki? And did
Makke know or not know about Sanna's other lover? Eki had
even gone to the trouble of helping Makke after Sanna's death,
ensuring he didn't face charges for involuntary manslaughter.
Still, even if Eki did kill Sanna, it might not have been on purpose. Perhaps he had just pushed her into the water during an
argument, and she was too drunk to resist the cold water for even
a moment to climb back out. Even a charge of manslaughter
would have ended his career.

Fortunately, it was Friday, and I didn't have to go in to the
office for another two days. I would have time to collect my
thoughts and formulate a strategy. Was Eki cursing his bad luck
for having made the mistake of hiring an enterprising ex-cop
like me? Armi and I would have met eventually anyway though,
and Armi would have talked to me whether I worked for Eki's
firm or not.

I picked up the skull from the floor, since Einstein seemed to have lost interest. I wondered what he might have smelled. Could he pick up the scent of the original owner? Was Sanna's scent still on it? And why did Sanna keep a skull on her desk anyway? Had she entertained the same thoughts as Hamlet—"To be or not to be"? But someone else had made that decision for her, and for Armi.

Armi and Sanna. Two different women, one hard and dark, the other soft and fair. Sanna, who broke every rule and never seemed to care what anyone thought. Armi, who was so desperate for respectability but had a curious streak and a habit of using information about people in odd ways. As far as I could tell, they hadn't much cared for each other, so it was ironic that Armi seemed to have become such a thorn in someone's side because of Sanna. But was that person Eki?

It was already a little past ten o'clock and the bus to Inkoo left first thing in the morning, so I needed to get to bed. Perhaps a nightcap would help me fall asleep faster. I turned off the living room light and admired the sunset still visible on the horizon, painting a red glow across the sea and coloring the few wisps of clouds hanging in the sky. We still had a few weeks until the solstice, so the light would continue increasing each night. I walked into the dimly lit kitchen and was just about to turn on the light when I heard a rustling at the front door.

Now my police instincts kicked in for real: I froze in place and groped for the nearest chair to use as a weapon. I heard a key turn in the lock, and then someone stepped in. I inched my way toward the knife rack hanging over the counter. A filleting knife trembled in my right hand as I lowered the chair in my left hand to the floor.

Fear gnawed at my throat as I tried to convince myself that it was only Antti, returned early from Inkoo for some reason. But I also realized how easy it would have been for Eki to swipe my keys, make copies of them, and return them to my jacket pocket. And today as I left the office, I even laughed with Annikki about my plan to spend a "glamorous" night at home, alone with my cat. Did Eki overhear us talking about where I'd be?

Steps moved through the entryway. I tiptoed to the kitchen door—I wanted to see my attacker. Hands shaking, I swore to myself that whoever he was, he was not going to get rid of me as easily as he had Sanna and Armi. Just as I was sliding toward the living room, I heard the sound of a light switch flipping on, and then someone spoke.

"Hi there, Einstein. Good kitty. Poor thing; didn't they take you with them to Inkoo?"

Just call me the queen of weak nerves. The lurker in the living room wasn't some bloodthirsty murderer, just my almost sister-in-law, Marita, who of course would have keys to her own parents' house. As I entered the living room, I intentionally bumped the door. Startled, Marita jumped up from where she had been petting the cat on the floor.

"Who...Oh, Maria! The whole house was dark, so I thought you'd gone camping with Antti. God, you scared me! I came to borrow Mom's blue silk blouse because mine has a stain, and I have not one, but three graduation parties I have to make appearances at tomorrow."

"At least the boys have summer vacation starting tomorrow. I bet that will be nice."

"I'm taking them to Inkoo on Sunday. I hope they'll be able to forget about Armi and Kimmo if we're away from all this and out in the country. They're just old enough to understand that this is real life, not a TV show. They know that someone killed Armi and that Kimmo is in jail because of that. Sanna's death was harder to explain to them because they were a year younger, and until then they always thought that only old people died." Marita sighed. Her large, slender hands fingered the hem of her shirt nervously. "And whenever I walk around downtown, I feel like people are staring. I know half of it is just me projecting, but now we can get away for a while, and I won't have to think as much. I feel bad about leaving Risto alone with Annamari, but she said Henrik is coming home next week. Did Mom move any of her clothes around when you guys moved in, or do you think everything is still here?"

"She took some stuff for the summer, but most of her things are still in the walk-in closet—let's go look."

We found the blouse she wanted, which looked too big for Marita.

"Won't that be too loose on you?"

"I'll try it on to see." Marita pulled it on over her head on top of her long-sleeved T-shirt. Raising her arms exposed the skin above the waistband of her pants, and I thought I saw bruises striping across her skin, right below her ribs, but I didn't get a good enough look before Marita pulled down her shirt.

"This should be just fine if I tuck it in. Do you know when Kimmo's case will go to trial?"

"It could be several months."

"That's horrible." She sighed. "I guess Henrik could take Annamari away with him to Ecuador. She doesn't start teaching at the community college until September, and even at that, she might want to consider taking a leave of absence, considering the situation."

"And leave Kimmo here in prison?" I said, feeling surprisingly angry. "Is that the way in the Hänninen family? Difficult family members are best forgotten? Just mentioning Sanna's name seems taboo."

She gave me a steely look. "Sanna's death was terrible for the whole family. I would expect a bit more tact from you of all people in a situation like this. I don't understand what you think you're going to achieve digging up the past. Sanna committed suicide; everyone else has learned to accept that. No one wants you to do anything except help Kimmo. That is what's important."

"I think I'll be the one to decide what's important and what isn't. Did you have a fall? You seem to have bruises all over your body."

Marita's face froze for a split second, but she quickly recovered, and then she blushed.

"A fall? Yes, I tripped after the party last Friday. That cognac was deceptively strong. And I bruise easily, just like Antti. Have you noticed?" Her explanation was more detailed and delivered faster than was necessary, and she immediately headed toward the door as if fearing I might start inspecting her bruises more closely.

I headed to the kitchen. My head throbbed as I poured myself a generous shot of Mother Sarkela's lemon vodka. Hell's bells! Why did everyone always have to tell me what I could and couldn't do? I wasn't rooting around in the Hänninens' dirty laundry for my own edification, after all. They should be happy I was the one doing the poking around and not Ström.

Speaking of whom, I would have given anything to know where his investigation stood. Unfortunately, the only person I knew in the Espoo Police Department was Herr Ström himself, so I didn't exactly have any back channels. I had no way of knowing if they had found anything interesting in Armi's house, or anything relating to Sanna. Did I dare ask Ström's Dennis the Menace subordinate for help? He had, after all, left that notebook for me, so maybe he would be willing.

My problem was that I lacked any authority whatsoever. I wasn't a lawyer yet, and I was no longer a cop. I had no power to interrogate anyone, to search Armi's house, or to pull rank on... well, anyone.

After scooping Sanna's papers from the living room floor, I read a little more of her master's thesis to help me fall asleep. The skull looked on, staring at me blankly from its perch on my desk. I thought about Marita's bruises. Could a struggle with Armi have caused them?

Sanna visited my dreams again. I hadn't even realized I was asleep when I saw her sitting next to my bed.

"Hi, Maria. I'm not sure anyone has notified you. I'm your angel," she said.

"Lucky me."

"I handled that thing on Monday pretty well, though, didn't I? You didn't hit your head and you didn't drown. Mind if I smoke?" She immediately rolled a cigarette and then blew bluish smoke straight into my eyes. I squinted a bit, but I wasn't about to flinch.

"Why did they make you my guardian angel?"

"I have to have something to do," she said, with a half smile. "Rub that skull any time, and I'll come visit you." Sanna turned horizontally and flew out the window. Her wings were brown at the tips, and as she rose, she nearly collided with an electric pole.

Some guardian angel.

11

I was lying on my back on a warm, smooth rock outcropping next to the water. The sun shone brightly, forcing me to keep my eyes shut as it caressed my naked body. As I stretched voluptuously, something cold and slimy landed on my bare stomach. Antti's hand, fresh from swimming.

"Aren't you going to say 'eek'?" Antti asked as he lay down next to me.

"Eek," I dutifully squeaked and then lazily kissed Antti on the shoulder. "You're so cold. Before you went into the water, you were as warm as a potbellied stove."

The entire morning we had been playing Adam and Eve on this uninhabited island a few miles southwest of Antti's parents' summer home. After rowing out in the evening, we set up our tent and sat up late around the fire with a bottle of wine, trying to solve all the world's problems. Far enough removed from murders, math, and the "joy" of cohabitation, our little island allowed us to find each other again, and at least for now, life tasted only of salty skin warmed by the sun and sweet white wine.

"Looking at the time is a shame since you seem to be enjoying yourself so much, but I promised Mom yesterday that we would be back for lunch."

"No way. We'll just say the oars fell off and the boat floated away during the night." Kissing him here and there, I nestled more closely into Antti's side, letting him know I wanted a quick reprise of what we had done earlier in the morning.

After noon, we began packing up our gear. As I was wrapping the tent stakes in the plastic ground cloth, I asked Antti, "Have you ever thought that Risto might be beating Marita?"

"No! Jesus, how did you get an idea like that?" Gradually, though, Antti's expression changed from one of stupefaction to one of concern. He said quietly, "I do know that Henrik hit Annamari, and sometimes even the children. Both Marita and Kimmo told me so."

I told Antti about Marita's bruises.

"I just know from my time on the force that these things have a nasty habit of getting passed down," I said. "You wouldn't believe some of the stuff I've seen. And the more respectable the family, the more likely abuse is to stay secret. Hearing your neighbors' fights is harder when you don't share a wall."

Antti looked distressed.

"Well, if that's true, we can't let it continue. I have to talk to Marita."

Antti's words reminded me of Armi's elderly neighbor's story: "I can't look the other way anymore; it just isn't right." Could Armi have been talking to Risto?

"These are just suspicions," I said, trying to reassure Antti. "Don't talk to Marita yet—I'll ask Kimmo first. But what do you know about his dad?"

"I don't know much about him." This conversation was clearly difficult for Antti. "Apparently he's violent when he gets angry, and when Risto was a teenager they had some serious run-ins. I also heard that Sanna got hurt pretty badly once trying to protect her mother."

I didn't bother being pissed at Antti for not telling me any of this sooner. At least he was telling me now.

When we finally glided up to the Sarkelas' dock, it was 2:05. In the driveway sat another car beside Antti's parents' Saab, and the commotion coming from the yard revealed that at least Matti and Mikko were present. My weird exchange with Marita on Friday at our house both embarrassed and irritated me, and I was also afraid that Antti wouldn't be able to act naturally around his sister after what I told him.

Around the lunch table, everyone was discussing Matti and Mikko's final report cards and their summer plans. Happy, random chitchat, I thought, as if Kimmo and Armi had never existed, never sat around the same table. I looked at Risto, trying to see any resemblance in his face to Sanna's. His eyes were the same shape as his half sister's, large and round, lending his angular adult face a certain childlike appearance. Sanna had always looked like a child, because of her big eyes and pouty lower lip. I realized that I knew much less about Risto than Kimmo or Sanna, despite the fact that he was the one I would actually be related to if I ever married Antti. Under his smooth, amiable exterior, there was still something distant, polished—one could almost say icy—about him. Perhaps his father was the same way.

"Is Grandpa bringing us real Indian bows from Ecuador?" Matti asked, his mouth full of ice cream.

"Don't be too disappointed if Grandpa doesn't remember this time. He had to hurry to come so quickly," Marita said. "Mikko, slow down. Don't take such big spoonfuls. Half of that is dripping on your shirt!"

"How long does Henrik plan to spend in Finland?" Tauno Sarkela asked Risto.

"It depends. Dad still has a lot of work to do on his Ecuador project before he retires, and I kind of doubt he will make time for a vacation."

"Yes, but doesn't he turn sixty-five this year?" Marjatta Sarkela asked, as she scooped a second helping of ice cream into the boys' bowls. "Take some more, Antti. You must be hungry from all that rowing. You too, Maria." My prospective mother-in-law passed the bowl of ice cream down.

"I did get my exercise," Antti said, kicking me under the table. We both giggled. I felt like a fifteen-year-old just back from a clandestine rendezvous in the woods to make love for the first time. The warmth running between us was still strong, and a furtive touch of our fingers on the edge of the ice-cream serving dish was full of tense anticipation.

Matti and Mikko shoveled their dessert down and asked for permission to go outside. After they left, the tenor of the conversation around the table changed, turning into more of an interrogation. Was Kimmo still claiming to be innocent? Why was I digging into Sanna's past? How soon would the trial be? Do the police make mistakes in things as big as arresting a murderer? By the end of the grilling, I was ready to take a vow never to marry into the Sarkela family.

"Of course, we all want to defend Kimmo," Risto said. "But we have to face the facts. Kimmo had these…deviant…sexual tendencies, and he was under the control of those feelings when he—no doubt unintentionally—killed Armi. At first I didn't want to believe that Sanna was an alcoholic or that she was mixed up in dealing drugs either, but I had to accept what was actually happening, not just what I wanted to be happening."

Matti and Mikko were playing cowboys and Indians in the front yard, with one energetically tying the other to a pine tree. I wondered whether any of the others were experiencing the same associations.

"Luckily, Annamari still has our boys." Marita sighed. "They can distract her and give her something positive to think about."

"What do you mean 'still'? Why are you all talking about Kimmo as if he's dead? Do you want to sweep Kimmo under the rug now just like everyone did with Sanna? I guess it would be a big relief for you if Kimmo would just hang himself in prison. Then the matter would be settled, and you could forget all about him!"

At this, I stormed away from the table like a teenager arguing about her curfew. I couldn't believe these people! Their own family seemed like nothing to them, like toys to be discarded. Oh me, oh my, this one broke—luckily, we have eleven more just like it. I could imagine what my parents would have said about me when I was born. Nurse, this child has a manufacturing defect; it doesn't have any testicles. Can we return this? I hoped my sister would produce the long-awaited boy child so we could all be done with it.

"Maria, wait!" Antti was coming after me, bounding over the roots and stumps in the forest as fast as he could.

"Who the hell do they think they are? It would be better if people didn't even have relatives! They're just as bad as my parents—I went to law school because they didn't think working as a police officer was 'smart' enough, or 'respectable' enough. No, our daughter has to get a fancy degree. How does anyone who's seen this shit ever work up the courage to have their own children?"

"Hey now, put on the brakes. Let's calm down and think things through," Antti said seriously.

"I can't stand their indifference. Could they take any less responsibility? You seem to be the only one really worried about Kimmo."

"That isn't true. They're just trying to prepare for the worst. Has it occurred to you they might be in self-preservation mode?"

"You mean they're bracing themselves for Kimmo languishing in prison for years? Or just the social stigma of having a convict in the family?"

"Maria, don't. I'm angry too. But it doesn't help. Finding some sort of certainty is the only thing that helps."

"I'm sorry," I said. "It just kills me that I didn't help either, that I didn't try to do anything for Sanna. Why couldn't I tell Armi needed something more serious than a girlfriend to gossip with?" I asked myself aloud, angrily kicking a moss-covered rock. It flipped over, and a couple of quick creeping things frantically swarmed away to conceal themselves under the next rock. I felt sorry for the little creatures. Who was I to go around exposing and frightening innocent things?

We spent a couple of hours walking in the woods before I had to leave for the bus. As I packed my things, I muttered a reluctant apology to Antti's family. In any event, Risto's attitude made me suspect that he was trying to protect someone other than Kimmo, but who? Himself?

I was set to see my old partner, Pekka Koivu, at eight o'clock that evening at the Corona Bar in the city. Since the bus deposited me a few blocks from my destination, I had a few minutes' walk through the stately old buildings of Helsinki and along a small, quiet park. For a moment, I longed for my old apartment, which was a short walk in the opposite direction. I heard the clinking of dishes in the university café and thought about all the happy times I'd had people-watching on the Esplanade.

In Tapiola, everything was different. With everyone so tight-knit and homogeneous, it was a completely different world from Helsinki, an international city constantly becoming more color-ful and diverse with every passing year. Tapiola might as well have been a walled-off village, because everyone there had gone to the same school or played basketball or hockey on the same team. Even Antti always specified he was from Tapiola, rather than the larger Espoo municipality. After a couple of months there, even I felt settled in, like I'd lived there much longer, perhaps because my home and work were so close to each other. Now I was seeing how oppressive that coziness could be.

When I arrived at the bar, my friend was already sitting at a table next to the window, sipping a pint. Seeing Koivu made a warmth spread through me that only increased when he noticed me and a broad smile spread across his blond bear-cub's face. If I had ever had a brother, I would have wanted him to be Pekka Koivu.

We started out by trading news. Koivu was still working in the same unit where we were partners the previous year. The problems in the department sounded even worse than usual. Good. I felt less bad about leaving.

"I've thought about transferring out into the country some-where to arrest drunk farmers," Koivu said. He was from a small country town just like I was, a little farther north but still in the economically depressed eastern region of the country.

"Big city lights losing their shine?"

"Yeah, I miss the woods. Besides, I met this nice girl who's graduating from nursing school next spring. She's from Kuopio and says she wants to work somewhere up that way."

"And you're planning to go with her? Whoa, Koivu, that sounds serious."

"Well, yeah. I guess it's about time to starting thinking about getting married, having a family," said this man four years my junior. Then he changed the subject back to work.

"So why did you want this Hakala guy's rap sheet?"

"Nothing anymore, since there's no way he can be my murderer. I guess I was just hoping for an easy solution to this mess. But I have a new theory." I began explaining the conclusions I'd come to so far about Armi's murder. Koivu and I used to be a good team, and talking with someone on the outside was nice, someone who didn't have any emotional connection to the events or people I was dealing with.

"Last winter I had to work with this Ström character a few times, and you're right about how difficult he can be," Koivu said. "I don't think he's necessarily a bad cop, but he's certainly not much of one for cooperation. And I would have loved to see you in all that leather," Koivu added, shaking his head sadly at my outfit of jeans, T-shirt, and sneakers.

"I promise to wear it to your wedding. So how does it sound?"

"No talking about weddings before I've actually even proposed to Anita. I don't want to jinx anything."

"I mean my theory, fathead! Does it seem possible that the same person who murdered Armi also murdered Sanna—and do you think my boss could be that person?"

"It's pretty far-fetched, but you know what, I've seen way stranger things in this job," Koivu said. "I've stopped making assumptions. So a couple of things come to mind. What about Armi's brother-in-law? If he really thought Armi was driving that car that almost ran them down and led to his wife's miscarriage, then he had motive. And then there are Sanna's abortions.

You should find out who the father or fathers were of those babies. Who would know that?"

At the memory that Eki had been the one to enlighten me about Sanna's abortions, I felt like vomiting. Was Sanna's final pregnancy Eki's handiwork?

"Sanna was Dr. Hellström's patient, so in a way she was also Armi's patient, because Armi had access to all her records and dealt with her at her appointments. That must be it: Armi knew who murdered Sanna because he was the father of her child! Koivu, you're a goddamn gem, you know that? I'll have to revisit that awful Hellström first thing tomorrow, although I don't fancy talking to the greasy letch about anything having to do with sex. Guess what I heard him say about me!" I told Koivu about the conversation I'd overheard at Risto's birthday party and my own intrusion. Koivu laughed so hard he almost inhaled his beer.

"I really miss you down at the station, especially when the boss man comes around stinking up my office with his cigar."

From the billiards side of the bar came a louder ruckus than usual, but we just ignored it. We started talking about his upcoming vacation.

"Anita and I are going to Greece for a week, to Skopelos. Then I've been thinking—"

An even louder bellow interrupted Koivu's sentence, followed by a crash and shouts. Over the general commotion came a bellow of, "Oh, so you think you're a big man, do you!"

I also heard a waitress clearly say to another, "He's got a knife. We should call the police."

Koivu and I weren't about to let this situation disintegrate. One beer wasn't enough to dull our edge. Giving each other a look, we rose at the same time. Koivu waved his badge at the bartender but still ordered him to call and request a patrol car immediately.

In the back room, we found the center of the floor empty, with people standing in a ring along the walls and next to the pool tables as if watching a boxing match. But no, this would be even less civilized: a good old Finnish knife fight. In the middle of the circle, a man lay bent over a table with the back of his head against the felt. A big, ugly man held him in place with one arm, while in the other hand glinted a sinister-looking jackknife pressed against the first man's throat. Just a tiny motion of the large man's hand and that throat would open up in a textbook butcher-shop cut. The men could have been brothers—the same robust, beer-infused physique, the same bloodshot drinker's eyes.

"This is the police. Put the knife away," Koivu said with calm authority. We're not both the police, I thought, but I could feel him tense next to me like a bear catching the scent of its prey, and I wasn't about to volunteer my actual career status to the crowd at that moment.

"This fucker cheated me at eightball!" The man with the knife spat in the face of his victim, who didn't dare move a muscle.

"I want you to calm down and put away the knife," I said, taking a few steps to the side and then two forward so the knife-wielder would be sure to see me. Usually troublemakers calmed down more easily when a woman was giving the orders. However, this time my attempt seemed unsuccessful. The man was obviously intoxicated, and drunks are way more unpredictable than other people are.

At least that was what they taught us at the police academy.

"If you come one step closer," he snarled at me, "I'm gonna cut this turkey's throat open!"

Sweat and tears of fear mixed with spit on the alleged cheater's face. Disregarding the threat, I took several more steps forward, extending my hand invitingly and trying to lock eyes with the attacker. At the same time, I saw that Koivu was slipping behind him. He didn't mean to rush him, did he? Given the likelihood of injuring the victim and himself, the risk was far too great. Persuasion was a much better tactic.

"I want everyone else out of here!" I yelled. "Clear the bar!" The crowd would probably just goad the knife-wielder into doing something even stupider than he already was doing, but with only a few people present, he would have an easier time giving up without losing face.

Although only a few dozen seconds passed, I had time to ponder how long the patrol car might take to arrive and how on earth someone could manage to cheat at pool. I mean, you knock the balls into the pockets, and everyone watches.

Of course, the curious crowd of onlookers had no desire to disperse. Why should they miss the free entertainment? They might even get to see live and in person how corpses got made. I heard someone whisper that this was just like a movie. Maybe they thought the guy lying on his back on the table had ketchup running through his arteries.

By now, I was close and began slowly circling the pool table, trying to keep all of the man's attention on me so Koivu could more easily slip behind him. For a big, muscular dude, Koivu moved silently—more like a giant cat than a bear.

"Fuck, girl, are you supposed to be a cop?" For the first time, the man with the knife turned his eyes straight toward me. "Do you have a gun? Are you gonna shoot me?" He was trying to sound sarcastic, but his tone contained a hint of uncertainty.

"If you do as I say, put the knife on the table, and let that guy go, then nothing will happen to you," I said, staring the man directly in the eyes like a snake charmer. I saw Koivu behind him now, poised to attack: as soon as the man let go of the knife, Koivu would tackle him.

The man holding the knife stared at me for a moment. Then came a sudden move of his hand, and the knife sank into the green felt of the table eight inches away from me. Giving in must have been a serious blow to his pride. I snatched the knife, tossing it out of reach and then rushing to Koivu's aid as he wrestled the man to the floor. We didn't have handcuffs or any other restraints, but between the two of us, we managed to keep him down for the two minutes until the patrol car arrived.

"What were your names again?" one of the patrol officers asked after getting the assailant buttoned up in the back of the cruiser.

"Officer Pekka Koivu and Maria Kallio, inactive reserve detective," Koivu answered briskly. "I work in Violent Crime—the switchboard can find me if you need any more information."

"So you intervened, even though you were off duty?" the other patrol officer asked with a hint of disbelief. Apparently, he hadn't listened closely enough to my "title" to notice the part about me being an ex-cop.

"Should we have stood by and watched while that other guy got a knife in the throat?" I asked, although I had clearly acted without authority.

The patrol officers thanked us coolly for the assistance, and we returned to the bar.

"Hey, Koivu, Red! The rest of the night is on the house," the bartender yelled.

"Great! You got Dom Pérignon? Well, OK, a bottle of Guinness if you're all out," I replied.

Koivu took a large bottle of domestic Karjala. Adrenalin was still coursing through my veins, making my whole body feel electrified. We cracked a few jokes with the servers, but the rest of the patrons in the bar wouldn't stop staring at us. I felt like a zoo exhibit. Perhaps police were like some sort of exotic, repugnant creatures to them—a police officer wasn't supposed to look like a normal person, at least not one having a beer in their bar. I wondered whether we should change taverns, but on the other hand, drinking here was going to be cheap.

Koivu raised his glass to me.

"Here's to teamwork." We clinked beer glasses, in complete violation of proper Finnish toasting etiquette. "Listen, Maria…I wish you were still my partner. Are you sure you don't want to be a cop anymore? You weren't afraid staring down that clown. I knew I could count on you."

"I was afraid. I was so damn afraid that other guy was going to end up as meat on a slab."

"But it doesn't alter your judgment. Take Saarinen and Savukoski. You know how they are; sometimes they're so weak at the knees I can barely get them out of the car, and Saarinen is so decrepit he can barely run. With your legal education, you could go far on the force."

"Why are you on this all of a sudden?"

I was bewildered. Too many people had voiced doubts about my choice of profession during the past few days. First Ström, whom I didn't much care about, and now Koivu. And I had to admit that sometimes I even did.

"You're one of the best cops I've ever met. And working with you was always fun." This was all so un-Koivu-like that I was starting to wonder where it was coming from.

"Are you taking some American-style self-improvement class that tells you to try to build up at least one other person a day? Twelve-step program? Emotional Intimacy 101?"

Koivu blushed adorably. "Well, since we're both dating someone now, I can compliment you without you thinking I'm trying to hit on you."

We continued talking about summer plans and agreed that he and Anita would come out to Tapiola for a sauna night sometime after their trip. Even though moving on to harder drinks would have been free, we decided to head home. I was tired from my short night's sleep in the tent, and my adrenaline crash was coming in the form of a pounding headache.

The evening was still light, so instead of walking to the bus stop, I continued past it to the main Helsinki city cemetery. I wanted to visit Sanna's grave. Based on what Antti had told me, I knew that Sanna had been buried in her mother's family's plot, in the older part of the cemetery. Although I found an appropriate grouping of Hallmanns, none of the surrounding stones bore Sanna's name. Of course not. The Hänninens didn't even want to remember Sanna's existence on a gravestone, I thought angrily as the stabbing pain worsened.

When I arrived home, Antti was playing the piano. The Scarlatti sonata calmed me in spite of the headache. I downed two ibuprofen, took a shower, and then read through Otso Hakala's and Sanna's criminal records, which Koivu had given me. Neither contained any stunning revelations, although Hakala's was even more impressive than I expected. Drugs, larceny, assault and battery. In a Dorothy L. Sayers mystery, he would have escaped without anyone noticing in order to kill Sanna and Armi and then cunningly returned himself to prison after committing his crimes. Or someone else entirely would be sitting in prison in his place, while the real Hakala was walking around having shaved his beard and dyed his hair. Disguised as Makke Ruosteenoja.

Antti opened the kitchen door just as I was making some chamomile tea I had found in his mother's amply stocked health-food cupboard.

"Teemu Laaksonen called—Mallu's husband. He said he was coming to Helsinki tomorrow and could meet with you then. How was tonight?"

Antti looked worried as I recounted the evening's excitement.

"Is it just me, or does your life seems more dangerous now than when you were a cop?"

"A leopard can't change her spots. I'm lucky enough to be trained to handle dangerous situations when I encounter them—it's not like I'm seeking them out."

"I don't want to lose you, Maria. Seriously. You could be a tad more careful, if only for my sake." As Antti looked me in the eyes, I could still see the warmth of our morning together in them. I didn't want to fight. Instead, I pressed up against him like a tame kitty cat.

"I'm going to see my advisor tomorrow to deliver another couple of chapters of my dissertation for him to look at," Antti said. "Unless he finds something big that still needs work, I can probably defend in November."

"Will you go back to the university after Christmas then?"

"I don't know. I'll still have a year and a half of fellowship funding left. In the beginning my plan was to go for a postdoc overseas, to the States or Denmark. My advisor and I are going to be talking about that tomorrow too."

"When would you leave? January?" I didn't want to put this conversation off, even though I wasn't ready and my head was still throbbing.

"Yeah, or the next fall semester. It depends a little on you. I meant to bring this up yesterday, and then this morning, but we were having such a good time I was scared to ruin the mood. If I go, what would you do? Would you come with me? Would you wait for me here? If I leave, does that mean it's the end of this?"

I didn't know how to answer. Up until now, we had been living without any particular plans, even moving in together practically by accident. I loved Antti, but how much was I willing to tie myself to him? And do you do that one day at a time, over and over, or once and for all?

"I just started a new job, so I'm not planning on going anywhere immediately," I said, not bothering to add that if Eki was indeed a murderer, I would be out of a job sooner rather than later. "Of course, at some point I still want to do my court internship. I can't just drop everything and follow you across the planet. And what do you mean by waiting? That you go gallivanting across the United States while I sit here hoping I'll still be good enough for you when you get back?" I regretted that last sentence before it was all the way out of my mouth.

"Don't be a jerk, I didn't mean that! I was just thinking… OK, maybe this isn't the time, since you're obviously in a bad mood."

"I'm sorry. My head just hurts."

We drank our tea in silence. I tried to think about something else other than our future.

"How well do you know Mallu's husband?" I asked after finishing my first cup.

"I've met him a few times. Why?"

"What kind of a person is he?"

"I don't know. Pretty normal. Nice, a little reserved. Like Kimmo. Or me. Not the murdering type. Is that what you're getting at? Is everyone a murderer to you this week?"

"I was thinking that maybe he did see Armi driving that car. But that's unlikely, because Armi didn't even have a driver's license."

"Where did you get the idea that Armi didn't drive? Of course she did. She used to drive me and Kimmo places all the time."

I took a deep breath and tried to focus.

"Say that again!"

"Armi had a driver's license. I know she did."

"So why on earth did Mallu say she didn't?" I asked, although I knew the answer. To turn suspicion away from herself. And, like an idiot, I didn't even check. I just took her word for it.

Despite the herbal tea and ibuprofen, my headache was getting worse. Tomorrow was going to be busy. I was so close to cracking the case I could smell it, despite the length of my list of possible suspects I still had.

"Seeing how much more interested you are in tracking down criminals than working on our relationship really hurts," Antti said as he rose from the table. "And your family. What time are your sisters coming tomorrow?"

Cursing myself, I realized I had forgotten all about Eeva and Helena's visit. On top of all my real work, I had to get ready for them, which at least meant cleaning the house and making dinner. I wasn't going to be able to do half as much as I wanted. I hoped I wouldn't have to cross paths with Eki at the office.

Before falling asleep, I thought about how wrong Antti was. It wasn't that I was more interested in criminals than in our relationship—my skills were just far better suited to one than the other. Puzzling out my own feelings was a much more difficult task than catching murderers.

12

Acting natural around Eki during our regular Monday morning meeting was a challenge. Albert was already out on vacation, so the only other employees present were Martti and Annikki. I tried to stay calm as we started reviewing Kimmo's case.

"I can't tell the police how to do their jobs, but I really think Kimmo Hänninen's alibi could bear closer scrutiny," I said. "Might it be possible for us to hire someone, a private investigator, perhaps, to interview the neighbors? We really need someone who can place Kimmo at home before one o'clock."

"Haven't the police found anyone?" Martti asked.

"I don't know whether they've even tried, and I don't have any time in the next few days to go around knocking on doors myself. The Palmgren case is going to court on Friday." I sighed. "I'll be tied up with that the last half of the week."

"Has the judge set a pretrial date for Hänninen's case?" Martti continued. Eki shook his head. I looked at him thoughtfully. Chubby, balding, and well past fifty. Not repulsive by any means, but not attractive, let alone handsome. Knew how to be coarse or courteous depending on the situation. Two adult sons just a few years younger than me. What would Sanna have even seen in Eki? Safety? A father figure? And what did Eki want from Sanna? Didn't he realize that getting involved with a client meant risking everything—his family, his reputation, and his career?

From out in the hallway came the sound of a phone ringing. Annikki grabbed the conference-room line, then handed the phone immediately to me.

"Teemu Laak—" was all she got out.

"Excuse me, but I have to go take this call!" I said, rushing out of the conference room. Mallu's husband didn't want to talk over the phone, so we arranged to meet at three thirty. Detective Ström was continuing Kimmo's interrogation at one o'clock, so I would still have time after our staff meeting to contact Dr. Hellström.

Back in the conference room, Eki was leaning back in his chair talking about the divorce settlement he was working on. Then he mentioned his intent to take some vacation time after Midsummer. Then he took a third piece of *pulla*. Then he asked after Annikki's aging mother's health. Was this supposed to be a cold-blooded murderer? Maybe I was the one too wrapped up with all this, with Sanna and Sylvia Plath and Poor Yorick making my imagination run roughshod over my good sense. Maybe Dr. Hellström would be able to help. Maybe Teemu Laaksonen was the answer and Armi *was* behind the wheel of that car.

When Eki left the office for the Helsinki District Court, I decided to check on his alibi for the morning of Armi's murder. Eki claimed to have left sailing first thing that Saturday morning. What did he mean by morning? For me noon could still be morning after a late night out. Exactly what time did he leave? Fearing my clumsy lie would be too transparent, I didn't dare meet Eki's wife face-to-face, so instead I called upstairs. Lying over the phone seemed easier.

"Hi, it's Maria down in the office. Did Eki already leave? Oh. Listen, you can probably help too. Kimmo Hänninen claims that he waved to your car when he was biking back from Armi's house on the morning of the murder, sometime around twelve thirty. Don't you keep your boat at the Haukilahti Marina?"

"Yes, but we didn't leave that day until nearly two thirty. Eki had a terrible hangover and didn't get out of the house to go to the liquor store until one. He was such a mess. I wondered whether he was even in good enough shape to drive. I imagine he could have taken the beer crate straight to the boat though. You should ask Eki when he gets back."

"It's more likely that Kimmo simply mistook someone else's car for yours. I wouldn't even bother Eki—Kimmo is so desperate at this point that he's started clutching at straws," I said in hopes that Eila Henttonen would forget all about my call. If I'd had more balls, I would have just asked her directly whether she knew about Eki's relationship with Sanna.

Next I dialed Dr. Hellström's number, where a machine answered and told me his next available appointment was at twelve o'clock. I decided to interview him then, convenient or not. For the intervening two hours, I attempted to concentrate on the rest of my caseload, suppressing the lingering shame I was feeling from manipulating Mrs. Henttonen. Researching the finer points of defamation law didn't help, given the accusations I was considering making against my employer. Since you always had to concentrate on several things simultaneously, police work had taught me a sort of beneficial schizophrenia. Those skills were an asset now, because between reading passages from my law books, I could also plan what I would serve my sisters for dinner that evening. Antti fortunately had time to clean the house after his meeting with his dissertation advisor. I didn't take all this multitasking to the point of trying to resolve the issues about where our relationship was going, though.

On the third floor of a drab gray office building in downtown Tapiola, Dr. Hellström's clinic smelled of disinfectant. The secretary shared by the various specialists in the building said that with Armi gone, she was handling all of Hellström's scheduling and a nurse from one of the other offices was assisting with exams. After the police had turned the whole clinic upside down searching for anything relating to Armi's death, the secretary told me, the office had been forced to call in a professional cleaning crew. Thus the smell.

"This whole thing is just so horrible. Erik looks like he's aged ten years," the secretary was saying as Hellström walked into the reception area.

"Dr. Hellström, do you have a minute?"

Hellström nodded stiffly and then blew his nose into a handkerchief.

"Still this cold," he complained. "I don't understand why I'm always the one getting sick around here. Come into my office."

With a desk and computer, bookcases, a couple of chairs, a sink, an instrument table holding forceps, cotton pads, and latex gloves, and a screen behind which loomed that hideous stirruped exam table loathed by women the world over, the room looked like any other gynecologist's. The thought came to me how silly patients undressing behind a screen out of sight of the physician was when he was going to come around and prod them in their nether regions anyway. As I sat down in one of the patient chairs, I almost expected Hellström to start asking me how I was doing with my menstrual cramps. But it was my turn to ask the questions.

"Actually, I came to talk about Sanna Hänninen. She was your patient as well, in addition to her mother and Mallu Laaksonen. Is that correct, Dr. Hellström?"

He sighed. "Please, call me Erik. I've known Antti's family since he was in diapers for goodness' sake." Hellström smiled, charming despite his red nose, which took me off guard. The light of the sun shining through the window on his hair illuminated the silver strands, momentarily creating a halo effect over his head. "Yes, Sanna Hänninen was my client. Why do you ask?"

"I understand that Sanna had several abortions. Dr. Hellström...Erik, do you have any idea who was the father or who were the fathers related to those pregnancies?"

"Come now. You should know I can't give out that kind of information."

"This is a murder investigation, Erik," I said, as I had so many times before, although realizing in the same moment that I still didn't have any right to demand this information.

"I also suspect Sanna Hänninen's death was a homicide," I continued. "I understand that this medical information I may need for my case is confidential. So are my suspicions. I still don't have any solid evidence to back them up. I need your help."

I found myself speaking more frankly to Erik Hellström than I ever had before. Perhaps the classic tableau was affecting me: the big leather chair, the white coat, the fatherly expression and graying hair.

"Sanna murdered? But why?" Hellström asked, looking interested. He was used to listening to women's cares after all.

"I suspect that she had a relationship with someone and it became problematic for him, possibly a married man. Did she ever mention a relationship of that nature to you?"

Now Hellström was the one who looked taken aback.

"With a married man? But before her death, Sanna was dating that"—he paused, searching for the name in his head—"Ruosteenoja. Kind of a bodybuilder? I think when she had her second abortion, she was with someone who went to prison for dealing drugs. Sanna was mixed up in that incident too. The first abortion? I don't know; the father was some other good-for-nothing. Of course, I was the one who wrote the abortion orders. I had to agree with Sanna when she felt she was in no position to have a child with her degree unfinished and given the type of men she kept company with."

"When was that second abortion?"

"Wait just a moment, and I'll check our patient files." Hellström turned away from me toward his computer screen and started typing.

"September two years ago. About six months before her death."

So just before Otso Hakala went to prison.

Did someone else come into Sanna's life after Hakala went to prison, and before she met Makke? Could she have turned to Eki for comfort when she lost Hakala?

"Did Sanna come to your office at all after the abortion? Perhaps needing birth control? Did she mention any serious relationships?" Something was stopping me from mentioning Eki directly, but I earnestly hoped Hellström would take my meaning. What did I know about the Tapiola good-old-boys' club? Did they brag to each other about their conquests?

"Of course Sanna came in for follow-up visits. And when she started dating again, I tried to make sure she was taking her pills."

"Was Sanna's suicide a surprise to you?"

"No, not really. Sanna was a hopeless case. I suppose most people close to her knew she wouldn't live long. No, I wasn't surprised. Sad, yes—surprised, no." Hellström's hands shook as he instinctively dug in his pocket for a packet of cigarettes, but then he presumably remembered he couldn't smoke in the clinic anyway.

"Of course the police interrogated Makke; it took a considerable amount of wheeling and dealing on your boss's part to keep them from charging him with manslaughter," Hellström continued. "But everyone who knew Sanna believed it was an accident or suicide. Henrik and Annamari wanted to believe it was an accident, of course. What does it matter now though whether her death was intentional or not? It's been so long. And why do you think Sanna's death has something to do with Armi's murder? Did you have a particular married man in mind?" Hellström looked at me pointedly.

"No. It's just a theory...and may be nothing. While I'm here though, I also wanted to ask about Mallu Laaksonen. You've worked with her quite a bit during her quest to have a baby, and then she had that accident and the miscarriage. Did she ever express any suspicions to you that Armi was responsible?"

Hellström sighed. "Mallu never told me about it, but Armi did. As far as I could tell, the whole thing was pure nonsense— no one in a situation like that would have had time to see the driver of the car, even if it hadn't been dark. I think it was some sort of reflexive fixation in Mallu's mind, a sublimated manifestation of the jealousy between two sisters." Hellström smiled faintly.

Then the telephone on his desk rang.

"Please excuse me, Maria, but my next client is waiting. Do call me or drop in again if you have any other questions."

Intended to be winsome, Hellström's parting smile dissolved into a fit of sneezing.

As I pedaled the four miles north to the Espoo police station, I thought about how Hellström didn't seem like the loose-lipped talker some of his former patients made him out to be. Too bad.

With a mental curse at the idiocy of the local traffic planners, I narrowly dodged a pair of old ladies bumping down the bike path. Why did the path suddenly end and then continue on the other side of the street? Why were the intervening curbs so abrupt that riding up them almost sent you end over end? Why was the city designed around the needs of automobile traffic? Didn't they know this was Finland? I sped up, trying to focus all my aggression on my upcoming meeting with Ström, forgetting that the prosecutor's office had begun deposing Kimmo.

The questions were just repetition now, seemingly without any other purpose than wearing Kimmo down in an attempt to make him trip over his words and incriminate himself. The investigation was clearly at a stalemate. No one could prove Kimmo guilty, but as long as the real perpetrator was a mystery, the police would continue holding him. The representative from the district attorney's office was more businesslike than Ström, informing me that the police had yet to find anyone who could remember anything concrete relating to Kimmo's movements during the hours in question. When I suggested taking an ad in the paper and pasting notices on utility poles, his attitude was dubious.

"We needed to have found eyewitnesses earlier. Now anyone could imagine having seen anything. Detective Sergeant Ström has reports of all manner of sightings, but none of them are reliable."

"He does? Why haven't you informed the defense? You know as well as I do that we have a right to know about any potential material witnesses for our case."

"Yes, I'll admit that Ström made a mistake there."

"He damn well did! I am sure you're just about to produce those for me, though, right?"

My vexed, slightly threatening tone produced results. Maybe I'd make a good lawyer after all. I now had Ström's list of potential witnesses, which included at least three people I wanted to talk to. One couple remembered seeing Kimmo pass them on a pedestrian bridge over the West Highway at 12:20, and a dog walker claimed to have sighted him a mile south near the swimming beach ten minutes later. The times didn't match up exactly, but this evidence alone should have been enough to win Kimmo release while things were sorted out. I was pissed at Ström for not considering this information worth revealing to us. The district attorney's representative also seemed to think it odd.

"Don't worry, Kimmo. You'll be out soon," I said when we sat down after the prosecutor left. "I'm going to go talk to these witnesses; and besides, I have so much material on other suspects that we'll nail someone soon."

Kimmo looked as though he needed cheering up. I hadn't seen him for several days, and he looked more depressed than ever. I knew that Risto and Annamari had visited him over the weekend.

"Dad is flying in tomorrow," Kimmo said. "And I hear Armi's funeral will be next Thursday. Do you think they'll let me go?"

"Of course. Even if you were still under arrest, you could go with a police escort, but you'll be out by next Sunday. I promise," I said, sounding like a mother talking to a child quarantined with the measles.

"You really think so? Maria, I've promised myself if I get through this, I'm never doing S&M again."

"Why? What do you have to punish yourself for? Oh, yeah, you're a masochist," I said, realizing as the words came out that it was a poor joke.

"I don't know how I'll go on living without Armi," Kimmo said, sniffing.

What could I say to that? Life always goes on, even if it isn't the same? Or did I have anything else equally banal to offer? Instead, I changed the subject and asked about Sanna's boyfriends.

"Sometimes they changed so quickly I couldn't keep up. Sometimes she lived in the city and sometimes with Otso. She didn't move home again until that last summer when she was totally broke."

"Can you remember who Sanna was going out with the winter before she died? Was she still dating Hakala when he was sent to prison? And then was there anyone between Hakala and Makke. You'd probably remember this one, and I'm sorry to ask it, but was there any cheating, maybe going with another man at the same time as Makke?"

Kimmo thought so intensely that I felt as though I could almost see the gears turning beneath his thinning blond curls.

"Are you getting at what Armi said about Sanna's death? That it was murder? Listen, lately I've been having some doubts too. Maybe it is possible. You knew Sanna. She was so manic she could make anyone insane. Like Otso. I only remember her going to see him in prison once. She wanted so badly to be done with him—and had for a long time. Him going to prison was a relief for her, I think, and I guess that's why she had the abortion, even though she said all the time that she wanted to have kids. But not with Otso. I do know she loved Makke. She thought she could start a new life with him."

His cheeks flushing pink, Kimmo seemed to gain energy as he thought, happy to get his mind off his own situation, no matter how unpleasant the subject.

"Sanna started dating Makke pretty soon after Otso went to prison. But I think she did have something else going in the meantime. I just don't know with whom. She was seeing someone, but obviously wanted to keep it private."

"Did you ever notice any tension between Sanna and Eki Henttonen?"

Kimmo looked shocked. "You mean the Eki you work for? The lawyer? Not in a million years! You think that he and Sanna...No, I don't believe it..." Kimmo shook his head.

Then, after a moment, he added, "But Sanna had been with older men before, even in high school. She always talked about her daddy complex."

I remembered Sanna's letter again. A daddy complex? Strange that I didn't have one myself, since my father never gave me his approval. Or maybe my issues manifested in some other way in me than getting mixed up with older men.

"One last thing. Are you certain that on the night of Mallu's accident Armi didn't go out driving?"

"I've gone over that night in my head a thousand times. Teemu and I drank way too much, and, to be honest, I got into bed and passed out right after Mallu and Teemu left. I had my dad's car parked in the driveway—wait, let me finish—but why would Armi have gone out, especially when she had been drinking too?"

"But in theory it would have been possible?"

"In theory; I was dead to the world, so I can't really know. But Armi wouldn't have done that. She hated drunk drivers. She was always preaching at Sanna about it. And Armi never would have left the scene of an accident. She was a nurse, for God's sake."

"OK, I believe you. What kind of car was it?"

"A white Opel Astra."

When I hugged Kimmo, I promised I would return the next day unless something massive came up. As I rode away, I was still cursing Ström for withholding information. Should I file a misconduct complaint? Did I even have the energy? Suddenly I felt overwhelmingly tired and decided to ride back to Tapiola along one of the city nature paths to reenergize myself. The last of the wood anemones were persevering along the edge of the forest, and birds hopped out of the way as if competing to see which could get closest to my wheels without injury. At the top of one of the hills, I stopped for a few minutes to eat a chocolate bar and socialize with a stray cat. It sported a red-and-white striped tail that reminded me of a candy cane. The chocolate and feline company did me good, and I felt ready to continue my work.

When Teemu Laaksonen stepped into my office at three thirty, I knew immediately why he hadn't returned my calls the previous week. His face tanned, Mallu's husband had clearly been somewhere far to the south of Finland. The hand that shook mine was hard and rough, and his manner was reserved.

"I'm sorry that getting back to you took so long, but I was in Ibiza for the week. I had to get away from things for a while, so some friends and I arranged a little tennis vacation."

"When did you leave?"

"Last Saturday. The same day Armi died. My flight was at four that afternoon. No one told me what happened, so I just got on the plane. Mallu isn't speaking to me, and my dad says he didn't want to spoil my vacation. How is Mallu doing? I've tried to call—when she hears my voice, she just hangs up on me. Her parents had to tell me what happened." Teemu stood and walked to the window, the suppleness of an avid tennis player apparent in his movements.

"When did you last see Armi?"

"That Saturday. Just a little while before she died, I guess."

Now I stood up too. "What? What time?"

Teemu stared at me, failing to comprehend the meaning of my question. Then his expression darkened. "If you think that I..."

"This isn't about that. I'm trying to prove Kimmo's innocence. What time did you see Armi? And why were you there?"

"I went there looking for Mallu sometime around twelve thirty. I wanted to see her before I left. She wasn't home, so I called her parents' house from a telephone booth. But no one answered there, so I decided to drop by Armi's."

"But Mallu wasn't there? Was anyone else?"

"No. She said Kimmo had just left and she had a guest coming. She actually brought up the accident again. She asked again why I thought I saw her behind the wheel of that car."

"And what did you say?" My mouth was suddenly dry.

"That I didn't even know myself. It was just a momentary impression, and I'd been drinking a lot. I even accidently left my keys at Armi's house. Luckily, Mallu had hers so we could get in at home. We had started to cross the street. Then that car came, and I remember Mallu slipping. She fell. The car just grazed her, but...The accident was our fault too, not just the driver's, but they should have slowed down when they saw us, and should have stopped after hitting her..."

I could hear in Teemu's voice that he had replayed the chain of events every day in his mind, always coming up empty. He still couldn't clear his conscience.

"What did you see, Teemu?" Even though this was a formal meeting, I realized I was using his first name. Our generation just didn't know how to stick to protocol with people our own age.

"Blond hair. I could have sworn the driver was wearing a red scarf exactly like Armi's. It was this sort of big cyclamen-red wool shawl she always wore in the winter. She bought it on vacation in Santorini. That was why I recognized it, because I'd never seen one like it on anyone else. I could always pick her out in a crowd when she was wearing it."

"And you thought Armi was on her way to bring you your keys but lost control of the car?"

Teemu waved in the air as if hitting an invisible tennis ball he wanted to lob as far away as possible.

"I know it couldn't have been her. Armi wouldn't have done something like that. Armi would have stopped even if it hadn't been her own sister. But how can I get Mallu to believe that?"

"Is that why you divorced—because you couldn't get Mallu to believe it wasn't her own sister who killed your baby?"

"We aren't divorced; we're just separated. And I don't want a divorce—I want my wife back!" Teemu stared at me, his face desolate. "Mallu's the one who kicked me out. She said she didn't want to try any more, not for a baby, not to make our marriage work, not for anything. Mallu needs help. I want to help her, but she won't let me. She makes up all kinds of crazy stuff. That I think she's worthless because she can't have a baby.

That I blame her for the accident. Nothing I say makes any difference."

Teemu waved his arms again. He made a gesture full of rage, as if he were trying to tear away a membrane isolating Mallu from him.

"And now you're afraid these delusions made Mallu kill Armi," I said, more as a statement than a question.

"I guess. And it's my fault. I was the one who said I saw Armi in that car."

Looking at Teemu, thirty years old and the picture of health and vitality, I remembered how happy Mallu was in the Christmas portrait she had showed me. They were a beautiful couple, like something straight from the pages of an Italian *fotoromanzo*. Their story just didn't seem to have a happy ending.

"Teemu, listen. It would be best for you to contact the police yourself and tell them you visited Armi at twelve thirty. This is a matter of life and death for an innocent man. It could set him free. Call the lead investigator"—I gave him Ström's direct number—"and say you have important information about Armi's murder. If you want, I can come with you to your interview. Now, when did you leave Armi's house, and where did you go?"

"I went to the airport at about twelve forty-five. It was an international flight and I wanted to make sure I had plenty of time."

"Twelve forty-five. So you were probably the last person to see Armi alive—except, of course, for the murderer. Can anyone confirm your schedule?"

"Wait...There was a traffic jam on Ring One because of an accident, so I was stuck in my car awhile. I didn't make it to the airport until two. My friends can back me up—they were pretty bent out of shape when I showed up at the last minute like that.

We still had to go through security and find the gate, and the lines were huge."

I thanked Teemu, and he left after giving me his new address. I sat down to think about his account of events. How strongly did he believe he saw Armi in that car? Teemu wanted Mallu back. Did he blame Armi for their separation? Could he have lost his temper and murdered her?

This all would have been easier, I thought, if Armi hadn't been so busy on the day she was killed. Quite a crowd had traipsed through her backyard that morning, and putting each visitor in order would have taxed even a certain fictional Belgian detective's gray matter. Kimmo said he'd left Armi's at twelve fifteen; Kerttu Mannila, the baking neighbor, tried to visit at one; and I came at two. Teemu and the murderer also visited. Then there were the phone calls. In homage to the esteemed Monsieur Hercule Poirot, I decided to draft a proper timetable of events:

12:15	Kimmo leaves for his house
12:30 (approx.)	Sari calls Armi
12:30 to 12:45	Teemu visits Armi, looking for Mallu
1:00	Kerttu Mannila tries to bring Armi warm pies and hears fight
1:30	Kerttu Mannila tries again by calling on phone, but no one answers
2:00	Maria arrives

According to my timetable, the murder must have occurred between one o'clock and one thirty. Simple. Now I would just have to ask the police to work out where each of my main suspects were during that half hour. But I already knew. Mallu,

Annamari, Makke, and Eki were all in downtown Tapiola. Teemu claimed to have been on his way to the airport, but no one had confirmed that yet for me. Perhaps the police would have a record of the accident on Ring I that had backed up traffic.

The office was already empty. Feeling the guilt an alcoholic must experience when opening a bottle after promising himself he was done for good, I walked over to Eki's desk. I wanted to see his calendar. Sanna's thirtieth birthday was the second of March. Pisces, like me, even though I don't put any stock in horoscopes. Would there be an entry on her birthday? Would there be records of other meetings with Sanna?

The old calendar was in Eki's top desk drawer. My hands trembled as I leafed through it. March, March second—

KENYA. Only one word written over the entire week. KENYA. Since I had seen the pictures, I knew what it meant— Eki and his wife had been on a safari that week in Africa. The greatest trip of their lives, they called it. So Eki couldn't have been in Finland to push Sanna into the water. Perhaps no one had been on the breakwater with her after all, and the old man just imagined the black-clad figure of Death. Perhaps he had an even more active imagination than I did.

13

Before making my tired way home, I had to stop at the grocery store. My sisters' visit had me wound up, and at the store, I came within an inch of losing it at a flock of bargain hunters jostling around the discount displays in the produce department like chickens. I hated food shopping, I hated my bike wobbling under the weight of the bags, and I hated the herd of little boys blocking the bike path.

I hated that I knew Kimmo was innocent but that I didn't have anyone to offer up in his place.

When I arrived home, Antti was busy cleaning the entryway, and I nearly tripped over the vacuum cord. Idiot—why didn't he vacuum before I came home? After shoving the dirty dishes into the washer, I started making a Greek salad and blue-cheese–pineapple quiche. Easy dishes even I couldn't screw up.

"Hey, can I talk to you?" Antti asked, cautiously poking his head into the kitchen. I couldn't help laughing. Apparently, he knew how to read my face well enough to tell when I was dangerous. "Is there anything else I can help with?"

"Could you get your parents' bedroom ready for Eeva and Jarmo and put the spare mattresses out in the living room? We'll put Helena and Petri out there. What did your advisor say?"

"He wants me to stay through the spring to teach a seminar on my dissertation topic and then recommended going abroad in the fall."

I continued chopping onions, and tears filled my eyes. Not until next fall. We would have time to figure out our options.

"Things are starting to look good for Kimmo," I said, wiping my eyes. "Mallu's husband can testify that Kimmo wasn't at Armi's house anymore at twelve thirty, and we have a couple of other witnesses who saw him on his way home."

"Have the police found anything else? Because if Kimmo didn't do it, then who did?"

"They have no idea," I said as I started in on the black olives. "But they'll have to start thinking hard about it now that they have to release Kimmo. Of course that means the whole rigmarole is just going to start from the beginning again if I can't come up with a solution."

"Kimmo going free isn't enough for you? Maria, when is it going to sink in—you aren't a cop anymore. You're a lawyer. Even though you knew Armi, solving this case isn't actually your job. Your job is getting your client out of jail and keeping him that way. And I don't want you taking any more risks."

"Yeah, yeah," I muttered at the salad dressing I was mixing. Continuing this discussion with Antti seemed pointless. Feeling mildly panicked, I did one last check of the house and changed my clothes. My sisters' train was already at the station, and their taxi would be pulling up at any moment. Why did I feel like I had to play the good hostess for them? In our family, I was the one who knew how to hammer, chop wood, and shoot a rifle. Eeva was the housewife type, and Helena was the beauty queen and the baby of the family. We each had a clear role.

Antti had met Eeva and Jarmo when we were cross-country ski-
ing at my parents' house earlier in the year. I still hadn't introduced
him to Helena and Petri. Maybe he and Petri would hit it off since
Petri was a mathematician too—he had just finished his teacher training and was looking for a job. Helena was almost done with her master's thesis and student teaching in English. I would have to remember
to ask her about some of the odd expressions in Sanna's thesis.

When I saw the taxi pull into the driveway, my anxiety
swelled. When I last saw Eeva, earlier in the spring, she was just
barely starting to show, and I hadn't seen Helena since Christmas,
when we were all—my sisters, their menfolk, and I—at our parents' house for the holiday. Antti hadn't joined me; he was here
in Espoo reprising his usual role as Santa Claus for Matti and
Mikko, and on Christmas Eve night, we exchanged several melancholy phone calls. Last Christmas wasn't the first when I was
the seventh wheel at my parents' house, but it was the first when
I'd had someone to make those longing calls to.

As I opened the front door, Eeva was just climbing labori-
ously out of the front seat of the taxi. An inch taller and usually a good ten pounds lighter than me, now she looked puffy
everywhere. Her belly was enormous, and her face was swollen.
Despite the two years separating us, she now looked older and
more regal than I ever did.

Rushing to help carry their luggage, Antti and I did our
best to be polite and formal. Eeva and Jarmo especially were
people who could handle any social situation. Eeva had been
teaching Swedish and German in their local high school for two
years now, which might have been the source of the slightly
starchy maturity she radiated. Jarmo was a chemical engineer
but worked in some sort of PR position, so he dealt with people
constantly, and it showed.

First, we gave them a tour of the house, admiring the view out the window of a pair of swans swimming on the bay and laughing at Einstein as he yowled in frustration watching the birds. All the while, I stared furtively at Eeva's soccer-ball belly under her tunic. This wasn't the first pregnant woman I'd ever seen, of course, but somehow the fact that she was my own sister made it infinitely more fascinating. Just think how many genes this baby and I would have in common! Maybe even my upturned nose. At first glance, Eeva and I didn't look anything alike—she resembled our mother, and I took after our father—but if you stopped to really look closer and took time to see them, the common features were there. The line of the eyebrows, the bridge of the nose, the grimace. Helena, on the other hand, was a simplified mixture of both of our parents and looked like a happy medium between us sisters.

"This is a really nice place; do you intend to stay here for a while?" Helena asked, attempting to conceal the tiny note of envy in her voice. She and Petri lived in a tiny two-bedroom apartment purchased using Petri's inheritance as a down payment and were now languishing under a mortgage loan that was too large given their income. I was familiar with Helena's taste in men, so I knew Antti was not particularly handsome by her standards and didn't dress the right way, but the Sarkelas' home clearly raised his stature in her eyes.

"It depends on Antti's parents' plans," I said quickly and then led everyone into the kitchen for dinner. They had already declined a turn in the sauna because they would have the opportunity on the cruise ship.

"How are you going to get along in Stockholm with that big belly of yours? Doesn't carrying it around wear you out?"

"Yes, I get more tired than usual. I'm just going to go sit in a café and let Jarmo run around to all the children's clothing boutiques. Did Antti bake that, or have you started cooking, Maria?" Eeva asked as I removed the quiche from the oven.

"That must be really rich. I'll just have salad," Helena announced.

"Yeah, you should fast now so you can eat more of the cruise food later," her boyfriend added. Of the three of us, Helena was the most slender but still dieted constantly. I thought bitterly about how pleasant lugging all of the ingredients home from the store had been just to have the food not be good enough for them. Even Jarmo just poked at his food. Maybe he didn't like blue cheese.

As the men talked soccer, I was surprised to find Antti joining in the conversation. I didn't even know he read the sports pages. Perhaps he had secretly been preparing for meeting my male relatives.

"Oh, Saku just woke up. Did you like the quiche, sweetie?" A moment passed before I realized Eeva was addressing the baby wriggling around inside her. "Don't kick so hard! Look, Maria, he's turning over."

Something was clearly moving inside Eeva's belly, the bulge deforming and seeming to swell.

"Go ahead and touch," Eeva said, laughing as she took my hand and placed it on her stomach. "There's Saku's bottom. And that's his knee. He's trying to use it to poke his way out. It's so funny, thinking that someone else is really living inside me."

"Isn't it scary?"

"How so? It's the most natural thing in the world." Eeva's smile conveyed clearly a knowledge of something I didn't have any hope of understanding. And she was right. How did I know what being pregnant was like? When you were healthy, you couldn't remember what a bad cold felt like, and in the summer, imagining the biting cold of winter was impossible.

"You're calling the baby Saku? So you're hoping for a boy?" I asked, looking at Jarmo.

"Just so long as the baby's healthy; that's all we care about," Jarmo replied, giving the expected answer. I didn't bother arguing, but I thought of my parents, because I knew they longed for a grandson.

"I could take Jarmo and Petri for a beer over at Hemingway's so you and your sisters can chat in peace," Antti suggested. I glowered at him angrily. That didn't fit my script for the evening in the slightest. Besides, I needed a beer too.

"Just one round—I want to get to bed on time," Eeva said, grimacing as she shoved salad into her mouth. "Of course this salad dressing would have vinegar. Say hello to heartburn."

"Sorry, I didn't know," I said. I was trying to be polite, although in my mind I was thinking that Greek salad dressing usually contained vinegar, and if someone couldn't eat it, they should take care of themselves. Was I supposed to be an expert on pregnancy diets all of a sudden?

The boys went off on their evening stroll to the pub. I made more tea and sat my sisters down on the sofa set in the living room. Einstein wove through us, first cautiously sniffing at Eeva, followed by Helena, who shrieked, "It bit me!" and shooed the startled cat away.

"He did not. He never bites anyone; he was probably just massaging his gums. You must smell really interesting to him. You didn't step in dog crap on the way over here, did you?"

I was steamed. My sisters couldn't have chosen a worse time to visit. What the hell right did they have to just announce that, hey, here we come? At that moment, I wished I had my own apartment where I could hide. Where no one could expect anything of me. I wanted to rip the phone out of the wall, pull the covers over my head, and hide far away from the big bad world...

"You and Antti seem pretty serious," Eeva said.

"And what did you mean when you said Antti wasn't very good-looking?" Helena asked Eeva. "He looks pretty good to me."

"Oh, he's just not my type—too tall and skinny. But Maria's always liked those sorts of chiseled, angular guys," Eeva continued.

"At least having different tastes means we don't have to compete," I said, making an old dig. Back in high school, my sisters had each had a crush on the same boy, and the combat was bloody. But as luck would have it, a third girl scooped him up, and my sisters made a joint resolution to abhor their previous heartthrob forever after.

Once again, I felt like an outsider. Eeva and Helena had so much in common, living in the same town, knowing the same people, visiting our parents on a regular basis. But why did they dislike me so much? And why did they have to come here and torment me?

"So what is your job like?" Eeva asked. "Is it like in *L.A. Law*? Is the pay good?"

"Well, I don't spend the day walking around in a snazzy suit defending celebrities, if that's what you mean. I mostly sit in my office pushing paper. The pay is OK—I get by." Though I was tempted, I didn't bother adding that it was better than a newly minted teacher's salary.

"So you're starting to settle down now too. You have a steady job and a steady boyfriend. And soon, it will be about time to start thinking about having kids. You're turning thirty next spring, and you should have some babies before you get too many wrinkles." Eeva laughed.

I made a face at her. People often mistook me for the youngest of us sisters. Probably because of how I dressed. My little sisters both looked like our middle-aged aunts by the time they turned twenty, while I was still wearing tennis shoes and letting my hair run wild.

"I don't get you two!" I burst out. "Why have you been in such a damn hurry to settle down? OK, fine, maybe that's your thing, but it doesn't mean it has to be mine."

"Oh, you've always known exactly how other people should live their lives," Helena countered. "Always commenting on what we do and bossing us around, and then getting mad if we don't do exactly what you recommended. The know-it-all big sister. Being a lawyer is probably perfect for you since you get to argue with people for a living."

I stared at Helena in amazement. In my mind, I was the one in our family who always had to conform to everyone else's expectations. "Maria, don't tease your sisters. They're smaller than you!" "Give the doll to Eeva, Maria; you're too old for that now." "Take those rugs out now since you're so big and strong." "No guitar practice now—Eeva and Helena are still doing their homework. They just aren't as fast as you."

Something I'd overheard my mother saying to one of her friends one day always stuck in my mind. I was never sure whether she meant for me to hear it: "Eeva and Helena need me. Maria never has; she's always been so strong and independent." I guess that was it—mothers loved the children who needed them most.

Still, I wondered what my sisters were supposed to need my mother for so much. They were the ones who were so good and obedient, while I tripped through my teenage years full of angst. But my parents took my leather jacket and rakish tomboy image seriously, without any attempt to look under the surface. They just assumed they knew me without knowing me at all. All they saw in me was what they wanted to see. But was I acting the same way, stubbornly believing that Eki was a libertine who meddled with young women and then murdered them?

"What do you two really think of me?" I asked defiantly. Perhaps finally letting out all the bitterness I harbored against my parents and sisters for ignoring me and shutting me out of their lives was best.

"Don't get upset, Maria. Helena and I have just been talking about this stuff a lot lately, about when we were kids. I guess these things just come to the surface when you're pregnant. You start worrying about whether you're going to make the same mistakes your parents made," Eeva said calmly.

"We both had a Maria complex growing up. You were so good in school, and you could stand up for yourself. You never came in crying from the playground because the boys were teasing you—"

"Oh, I would have, but I wasn't allowed," I said, cutting in. "I envied you—especially you, Helena, because you were always the tiny one who needed taking care of. They just pushed me out the door and told me to fend for myself."

"You always interrupt me! Let me talk for once! Do you think learning to be independent has been easy for me after always being the baby? You think I'm brainless, and Eeva thinks I'm a helpless glamour girl who doesn't even know how to boil water. And then everyone was surprised when I didn't fail my exams after all and actually got into college. Shocking! I have a brain!"

On the verge of tears, Helena's mascaraed eyelashes fluttered violently, as did mine.

"I was relieved when you went to the police academy and not to medical school or something," Eeva said. "You weren't as special as everybody thought after all. I remember how disappointed Mom and Dad sounded when people asked where you were studying and they had to say you were there. Don't say anything, Maria. I don't think parents should get to set expectations like that for their children either, but it was still a relief for Helena and me. My test scores weren't all that great, but I got into the university on the first try anyway, so they had someone to be proud of—and then Helena got in the next year."

"But then you had to go to law school, and that's almost as fancy as medical school," Helena said, picking up the thread. "A degree in Germanic languages or English isn't anything compared to that."

Had it really been like that? I had no idea. "I never wanted to give anyone a complex," I said. "Don't I have a right to live my own life? All I want is to be left alone!"

"Do you even want to see us, ever?" Helena asked, growing shrill. "Does having sisters mean anything at all to you?"

I looked past them out onto the bay where a duck, out abnormally late, swam toward the reed beds along the shore now painted the color of plums by the setting sun. The image began to cloud, the reeds becoming a blurry violet mass.

"Why would you ask something like that? You can't just erase your family. It's always there, even if you try to forget. I don't have anything against you. I've just always thought that... that you never had any conflict with Mom and Dad. That *I* was always the cause of the conflict. Because I dressed wrong. Because I had the wrong friends. Because I wasn't a boy—"

The door opened, and the three men came clomping in. In a moment, the mood changed to one of restrained bonhomie. I started bustling around, getting beds ready, trying to figure out at the same time whether I was irritated or relieved about the interruption of our conversation. What had just come out would take me plenty of sleepless nights to digest.

"I'll be in and out of the bathroom all night. Hopefully it won't bother you," Eeva said from the bedroom door.

"Don't worry. We can't hear much from our room. Good thick walls. How is Saku?"

"He's doing his bedtime gymnastics."

Suddenly I felt like hugging Eeva. My sister looked so beautiful with her huge belly and swollen nose.

"Can I touch again?" I put my hand on Eeva's stomach, after a moment feeling a strong churning and bulging.

"Hi, baby. It's Aunt Maria," I found myself saying. "Remember to let your mommy sleep a little."

"I don't know what you were all uptight about. Your relatives are fine," Antti said as I flopped down next to him in bed. "Did you gals have a nice time together?"

"Nice isn't exactly the word. I'd say 'enlightening.' Too tired. Let's talk about it tomorrow," I said, turning off the lamp.

The room was still bright though, the diffuse summer evening light penetrating the thin curtains and illuminating Einstein as he hopped up onto the foot of the bed below my feet and began preening his coat. He began at his left-rear paw. I pushed my foot down next to his tail and concentrated on listening to the steady lapping sound of his tongue and Antti's quiet breathing at the base of my left ear. I tried not to think of my sisters, instead concentrating on Armi, Sanna, and Kimmo.

Kimmo would be free soon. How had he felt when his sister died? A mixture of sorrow and relief? Did he miss her? Perhaps relating to a brother would have been easier than sisters; perhaps a brother wouldn't be such a mirror. Or would I have been even more jealous of a younger brother? Probably. Did siblings ever hate each other enough to kill each other?

I thought of Mallu—could I become that obsessed with Helena or Eeva...?

Before falling asleep, I tried desperately to imagine how having a baby rolling around in my own belly would feel.

14

By morning, no traces of the previous night's emotional storms remained. We were all hurried and reserved but not shouting at each other. It reminded me of those mornings before school when we all lined up for the only bathroom in the house.

"Come see Saku when he comes!" Eeva had called from the taxi window. We promised to come in the middle of July, when I would have a week of summer vacation.

Since my sisters hadn't caught their taxi until just after nine, I was so late to work I didn't even try to make up time. As I leisurely biked past the shopping center, I noticed that the door of Makke's store was open, so I decided to drop in. No one was around, just the radio blasting Mauno Kuusisto's Finnish rendition of "Just Say I Love Her."

All of a sudden, Sanna was in my head again. She had been there the one and only time I worked up the courage to sneak into a bar as a teenager; in that case, a seedy dive in our hometown where the management didn't care how old we were. The rest of the group was already old enough to drink legally, and I just slipped in with them. Sanna had played this same song over and over on the jukebox, which surprised me. I had imagined her more as a heavy-metal or maybe a Dylan type. In my mind's eye, I could see Sanna's mocking smile, the glass of beer in her hand, the hair hanging down in front of her beautiful eyes.

Why had Sanna liked this song?

"What can I do you for?" Makke came out of some back room with an armload of soccer shoes. "We've got good cleats on sale right now."

"I haven't joined the powder-puff league yet, although maybe I should."

Makke froze, possibly recognizing the song.

"Wasn't this one of Sanna's favorites?" I asked. When Makke nodded, I continued. "This is the last time, and then I promise I'll never talk to you about Sanna again unless you want to: What drugs was Sanna using? Weed? Something stronger? Prescription stuff? Where did she get it?"

Makke brushed his bangs back off his brow. His cheeks were tight, his fingers nervously exploring the spikes on the bottom of the soccer shoes.

"She didn't use drugs anymore when we started dating. She drank plenty and took some sedatives—Valium, I think. I don't know where she got them. But all you have to do is go into a doctor's office and tell them you are achy, or a little depressed, or can't quite sleep—they don't care."

"Can you get that sort of thing at the gym? I know stuff moves through there."

"Gosh, no one has ever offered me any," Makke said testily.

"And Sanna didn't get the Valium from Armi?"

Makke looked at me as if I were a half-wit.

"From Armi? No way was Armi pushing pills. She wasn't the type."

"I'm not sure of anything anymore," I said, hoping it didn't sound too dramatic, and then left.

What if Armi's and Sanna's deaths really were two separate crimes and Mallu's car accident had absolutely nothing to do with either of them?

Maybe I was imagining things again.

When I arrived at work, Eki was sitting in the conference room eating a chocolate jellyroll. I kicked myself in the mental ass.

That was the man I suspected of killing two people?

"The police called. The Hänninen case is going before the judge again today. New witnesses have come forward, and, in the light of their testimony, it looks unlikely that Hänninen was at Mäenpää's house at the time of the murder," Eki rattled off like a man who had never thought anything else.

"So Teemu Laaksonen has been in touch with Detective Sergeant Ström already. Good. What time is the hearing?"

"Three. How about I go, since I'm a friend of the family and the head of the firm? I'll need you to bring me up to speed a little, though."

Dumbstruck, I stared at Eki. Are you kidding me? I was the one who did all the work, and now this old man was going to swoop in and take the glory for himself! After kicking myself yet again to keep from exploding, I then told Eki the bare facts, and the bare facts only. No one else was going to get anything more out of me until I was completely certain of what it all meant.

Still, losing this opportunity was a distressing setback. I had already played through the scene, how I would free Kimmo and then we would walk out of the courthouse arm in arm. How stupid I had been! Eki hadn't even believed Kimmo was innocent. Maybe I should check the dates of that Kenya trip after all...

Fortunately, one of my clients called, forcing me to move my mind onto other matters. The case was about the division of an estate involving an illegal concealment of property. I wondered whether my sisters and I would be at such loggerheads divvying up our parents' effects.

Which gave me an idea.

"Hi, it's Maria Kallio."

Mallu's response to my greeting was less than enthusiastic.

"Listen, I have to ask you a weird question. Did you ever get any sedatives from Armi without a prescription; maybe she gave you a sample pack or something like that?"

"Sedatives? Maybe once or twice when I couldn't sleep. I had a prescription though, and it was just for small amounts. Why would you ask me something like that?"

"I just thought—"

"And why did you talk to Teemu about me? What on earth have you been telling him? I never wanted to see him again, and here he showed up today at my door thinking he was some knight in shining armor. I told him to go to hell!"

"Did Teemu tell you that Kimmo is being released today because of his testimony?"

"I don't have time for this bullshit! I have to be at Dr. Hellström's office in half an hour for a checkup. I'm really looking forward to him telling me—yet again—that I can never, ever have children," she said sarcastically.

"Mallu, we have to talk! How about if I come see you later, like around five?"

"Why? What could we possibly have left to discuss? Oh, yes, because now that Kimmo is getting out, you need someone else to blame for my sister's murder. Come on over. Having someone accuse me of murder is about all my life is missing right now."

Mallu slammed the phone in my ear.

For the next two hours, I worked like a madwoman, and decided to burn off some excess anger and energy by spending my lunch hour at the gym. Grimacing at the reflection of my legs in the mirror whipping a seventy-five pound stack of weights up and down on the leg abductor, I cursed in rage. Let Eki take all the glory for freeing Kimmo! Let Ström solve the murder case on his own! I would have to come up with some excuse to see Ström so I could gloat over his embarrassment after arresting the wrong person. Although, I had to be careful. I could see where he might turn his sights on me next because I was the first one who had arrived at the scene of the crime. Had the police ever found Armi's dishwashing gloves or confirmed that the murderer was indeed wearing rubber gloves?

I closed my eyes, and images flashed through. Seeing Armi splayed on the grass, her face that blotchy purple. Seeing Sanna emptying her bottle of vodka and slipping into the water. Seeing the car that hit Mallu speeding along the glistening black street driven by a blonde girl with a red shawl.

Start at the beginning, Maria, I said to myself. Start from Armi. Your first assumption was that Armi died because she knew something someone didn't want her to tell you. What did Armi know? What did she want to ask for advice about?

The magic of the weight room worked again. An hour after my self-inflicted flogging, my body felt wobbly, but my mind was clear. Back in the office now, I was slurping nonfat cherry yogurt straight from the paper carton and preparing for a court session the next day when a knock came at my door.

"Maria! Why are you here? Kimmo's hearing is about to start." Marita's voice sounded confused, and I saw Risto peeking curiously around her.

"Eki went. He doesn't need me there," I said bitterly.

Risto smiled. "I hear they're going to let Kimmo go. All thanks to you, Maria."

For some reason, Risto's thanks irked me. And forget about me, what were they doing in our law office instead of rushing over to the courthouse to roll out the red carpet for Kimmo and Eki?

"If Kimmo is innocent, then who did this? Who strangled Armi?" Marita finally asked.

"Don't you know? Ask Risto," I said angrily.

Suddenly Marita looked scared and confused. Under her ear, the yellow hint of a bruise was still visible, but thankfully, I didn't see any new ones. Or were they hidden under her clothing?

"What am I supposed to know about it?"

I had never heard so much menace in Risto's voice as at that moment. I stood up, waved them into the room and closed the door. Martti had a client in his office who didn't need to overhear this conversation.

"Armi was murdered because she had information. She knew that someone killed Sanna. And she may have known even more. Maybe Armi and Sanna's killer had a habit of beating his wife—like you do, Risto. Was it your father who pushed Sanna off the breakwater that night? Was it an accident? They argued over something, and Sanna was drunk? And then, maybe he just watched her sink, and thought, 'Good riddance.'"

Marita's face flushed, and Risto's face filled with anguish and confusion.

"Stop bringing Sanna into this! If you think you can wildly accuse people of horrible things without losing your job here, you're out of your mind!"

"You aren't going to hit me though, are you, Risto? Or strangle me, like you strangled Armi?"

I heard a horrified intake of breath from Marita, who took a step toward me as if seeking protection from Risto. Risto stared at his wife for a second and then realized that she must believe me.

"Marita! Don't believe a word she says! What have you been telling Maria?" Risto's voice was so threatening that I would have been afraid too, if I were Marita.

"Marita hasn't said anything to me. I drew my own conclusions from her bruises. Why do you hit her? Does it make you feel better about yourself?"

"Hit? Everyone has fights sometimes. And our marriage is none of your business, Maria. Not as an attorney or as my brother-in-law's girlfriend. You aren't even a part of this family."

I looked at Risto's hands—the hands of a man who worked at a desk. Sparse black hairs grew on their backs, and his wedding band was nearly a quarter of an inch thick. Were those the hands that strangled Armi?

"Risto, if there is any truth to what Maria is saying, you have to tell me now," Marita whispered, as if forcing the words out of her mouth only with supreme difficulty. Risto stared at her as Marita withdrew from him and stepped closer to me.

"I don't know anything about anything, and I'm not going to stand here listening to either of you. I'm going to go get my brother out of jail!" Risto bellowed before slamming the door open and storming out. Marita collapsed into a chair and didn't start talking until she heard the screeching of car tires pulling out of the driveway.

"It isn't what you think, Maria. Risto doesn't hit me very often. He's just been under so much stress lately. Things are going poorly at his company and he's been on a hair-trigger.

He doesn't mean it, he didn't mean to hurt me, and I bruise so easily."

"Jesus Christ, Marita! You can't really believe that! You have to get help. You can't let him get away with hitting you. Does he abuse the boys too?"

"No! I wouldn't let him." The way Marita shook her head reminded me of the same movements Antti made when he was distressed. "You don't know what it's like, Maria. Risto is so wonderful most of the time. And then sometimes I get worked up and start nagging him about something, and then he hits me."

"Don't you dare blame yourself! Have you talked to anyone about this?"

"Well, I tried to get us into family therapy when Sanna died, because Risto was so depressed. He wouldn't go, though, because he was afraid of having it come out somehow and hurt his reputation. Antti doesn't know about this, does he?" Marita looked more afraid of that than the prospect that her husband was a murderer.

"Yes, he knows. And he wants to talk to you about it."

"Do Mom and Dad know?" Marita sniffed.

"No. Did Armi?"

"Yes." Marita shook her head, looking like Antti again. "Armi was the one who encouraged me to go to therapy. She said that Risto could...get better...that hitting in a family was like an infectious disease that Risto caught from Henrik. She said that therapy could heal it before it spread to the boys, and that Sanna and Kimmo had their own symptoms. What did Armi mean by that?"

"Sanna always looked for men like her father, men who would hit her. And Kimmo...Well, we all know about Kimmo now. That was probably what Armi meant. Is Henrik's abuse the reason he and Annamari live apart? Is that why Annamari is so skittish?"

Marita nodded. Tears filled her eyes, and dark rivulets of mascara began snaking their way down her pale cheeks. I dug a tissue box out of my desk drawer for her before continuing.

"I think that Sanna died because she wanted to get better. She wanted to get away from all the anger and humiliation she had been living with. She had finally fallen in love with a man who didn't want to rule over her or smack her around. But that didn't fit with someone else's plans."

"Do you mean Risto?"

"I'm not sure yet, to be honest. In the meantime, Marita, we have to put a stop to this abuse."

I thought of Antti and all the pressure he was under because of his dissertation, wondering whether I dared put this load on his shoulders as well. But she was his sister. "Talk to Antti. He'll help you. Go to our house right now. Usually he takes a break from work around this time."

"Maybe I will." Marita wiped her eyes and stood up, her upright posture determined. "Antti is nice," she said, sounding like a child. "You be nice to him too."

"Tell him I'll be home by seven at the latest," I said as she left.

Still hungry after my workout and needing to get out the door, I sucked the last of the yogurt out of the carton and grabbed the last hunk of chocolate jellyroll from the conference room. Cramming it into my mouth, I hoped I would be able to get some coffee from Mallu.

At exactly five o'clock, I was at the door of Mallu's apartment pressing the bell. The yard outside was completely deserted, making the afternoon feel as though time had stopped. The doorbell trilled, echoing hollowly in the apartment. I remembered the bare walls, the unmatched furniture.

No answer. I pressed the bell again, recalling with a sick feeling how I had rung Armi's doorbell and no one had answered then either. A wave of fear washed over me as I walked over the lawn. Nothing. I peered in through the kitchen window. No one. I walked around to the backyard to look through the large living-room windows. All I saw was the partial sofa set and the lonely television set. No movement. I rushed to the bedroom window. It was higher than the kitchen window, and I had to half climb onto the sill to see in.

Lying supine on the bed, her eyes closed and body limp, I saw Mallu surrounded by the classic signs of suicide: pill bottle lying on the floor, half-empty bottle of wine, scrap of paper.

I ran back to the living room window, grabbed a large stone that was being used as an edge for a flowerbed, and yanked. It pulled out easily and I hurled it straight through the lower pane. Most of the window was gone now, and I pushed the remaining large shards in with the tip of my shoe and crawled inside. Grabbing the phone, which fortunately was cordless, I dialed the emergency number, 112. Before the operator picked up and I ordered an ambulance, I had time to glance at the label on the medicine bottle and feel Mallu's pulse. Her heart was still beating, but slowly, and her breathing was halting. Trying in vain to wake her, I noticed the piece of paper still lying on the floor. Picking it up using the tail of my shirt, I read Mallu's tiny, sharply slanted handwriting: *I can't take it anymore. Armi's death was my fault. Mallu.* I considered whether I could rip the second sentence off while leaving the first and the signature but realized it was impossible. So I shoved the note in my pocket. When the paramedics arrived, I immediately gave them Mallu's parents' phone number and handed them the pill bottle. Neighbors were beginning to congregate now, curious about the flashing emergency vehicle in the street. Someone promised to call the janitor about the broken window.

When the men began lifting Mallu carefully onto the stretcher, I rushed out the door. Mallu's suicide note was still in my pocket. I should take it to Ström. But no—I still couldn't believe that Mallu was the murderer I was looking for.

I jumped on my bike and rode off without any specific destination in mind. Something red and sticky fell onto my pale-brown sandal. I glanced at my hands. A gash on my left wrist was dripping blood. I must have hurt myself climbing through Mallu's window, though the cut didn't hurt much. I would need to find a towel, I thought to myself.

Surely Mallu knew that one little bottle of mild sedatives and some white wine wasn't going to kill anyone. What was she doing? And what did her note mean?

I had to have time to think. Instinctively I rode toward the sea, first through a bicycle and pedestrian tunnel under the West Highway, then along residential streets past a clam-shaped community center, and finally along park paths overgrown with grass to the breakwater.

Antti once had told me that as a child he had a habit of sitting at the end of the jetty and imagining he was on the bow of a pirate ship, bound for new adventures. But Sanna's adventures had ended here. How cold and dark that night must have been without any snow or ice illuminating the dreary March landscape. She must have gone numb almost immediately in the frigid water, especially drunk.

Walking halfway out on the breakwater, I found a small, sheltered recess where I could curl up to think. The ruddy granite was cool under my fingers, and the green moss protruding from the cracks between the roughly quarried boulders was as soft as Einstein's fur. Out to sea, two or three sailboats were visible along with a lone windsurfer.

Was Mallu's suicide note a confession or a hint about Teemu? I dug the paper out of my pocket, but no matter how many times I read the words, it never told me anything more. *I can't take it anymore. Armi's death was my fault. Mallu.* Had someone tried to stage Mallu's suicide in hopes of covering his tracks? But who?

I pressed my cheek against the bronze-colored stone with its blooms of lichen, and I thought. Facts streamed through my mind like the patterns of a kaleidoscope. The person with Sanna on the breakwater was tall and wore a black coat. Sanna's lover. Valium. Herr Enemy from Sanna's graduate thesis. A blond driver wearing Armi's scarf. A strangler Armi must have known, or she wouldn't have offered him a glass of juice. The group of men standing around talking about me at Risto's birthday party. The warning voice on my telephone.

Men's faces danced in my mind as Sylvia Plath's poem hammered on the inside of my skull. As I brushed my windblown hair out of my eyes, I began to see the kaleidoscope slowly come into a focus, now a crisp, clear, beautiful picture.

Herr God, Herr Lucifer, Beware, Beware. Now I knew what had happened. I stood up and headed off to meet Armi's murderer.

15

I arrived at the murderer's door out of breath. Pressing the door-bell insistently, I forced a smile when he appeared.

"I'm glad you're home. May I come in?"

The house was quiet in a way that suggested no one else was present.

That was fine with me. I didn't want any spectators for this portion of the show. The man led me into the kitchen. Sitting down on a hard chair next to the door, I switched on the tape recorder in my bag.

Keeping my composure was difficult. When I first realized what was going on, I was thrilled to have finally figured things out. Then came the rage. This man denied life to Armi and Sanna. What right did he have to turn upside down the lives of so many? I had vowed to catch him, but I knew that wouldn't save the rest of us. Murder always left its mark on everyone involved.

"Would you like some coffee?"

I shook my head. The man poured himself a large mug and then removed a bottle of cognac and two snifters from the cupboard.

"And cognac? Certainly your client's release is cause for celebration."

The man poured himself more than half a glass of cognac and threw back his first slug without savoring. His hair glinted in the sunlight shining through the window.

"Thank you. Yes, I could take a drop."

I watched as he poured a generous amount of the liquid, the same color as my hair, into the expensive-looking stemware. I tasted cautiously: I had to stay ready for anything. The gash on my arm had stopped dripping now, and I gingerly ran a little cognac over the wound, making it sting a little.

"I think I'll wait to celebrate until the truth comes out," I said, staring the man in the eyes. Long black eyelashes fluttering, he averted his gaze.

"Do you think I can help with that somehow?" The man attempted to look amused, but I saw his body tense.

"This day hasn't been all good news. A few minutes ago, I put Mallu Laaksonen in an ambulance. Attempted suicide. But don't worry," I said when the man jumped out of his chair as if he would run headlong to Mallu's side in the hospital. "She'll pull through."

"But why would she attempt suicide?" The man drained the rest of his glass and then poured himself more.

I related the contents of Mallu's suicide note.

He looked aghast. "Did she really kill Armi? But why?" I noticed his shoulders begin to relax.

"No. Mallu thought someone else killed Armi because of her. She wanted to protect her husband." I sipped from my own glass, trying to think how best to weave this net of words. "Mallu thought Armi was driving the car that ran her off the road and caused her to have her miscarriage."

"And someone killed Armi because of that?" His tone was dubious.

"No. Armi wasn't the reckless driver—the driver was the one who killed Armi. Of course Armi knew who could have had her red scarf at the time of the accident."

The man looked at me dubiously. "Surely no one would kill over a traffic accident."

"That wasn't the only reason for Armi's death. She also knew something else about this man. She knew that he was Sanna Hänninen's lover and killed Sanna because she wanted to end their relationship. I'm not sure what finally made Armi speak out, but it may have been the Laaksonens' separation. Maybe Armi thought that Sanna was at least partially to blame for her fate, but the Laaksonens were innocent."

The man stared at me, his eyes darkening. Again, I saw the muscles in his neck tense, but when he spoke, he struck a cheerful tone.

"A very imaginative story. I can barely wait for you to tell me who the bad guy is."

"Don't you know, Herr Doktor? I feel like an idiot for not guessing right off that you were Sanna's lover."

I stared at his salt-and-pepper hair, the gray at his temples, the wrinkled yellow backs of his hands. Herr Doktor, Herr Lucifer, Herr Death. I flinched at a sudden movement of his hands, but he was only reaching for the package of cigarettes in his shirt pocket. Lighting the cigarette took a few moments because his hands were trembling. Yet his voice remained controlled.

"Kimmo Hänninen's defense must have left you completely exhausted. Wouldn't it be best to leave the investigation to the police? Perhaps they'll be able to come up with something more convincing." Dr. Hellström spoke evenly, as though he were advising a patient on a new prescription.

"Take a few Valium and all these pesky figments of your imagination will go away—is that it?" I said. "Of course the pills Sanna Hänninen was using came from you. How could you be so stupid to get mixed up with your own patient? You fucked her and supported her drug habit. I knew Sanna, and, yes, I can remember how attractive she could be, but even so…"

Instead of answering, he just stared past me into the distance. From outside came a commotion from a group of boys on their bicycles. I heard mostly Swedish, interspersed with Finnish swear words.

"Did Sanna threaten to expose your relationship? That would have been dangerous—no one could know you were taking advantage of your own patient. Did she want to have sex with you, or did you force her in exchange for the drugs? I imagine it all started with that second abortion when Hakala was on his way to prison. Sanna couldn't get along without her sedatives, and she had no difficulty convincing you to give them to her."

"I did obtain access to medication for Sanna. But there's nothing illegal about that; I was her doctor—that's just part of my job."

"Yes, but sleeping with mentally unbalanced patients isn't."

"Sanna knew what she was doing!" Hellström's self-control was starting to crack. "She was using *me*. She said I was like the father she never had! But she just wanted the pills, not me. And then she ran into that Ruosteenoja punk and decided she was going to start a new life without me. As if she could stop just like that!"

"At least she wanted to try, but you didn't give her the chance." I felt my anger rising again. Hellström stared at me curiously, his eyes narrowed, as though waiting for my next sentence.

"What about the car accident then? What explanation have you dreamed up for that?" His tone was one of forced amusement, but anger boiled beneath the surface.

"Teemu Laaksonen claimed to have seen a driver with blond hair wearing Armi's red scarf. When the light hits your hair just right, the gray stands out enough that it almost looks white. When you were tending to Mallu on the morning after the accident, you complained of a cold. I imagine you accidentally left your own scarf at home and found Armi's in your office. And when Armi started thinking about it, she remembered leaving it at work that same day."

"So you think I put on a scarf and drove into a couple of people and didn't bother to stop? I am a doctor. I would have stopped if someone was hurt, no matter what."

"Of course you would have, unless you were drunk. Word has it Sanna wasn't the only one with a substance-abuse problem. You were probably self-medicating with booze and pills and weren't in any shape to drive. You probably didn't know what happened to Mallu or even notice that it was Mallu at all. Failure to stop and render aid is a serious crime for anyone, but especially for a doctor."

Remembering Mallu's prematurely aged face and the stink of stagnation in her apartment, I finally understood Armi. She had to do something for her sister, and she needed to ask me how to proceed.

Hellström fumbled for another cigarette.

"You can't prove any of this." Now he sounded afraid.

"I have two witnesses. One saw you kissing Sanna Hänninen in your office, and the other saw you with Sanna on the breakwater. I think he'll be able to pick you out of a lineup. And then it's going to look pretty strange that you never told anyone about seeing Sanna on the night of her death."

"Recognizing someone you saw from a hundred meters away more than a year later? I doubt it. That old man couldn't have seen anything in all that fog."

"How did you know my witness was a man?" I squeezed the strap of my backpack, which contained the voice recorder. Hellström had gone for the bait on the very first try, and I had it on tape.

"Man or woman—it's all the same. You of all people should know that won't hold up as a confession in court."

"We have other evidence too, like a draft of Sanna's graduate thesis. One of the main characters in a poem she analyzed was called Herr Doktor, Herr Enemy. Next to that Sanna wrote: 'Like me and E.' E as in Erik. Read the right way, Sanna's whole analysis is proof of your relationship with her. That was why the poem was out on her desk. It wasn't a suicide note—it symbolized the beginning of a new life to her."

"Bullshit," Hellström said dismissively, as if addressing a hypochondriac complaining of uterine cancer. "So what was Armi supposed to have known about all this? Why didn't she tell anyone about Sanna's murder earlier?"

"Armi was in charge of keeping stock of your drug supply and prescription records and did the math. She knew there were way too many pills flying around your office, and she knew about your relationship with Sanna. She even tried to tell Annamari about it, but Annamari wouldn't believe her. Now was just the right time for Armi to use the information she had been storing up. You know why better than I do."

I stared into Erik Hellström's brown eyes. We weren't in his medical clinic anymore—now it was my turn to render a diagnosis. I had finally put all the symptoms together.

"The whole time I had this feeling that Teemu Laaksonen told Armi something really important on the day of her murder. What? He told her again what the driver of the car looked like. Armi must have been too careless though. After Teemu left her house, Armi called you and told you she was sure now that it had been you. You couldn't let Armi talk, so you rushed over to her house and, after trying in vain to persuade her to remain silent, you strangled her. You happened to have a pair of exam gloves in your pocket—every good doctor carries them wherever he goes. Of course, that pair is either burned or in the landfill by now. You were just lucky no one saw you."

"Do you really intend to present this ridiculous story to the police? Who do you think will even believe you? When the police find Mallu Laaksonen's suicide note, they'll think she did it…"

"Did she tell you today that she thought Teemu was guilty? Did you encourage her suspicions?"

Hellström's expression told me I had guessed right again.

"And did you give her some sedatives to help her on her way? Of course you did, you bastard! But, Herr Doktor, the police aren't going to find any note. I took it."

Hellström glanced around, looking so angry I thought he might be on the verge of attacking me.

"Keep listening! I don't have it on me anymore; it's in safe-keeping," I lied. "And I'm not going to tell you where it is, so keeping me alive is in your best interest. That's what you're thinking now, of course: How do I get rid of this bitch too?"

Hellström dropped his cigarette on the floor, seeming not to notice as he did. His self-control was breaking down the same way it had when he had killed Armi and Sanna. I knew it was a matter of seconds before he would get violent. I wished I had my old service weapon. Even with an empty revolver, I could have at least threatened him.

"Detective Sergeant Ström isn't stupid. Once he hears what I have to say and interviews the right witnesses, you're through. And I don't think Mallu is in any mortal danger—Valium wasn't nearly enough to do the job properly. When I arrived, she had probably only just lost consciousness. A little stomach pumping and she'll be as good as new. And when Mallu tells the police why she attempted suicide—she thought Teemu was guilty— then your game will be up."

Hellström mechanically lit another cigarette. The smoke in the room was becoming thick enough to bother my lungs and cling to my hair.

"The rambling of two hysterical women against a respected physician? Who will believe you? And if you're so smart, why did you come running over here alone and play your whole hand? You're as big an idiot as Armi. She didn't exactly try to blackmail me, she just asked which of us would go talk to the police. I had no idea she knew about Sanna until that morn-ing—I thought she just wanted to confront me, finally, about Mallu's accident. And I knew no one would have been able to prove that. But the relationship with Sanna was different. Armi had one of Sanna's last diaries, which she stole from Kimmo. Sanna was right about one thing. Armi was a military-grade pain in the ass."

Hellström tried to laugh. Cautiously, I rose to my feet, preparing to make a run for it. I bolted, but hadn't made it as far as the kitchen door before he rushed me. Dr. Hellström was a good seven inches taller than I was and probably sixty pounds heavier. When he lunged for me, I jumped to the side, and he crashed to the floor. I think I had taken him completely taken off guard: I was faster and in better shape, and Hellström had no idea how strong I was, given my height. As we backed out of the upstairs hallway into the library, he grabbed my calf and tried to pull me down next to him, but I kicked him in the jaw. The crunch as it broke made me cringe, but he continued clutching at my leg all the more violently. Sweeping the glasses from his eyes, I tried to make for the front door, but he caught my ankle and held on.

As I attempted to kick and wriggle out of Hellström's grasp, a wave of rage washed over me. Rage for myself. Rage for Armi and Sanna and Mallu. I had to make it through this alive for them. I bent over and bit the hand holding me, and Hellström reflexively let go of my leg.

Casting about for an appropriate weapon with which to knock Hellström out, I saw a bronze statue standing on a bookshelf. Realizing what I meant to do, Hellström tried to reach my outstretching hand. I kicked him to the ground, and my next punch landed on his already injured jaw. This last blow did the trick, so I didn't need the statue after all. Hellström fell into a heap on a crimson rug in front of the bookshelf.

Using wire ripped from his stereo speakers, I tied Hellström's hands behind his back and then went to the phone. Hellström's breathing seemed normal, and he would probably regain consciousness soon. The emergency operator promised to dispatch a patrol car and inform Detective Sergeant Ström.

Hellström jumping out a second-story window seemed unlikely, so I began grabbing my things—hopefully the tape recorder was intact! The door to the library had a lock that could be opened only with the key protruding from it. Removing the key, I closed and locked the door from the living-room side and headed downstairs in search of proper restraints and a real weapon.

I had just found a gruesome-looking bread knife in a kitchen drawer when I heard a crash from the entry-way. Somehow, Hellström had managed to worm his way free. Cursing myself, I realized I hadn't checked his pockets. I clutched the knife tightly, but Hellström ignored me as he raced toward his car, blood streaming from his mouth. Hellström slammed the front door of the house in my face, and although he had only a ten-yard head start, I didn't reach him until he was closing the car door. Automatically I jumped out of the way as he accelerated out of the driveway onto the street. At the first intersection, Hellström noticed the approaching police cruiser and sped up. Taking several critical seconds to grasp the situation, the driver came to a full stop. I yanked the passenger door open and jumped inside, screaming at him to follow that car.

Hellström's most likely escape route would be to the west, away from the city, because the beltways and downtown Helsinki would be jammed with traffic at this hour. The patrolman in the passenger seat broadcast Hellström's license plate number and a description of his BMW across the metro area.

Then, suddenly, Detective Sergeant Ström's voice came over the radio.

"Goddamn it, where is that Kallio bitch?" I grabbed the hand microphone and, holding it and my tape recorder close to my ear, played Ström a few crucial snippets. Ström listened, cursing to himself. I wondered why I didn't feel triumphant.

"I would have checked Hellström next too, since we had to release Hänninen," Ström shouted after I finished. "Why the hell didn't you take me with you?" he barked. "Didn't you learn anything at the academy? When do you go to make an arrest without backup? You don't!"

With that, a report that the doctor's BMW had just turned northeast onto Ring III interrupted our pleasantries. Since he was coming in from the north, Ström announced that his car would move to intercept. Before signing out, he added, "Maria, you might be interested to hear the latest word on Mäenpää's sister: she's conscious and we'll be able to question her tonight."

I leaned back and swallowed my tears. At least someone had escaped Hellström's clutches alive. After cutting northwest toward the suburb of Kauklahti, we had just arrived at the Ring III on-ramp when Ström's agitated voice came over the police radio again.

"Subject passed car two, about one kilometer south of Kauklahti. All cars, proceed toward Kauklahti intersection."

The signal crackled and cut out. Ahead we saw a roadblock hastily constructed from a spike strip and two police cruisers. Sirens blaring, we maneuvered past the backed-up traffic. Trying to find Ström among the police officers waiting in their cars, I suddenly heard his voice over a megaphone.

"Everybody ready—here he comes!"

Stop signs and weapons came out, with three megaphones blaring orders to halt as the white BMW careened around a bend in the road, with at least two police cars trailing. Everything happened fast. The BMW failed to stop, despite the crowd of police.

Noticing the spike strip, Hellström turned his car straight into the forest. At no less than ninety miles per hour, the car plowed through several dozen yards of brush before a stone retaining wall checked its progress.

By the time we reached the vehicle, it was too late to do anything. The car was now half its former length. I didn't even want to know how much of Dr. Erik Hellström remained.

16

Sun filtered through birch branches bent under full loads of mature leaves, the patterns of shadow cast on the sand of the old cemetery's central path shifting and rippling in the wind. As we walked between the rows of graves, light and shadow interchanged constantly, making the fur of a squirrel suddenly change from red to black and black to red as the animal jumped from headstone to headstone.

We were looking for Sanna's grave. Having been present at her funeral, Antti said he would recognize it when he saw it. Occasionally, I would see a familiar name as I looked at the faded letters on each stone. I sat down for a moment on a rusted bench and let Antti continue looking.

The past few days had been pure hell. If not the third degree, Ström had put me through at least a second-degree interrogation as soon as they finished scraping Hellström's remains out of the car. After throwing me in the back of his cruiser and speeding back to the station, he made me explain everything to him at least five times. Then he threatened to toss me into the same cell he had let Kimmo out of a few hours earlier.

"Kallio, I can't even count how many things we could charge you with: interfering with a police investigation, withholding evidence, assault on Dr. Hellström, false imprisonment. It's a pity we can't charge you with endangering your own life too. Why didn't you let us do our job? You're always so goddamn impatient. If you would have just waited another couple of days, we would have caught up with the doctor too."

"If I had waited any longer, Mallu Laaksonen would be dead."

"Maybe Laaksonen wouldn't have tried anything if you hadn't been bumbling around. Without you, the goddamn gynecologist would still be alive and we could put him on trial."

"So charge me with murder! I wasn't expecting a pat on the back anyway. At least in a cell I could lie down and get some goddamned rest. I'm exhausted from doing your job."

"You're still playing the tough guy, just like at the academy. Listen, Kallio, you're living in the wrong country. We don't need private detectives in Finland. If you want to go sticking that cute little button nose of yours into other people's messy business, why don't you come back to the force?"

"I've already told you twice that it just isn't my thing. Especially since I'd have to work with shitheads like you."

I heard a snort from the direction of the clerk and then watched as Ström drew in a breath and mentally counted to ten.

"It doesn't matter what I say, does it?" Ström yelled, his face glistening with sweat. "Just don't expect me to cry over you when we have to pick you up in pieces on the side of some road because you've been digging around in things that don't concern you."

Something clicked in my head as I remembered the raspy voice warning me on the phone. The same phrase: digging around in things that don't concern you.

"Ström, you talk big. What, you think I don't still have my recording of a certain threatening phone call?" When Ström's face suddenly went blank, I knew I had hit the bull's-eye.

"Today must have been hard on you, little girl, since your memory is acting up now. Puupponen, take her home," Ström snapped at Dennis the Menace.

Puupponen said he would be by again the next day with the interview record for me to sign. I assumed Ström would try to lie low, and that was fine by me. I considered whether he might have tampered with my bike too. Somehow, verbal intimidation seemed more his style. Perhaps Hellström was to blame. I would probably never know.

I came home to a scolding from Antti. Lecturing me about taking unnecessary risks, he marveled aloud why I hadn't taken him along as protection.

"I get along just fine without a man as my bodyguard!"

"So is life with you always going to be a roller coaster like this?"

"Find out if you dare!"

Slamming the door, I stormed out into the bathroom, tore off my dirty clothes, and let the shower wash my tears away. When Antti came to make peace, we made love for a long time while the shower continued to run. That was the end of our fighting.

Armi was buried yesterday. Following Kimmo's release, the investigation into Armi's murder wrapped up quickly, since several of her neighbors remembered seeing Dr. Hellström's BMW in the parking lot of a nearby school the morning of the murder. After searching the house again, the police finally found Sanna's diary in a plastic bag hidden in the basement behind some jars. It confirmed Sanna's relationship with Dr. Hellström.

Eki contacted Hellström's wife in Nice. She had also known about her husband's relationship with Sanna and had told Eki about it during discussions about her divorce options. Eki had wrung out of Sanna that Hellström was writing her prescriptions for sedatives whenever she asked. The notes from that conversation were what Eki tore from Sanna's file. He claimed he was positive that it had nothing to do with Sanna's suicide or Armi's murder. I suspected that he had actually guessed the truth and wanted to protect Hellström for some reason. I also suspected that I wasn't going to want to work for Henttonen & Associates any longer. Even so, I thought I should take my short paid summer vacation before resigning.

Doris Hellström had happened to be in Finland the previous March. She remembered her husband coming home drunk and sick with a cold the night before he had to go care for Mallu Laaksonen at the hospital early the morning of her accident. She also remembered an odd, cyclamen-red scarf around her husband's neck.

"Gathering information and making sure of everything before acting was so typical of Armi," Kimmo said at her funeral. "I'm sure she smelled something rotten in Sanna's death from the very beginning. In retrospect, I can see how she was constantly hinting at that. That was probably why she stole the diary. Armi was there when we burned all of Sanna's papers. If only I would have listened."

Kimmo hadn't really been able to begin mourning Armi until he was released from jail. Time might be able to wash away his sorrow, but it wasn't going to happen any time soon.

After hearing that Hellström had killed both Sanna and Armi, I didn't know which was worse for Kimmo—finding out about the murders or the fact that Hellström was already dead. Kimmo would have gladly tracked him down and killed him himself. Although Kimmo was clearly in agony, his rage also startled me: here I had thought him incapable of murder. But I guess anyone could kill. I remembered groping for Hellström's bronze statue to knock him out. As if that would have been the only possible outcome.

Even so, I wanted to assuage Kimmo's guilt if I could.

"Armi was a little like me, I think. Maybe she would have listened to your advice about what to do in the situation, but then done exactly as she pleased anyway."

"No, she was more like me," Mallu said, coming up behind us.

"She got fixated on things. Armi was convinced that she could make Hellström pay for his actions. Armi was like that even as a child. She might have been a bit of a sissy, but she always wanted to help people who got teased get even. I guess now she wanted to get revenge on Hellström for Sanna and me."

"And Maria Marple finished the job," Antti interjected. "Was your ingenious deduction based at all on the fact that male chauvinists are generally evil?"

I was already making a face at him before I realized that was inappropriate behavior at a funeral.

"No, it was based on the fact that there wasn't anybody else left it could be."

Only once I left Mallu's apartment after turning her over to the paramedics did I realize that the role I had constructed for Eki actually fit Dr. Hellström even better. Sanna and a doctor—of course! Teemu Laaksonen had confirmed my theory about the scarf. On the day before the accident, he had run into Armi while she was wearing the scarf, which was probably why his subconscious made him see Armi's face in the car. Mallu and Teemu had each suspected the other, and Hellström egged Mallu on.

"After Armi's death, I went completely out of my mind," Mallu explained. Now, after her brush with death, her eyes were still red and she seemed even thinner than ever, but the deep anguish was gone from her gaze. Maybe she was ready to get back to living.

"In the end, all I could think of was making all of this go away…"

You knew I was coming to visit at five o'clock though, I thought, but I didn't say it. Mallu and Teemu had decided to reunite their half sets of furniture. I didn't know whether to think they were crazy or brave. At least they seemed to need each other, clinging to one another like frightened children hugging their teddy bears.

Armi's parents' house was crowded with funeralgoers. Outside, the sounds of life had returned: Makke had taken the twins out in the yard to play soccer. The truth of Sanna's death had given him another rough ride. In the gym together one night, I almost had to drop a hundred-pound plate on his toes before he would believe that Sanna's death didn't have anything to do with him being passed out drunk—Hellström would probably have tried to kill Sanna sooner or later anyway. Myself, I didn't know whether that was true or not.

Sanna's entries about Makke in her remaining diary, which ended two months before her death, were touching. He was the personification of youth and purity, the savior who would free her from men like Otso Hakala and Herr Doktor, Herr Enemy.

"Armi was always going on about how happy I made Sanna," Makke said, biting his lip, when I told him about what was written in Sanna's diary. "I asked her how she was supposed to know, and she wouldn't tell me. I thought she just wanted to comfort me."

That shadow would probably never leave Makke's eyes. He didn't need to forget Sanna though, and Kimmo didn't need to forget Armi. They just had to learn to live without. Did believing that mean I had never really loved?

"There it is," Antti said, snapping me out of my reverie and then leading me along the smooth-raked path. A blackbird sang in an elm tree next to the grave. A fresh-looking bouquet of lilies of the valley accentuated the dark color of the stone, which was nearly my height. At Armi's memorial, Annamari had remarked that it was high time to have Sanna's name carved on the tombstone. That made me happy—perhaps I had succeeded in making Sanna more visible.

Antti had moved away a little and was feeding nuts from his pocket to greedy squirrels trying to climb his pants legs.

I set my own bouquet of poppies carefully on the grave. Although I didn't believe Sanna was under that stone watching me, I didn't know where else I could send her my greetings. And how did I know she couldn't see my flowers?

Sanna appeared for a moment on my internal video screen, the perennial cigarette hanging from her lip, her black hair tousled, extending me that bottle of rowanberry wine. I wanted to imagine she was offering me a drink in thanks. As we were in the shop buying the flowers, I had thought I was finally getting over Sanna. Standing at her grave, however, I realized I would never be free of my guilt. What I did after her death didn't mean anything to her. I should have shown her when she was alive that I cared about her.

Love was such a terrible risk. If you cared about someone, you could spend the rest of your life afraid of losing them. Turning away from Sanna's grave, I realized that I was more afraid of that than I would be meeting up with ten armed murderers. That was why I didn't dare commit to Antti, to promise to go with him to America or to wait for him in Finland. It wasn't a healthy desire for independence—it was simple cowardice.

It was getting late as we set off walking along the shoreline path. The cemetery would be closing soon. The sun was still shining over the neoclassical outline of the Lapinlahti psychiatric hospital, but the shadows of the trees were lengthening. The wind had died down. A hedgehog rustled in the grass. Someone had left a plate of milk for it next to a fir tree.

The fountain was still working. We sat down on a bench next to it, watching the shafts of sunlight on the bay, the silhouette of the hospital, and a full moon rising to compete with the sun. Antti wrapped his arms around me.

I thought of Makke and Kimmo, the firm hugs they both gave me at Armi's funeral. Apparently, they were holding a sort of two-man therapy group at the gym. I thought of the Laaksonens, who wanted to try again. No, they weren't crazy. They were brave. I tried to gather my own courage.

"Antti, I've been thinking…Your trip to America isn't the end of the world. I can wait." I saw in Antti's eyes that he understood what I wanted to say. "If I get too lonely, I'll take a vacation and come see you."

As we kissed, a nightingale alighted in a nearby maple tree and began trilling wildly.

ABOUT THE AUTHOR

Leena Lehtolainen was born in Vesanto, Finland, to parents who taught language and literature. A keen reader, she made up stories in her head before she could even write. At the age of ten, she began her first book, a young adult novel, which was published two years later. Besides writing, Leena is fond of classical singing, her beloved cats, and—her greatest passion—figure skating. She attends many competitions as a skating journalist and writes for the Finnish figure-skating magazine *Taitoluistelu*. *Her Enemy* is the second installment in her best-selling Maria Kallio series, which debuted in English in 2012 with *My First Murder*. Leena currently lives in Finland with her husband and two sons.

ABOUT THE TRANSLATOR

Photo © Pekka Piri, 2012

Owen F. Witesman is a professional literary translator with a master's in Finnish and Estonian area studies from Indiana University. He has translated over thirty Finnish books into English, including novels, children's books, collections of poetry, plays, graphic novels, and nonfiction. His recent translations include the first novel in the Maria Kallio series, *My First Murder* (AmazonCrossing), the satire *The Human Part* by Kari Hotakainen (MacLehose Press), the thriller *Wolves and Angels* by Seppo Jokinen (Ice Cold Crime), and the 1884 classic *The Railroad* by Juhani Aho (Norvik Press). He currently resides in Springville, Utah, with his wife and three daughters, a dog, a cat, and twenty-nine fruit trees.

Made in the USA
Charleston, SC
20 April 2013